I0685683

TAKEN BY THE WOLVES

A PARANORMAL WOLF SHIFTER REVERSE HAREM ROMANCE

STEPHANIE BROTHER

1

SCARLET

Never trust a stranger—friend;
No one knows how it will end.
As you're pretty, so be wise;
Wolves may lurk in every guise.
Charles Perrault, Little Red Riding Hood.

The small-town bar in Braysville is no better than the run-down motel I checked into an hour ago, its sagging porch and weather-warped sign doing little to inspire confidence. As I push open the doors, the interior greets me with the same weary air of neglect. It's rustic, but not in the way the word is usually meant. It's the kind of rustic that smells faintly of mildew and wet dog, with mismatched furniture that creaks when you lean on it and walls stained with the smoke of a hundred thousand unfiltered cigarettes.

I pause inside, my nose wrinkling instinctively as I inhale. My sense of smell has always been bloodhound sharp, according to my mother, and right now it's not doing me any favors. My stomach chooses that moment to growl, a loud, awkward protest, reminding me that I haven't eaten since breakfast. I almost turn around and leave, but there are few options in this town, and the receptionist at the motel, a tired-looking woman with too much eyeliner and too little patience, assured me this was the best place.

If Doug's Place is the best, I don't want to experience the worst.

Heads turn as I make my way toward the bar, masculine eyes, narrowing with interest or suspicion, tracking me like prey. I'm not surprised. In a town like this, where everyone knows everyone and outsiders are a rarity, I must look like something exotic blown in on the wind. My hair, a thick curtain of red that falls past my waist, tends to catch attention wherever I go. With skin as pale as porcelain and a frame that's more willowy than muscular, I know I don't blend in easily.

The man behind the bar, who may or may not be Doug, saunters towards me as though he has all the time in the world. "What can I get you?"

"A beer," I say without hesitation. His eyebrows lift slightly, as if he expected me to order a glass of chardonnay or something with a slice of citrus on the rim. "And a burger. If you serve them."

"It's our bestseller," he says.

As he turns to relay the order to the back, I glance around, finding myself under the weight of several more stares. All male. In fact, I think I'm the only woman in the place.

"That'll be twenty bucks," he says as he returns.

I hand over the cash and try not to notice the grime beneath his chewed fingernails. I silently hope he isn't also the cook and briefly pray that my burger comes straight from a factory freezer, untouched by human hands. It might be the only thing that saves me from food poisoning.

At least the beer is cold.

As I wait for my meal, I take a seat at the bar. I like it better perched high with my back to the strange-looking, overly observant crowd. I scroll through the emails on my phone, letting the low hum of conversation and twang of country music fill the space around me. There's a strange, charged energy in the air, like something's about to happen. I try to ignore it.

My thoughts drift to the reason I'm here: a new commission, a full dining room suite for one of my most high-end clients. They've bought a sprawling log cabin in Aspen, and they want it furnished with custom pieces that are as wild and authentic as the mountains themselves. Rustic chic, they call it. And I'm known for that.

Which is why I'm here.

Furniture is all about the materials. Find a good quality piece of slow-grown wood, and you're halfway to something exceptional. Braysville might be an armpit of a town, but it is famous for its lumber.

And its lumberjacks.

A few online reviews even mentioned the legendary hospitality of the locals, in and out of the bedroom. I fan my hand in front of my face as a flush blooms across my cheeks. It's been a while since anyone provided me with any kind of bedroom hospitality, and the thought of a sexy woodcutter has my lady parts warming in addition to my face. Unfortunately, this bar isn't where the gorgeous, hospitable locals hang out. It's more Deliverance than a romance novel.

3

Keep your mind on the job at hand, I tell myself.

After my last boyfriend dumped me for my best friend, I locked my heart away. It was humiliating. Not just the betrayal, but how easily it could happen, and while I've rebuilt myself piece by piece, there are cracks now that didn't exist before. Trust is a fragile thing, and once it's broken, it doesn't reform with the same strength. I've found satisfaction in my work, particularly in meeting new clients and suppliers. My family has been amazing at supporting me.

Still, there are nights when I crave more than solitude. Nights I lie awake aching for arms around me, for the weight and warmth of another body, for something wild and sweet and desperately needed. I hate that my body doesn't understand the rules I've set.

The burger arrives, looking surprisingly edible. The fries are crisp and golden, and when I take a bite of the burger, it exceeds all expectations. My stomach hums in satisfaction as I devour it.

"That looks good."

The voice comes from my right, deep and amused, and I glance up to find a man with an empty beer bottle standing beside me. He's handsome in that roughneck, blue-collar way, with dark hair, dark eyes, a day's stubble on his jaw, and a plaid shirt that hugs a broad chest. His hands are big, calloused, but clean.

"It's good," I admit, swallowing quickly. "Better than expected."

"I've had one before. You're safe."

His gaze flicks to my blouse, lingering a moment too long. I shift slightly in my seat, the air between us cooling. He's not subtle, but he is my type.

4

"You new in town?" he asks.

"Just passing through. Business."

"What kind of business?"

"Furniture," I say. My tone is clipped now, a little defensive. Something about his presence grates. *Beware of strangers,* my mom's voice echoes in my head. She's obsessed with warnings about danger. When I was a kid, it was about men who would come and take me away with sweet temptations or maybe cute puppies. When I was a teen, it turned to men who were going to come to steal my innocence. In recent years, there have been warnings about men who will hurt me. Mostly, I've brushed it off, much to her annoyance. She tells me that I won't understand how hard it is until I've had a child of my own. I haven't told her it's never going to happen. There's a niggle inside me, though, a niggle that makes me wonder if maybe she senses something bad in my future.

He lifts an eyebrow. "Buying or selling?" He gulps some of the beer the barman placed in front of him. He must have a tab because he isn't asked to pay.

"Making. I'm here to buy raw materials."

He laughs, a low chuckle that vibrates in his chest. "You don't look like a carpenter."

My hackles rise immediately. What the hell is that supposed to mean?

"And what does a carpenter look like?"

The guy leans forward, his eyes leering and expression hungry. Call it intuition, but I don't like him. I've met men like this before. Men who poke your sensitive places to get a response. Men who end up trying to destroy you in the end. "They're usually bigger, with more facial hair than you."

5

"Looks can be deceiving." I take another bite of my burger to stop myself from saying more. I don't need an altercation with this man in a strange bar in a strange town. I need to keep my wits about me.

I nod, still chewing. I wash it down with a long slug of beer, hoping he realizes from my food and my drink choices that I'm no salad-eating, mimosa-drinking wallflower. I wish I had the guts to tell him to leave me alone now. His presence is taking the edge off my delicious meal and leaving me with a sour taste in my mouth.

"I bet they can," he says, eyes gleaming. "You, for example. You wear your clothes crisp and white, but I bet you're nothing like that underneath."

"What I am underneath is none of your business," I say coolly. "And now I need to eat my burger. Enjoy your night." I swivel a little on my stool so my back is directed toward him, hoping he'll take the hint.

"Oh, it's like that," he says, laughing ominously. "I wouldn't have expected anything else."

I don't reply and use my phone as a distraction while I chew a mouthful. Mom has sent me a message to ask me if I'm okay. Her Spidey sense is working in full force. I wonder what she'd say if she could see me now. She'd probably lock me in her basement and throw away the key. At least until my handsome prince comes knocking.

I type back, 'All well. I checked in at the hotel. I'm having dinner.' She sends me a smiley face emoji that makes me laugh. Until last month, Mom didn't know what an emoji was. Now, she's at the point of overusing them.

I don't turn to check if the man has gone. I know he has. It's strange how deeply I sense his absence, like the air around me shifted back into place. He never touched me, but there was an unsettling clash between his presence and my aura.

The burger and fries hit the spot, and the beer warms and relaxes me. The clench of anxiety he left behind eases. No one else bothers me while I eat, and by the time I'm done, the bar is busier and noisier.

It's time to leave. I don't want to be here when the night turns rough.

Sliding off the barstool, I tuck my phone into my purse and sling it over my shoulder. My thoughts are already with the creaky motel bed that waits for me like a quiet reward.

Eyes trail me to the exit. Men always look. It's instinct. Predator to prey, desire disguised as curiosity. My ex used to do the same. Always watching other women, thinking I wouldn't notice. He called it harmless. He accused me of being paranoid, then he proved me right.

My skin prickles, a warning wrapped in a memory, and I can almost hear their thoughts. *What does she look like under that blouse? How tight are those jeans when they're peeled off? Do those spiked boots mean she wants to be handled roughly?* The man at the bar certainly thought so. He looked at me like I was something to unwrap and consume.

Truth is, I don't know who I am when I'm naked anymore. With Kade, sex was a performance. Something choreographed for his benefit, full of fake gasps and gentle submission. I played the part. The demure girlfriend. The grateful lover. But it was never about me.

The first gust of fresh air hits me as I push through the swing doors. The sky has shifted into full darkness, and Braysville is wrapped like a forgotten town tucked beneath a dark blanket. The lights outside the bar are dim and few. I should have driven, but the night felt mild earlier, and I needed to move after the long haul on the road.

I head toward the lot, heels clicking against the uneven gravel, purse tucked close. It's not far to the motel, and once I'm there, I'll be safe. The wind picks up, brushing strands of red hair across my face like warning banners. I smooth them away with one hand, senses on edge. The woods flank either side of the road, thick and close, their shadows dancing with the wind. Every rustle is a whisper, every creak a warning.

A twig snaps behind me.

My heart skips a beat.

I know there's someone there before I look. The prickle of unease I had in the bar returns tenfold, and I whip my head around, finding the creepy man behind me by only a few paces. Was he waiting in the undergrowth for me to pass, or had he followed me all this time? That same rotten energy brushes up against mine. He's too close. Too quiet. Too intentional.

Don't trust strangers, my mom's voice screams in my mind.

"Hey," he calls out, casual and smooth. "You want me to walk with you? It's not safe out here."

"It's okay," I say, trying to sound light and breezy, like I'm not unraveling inside. I wave a hand, dismissively. Keep it friendly. Don't escalate. But he doesn't fall away. His stride matches mine, unhurried and too confident.

"It's no trouble." He smirks like a wolf.

"I'm fine," I say firmly. My feet are burning from the heels. I wish I wore sneakers, something I could run in. I quicken my pace, and he keeps up easily.

"I guess what they say about redheads is true," he mutters.

I don't take the bait, but it's hard. Every word from his

mouth grates like sandpaper across my skin.

"What's that?"

"Feisty," he says, and that's when his hand clamps around my wrist.

I gasp, twisting my body away, trying to yank free, but his grip is solid, snagging my skin and bruising my bone.

"Let go of me," I hiss, yanking my arm back again, but he grins, his yellow teeth turning my stomach.

"Don't be like that," he croons. "I'm looking out for you."

"I know," I lie, gathering my senses. Rage won't help me here. He wants the struggle. His eyes light up with it, bright with the thrill of dominance. "But I don't need looking after. My husband's back at the motel. He's waiting for me."

He turns my wrist, inspecting it like he owns it. "No ring," he says, voice thick with amusement. "And no man in his right mind would leave you to walk alone. Not looking like you do."

I have no comeback. Nothing will work. He doesn't care what I say. He's already made his choice. He's going to take what he wants unless I stop him.

So I scream.

I scream with everything I have. My lungs tear with it. He tries to shut me up, lunging with his other hand, but I twist, kicking and thrashing, refusing to make it easy. We stumble off the road and into the woods. My ankle catches on something, and I crash forward. Still, I scream.

"Shut up," he barks, yanking my hair, turning my face roughly. His hand clasps viciously over my mouth. I bite. I bite so deep, I taste blood.

"Bitch." He slaps me around the back of the head, pain exploding in white stars, and I blink furiously through the haze. Then something moves. Low to the ground. Fast.

A growl splits the night.

He spins.

Wolf.

His grip slackens. There are two of them. Massive, muzzles low, yellow eyes trained not on me but him. Saliva threads from the jaw of the closest one, its lip curled in a silent snarl.

I stumble back, tripping over a fallen log and twisting my ankle. When my ass hits the ground, all the breath is knocked out of me, and a white-hot scream of pain flashes through me.

The man backs away, his bravado gone. Now he's a scared animal in the sights of something bigger, stronger, and more deadly.

The wolves look hungry and angry, like they want to tear the man limb from limb, not for food, but for pleasure.

But wolves don't attack humans. I know that much from school. They're shy, reclusive creatures, except these ones don't seem that way. They are monstrous in size, intelligent in the tilt of their heads, in the stillness of their poised bodies. They're not interested in me. Only him.

The wolves prowl after him until they're lost to the gloom, the sounds of his scrambling feet and their giant paws in the dry leaves the only indication they were ever here. Then they vanish into the dark with him, swallowed whole.

I crawl to the side, heaving with panic. My phone is useless. No signal. My boot is off, my ankle is swelling, and the pain is biting deeper.

I try to breathe. Try to think.

The branch nearby is long and sturdy enough. I drag

myself upright, testing weight on one leg. It's bad. But I can make it. I have to make it.

Then a shadow moves between the arching trunks.

My heart stops.

A man emerges from between the trees. His hair is dark as the night, his eyes sparkle like blue diamonds even in the low light of the forest. His beard frames a mouth too soft for this wild world. His shoulders stretch the fabric of his shirt, and his arms look carved from stone.

I freeze. My heart thunders.

"Hey," he says, raising his hands. The moment our eyes lock, light erupts between us, like a flash of lightning or a falling star. I blink, dazed, and he stares back, just as stunned. Something passes between us. Some recognition I don't understand.

We're still as tree trunks, whipped by the wind that rustles the leaves, an eerie soundtrack to our encounter.

"I was attacked," I finally choke out. "He... he was chased off by wolves."

The man's eyes narrow, his gaze sharpening. "You're safe now."

I want to believe him. God help me, I want to believe he's a hero because the alternative is too terrible to contemplate.

2

SCARLET

"Do you need help?" He makes his way closer, his eyes roaming my leg and foot to where I've been keeping my weight off my swollen ankle.

"I twisted it," I say. "It hurts to walk."

"Here...let me..." He reaches for the makeshift walking stick I'd been leaning on, his hand brushing mine for the briefest moment. I expect him to drape my arm over his shoulder or offer a slow, awkward hobble back toward safety. But he does none of that. Instead, with a swift movement and effortless confidence, he lifts me into his arms like I weigh less than air.

I gasp as I cling to him instinctively, worrying he might drop me. My face flushes hot, blazing like a sunset. His arms are like sculpted stone wrapped in heat, and his chest is a wall of muscle that smells like pine needles crushed beneath boots, like cedar smoke curling in the wind, like leather warmed by sunlight. It's woodsy and earthy and perfect for this lumberjack look-alike.

"You don't have to carry me," I stammer, though I make no move to escape. My hero doesn't seem to care, and it feels too good, too safe, to be held like this.

"Shoes like that don't do well in Braysville," he says, his mouth quirking slightly.

"You have roads and sidewalks," I mutter. "And I can walk fine when I'm not being ambushed by hillbilly assholes."

He chuckles, walking carefully as he weaves through the thickening darkness of the forest, always careful to keep me clear of low-hanging branches and twisted roots.

"What's your name?" It seems the polite thing to ask.

"Nixon," he says. "And yours?"

"Scarlet."

His gaze dips to meet mine, and in the shadows, his eyes catch what little light remains, twin points of gleaming sapphire. "Red," he says, a slow smirk blooming on his mouth. "Like Little Red Riding Hood?"

I roll my eyes with a sigh, too tired to be offended, though the comparison grates. "No. Like Scarlet. No muffins in my basket. Just chisels and screwdrivers."

"Red Riding Hood was dumb. She did everything her momma told her not to, and the only reason she survived was because she was rescued by a man." Even as I say it, I realize that I'm pretty much in the exact same situation.

Woodcutter and wolves to the rescue.

His eyebrows rise, but he doesn't ask me what the hell I'm talking about. He's clearly not the kind of man who wastes words unless he has to.

"I'm staying at the motel," I tell him. "The one on the edge of town. My car is there, too."

He tightens his grip a little, and I'm drawn even closer

against his chest. The motion makes my breath catch. His heartbeat is slow, steady, and calming.

"You know," I say, trying to get a handle on the weird energy between us, "if you're getting tired, I can walk... with help. Rest my arm over your shoulder."

His jaw ticks like I've challenged him. "Do I look like I'm getting tired?"

Wow. Fragile male ego. That didn't take long. Still, there's no strain in his steps, no sag in his posture. He carries me like I'm made of down feathers and light.

"No," I say carefully. "But if you do... You know, just tell me."

"I won't."

That's it. Two words. Ironclad.

And maybe it's the way he says them or the way the trees part for him like they're not foolish enough to get in his way, but I believe him. I think he'll carry me all the way back to the motel and won't slow once. I believe he'd run through fire if he needed to. There's something otherworldly in him. Not only strength, but purpose.

It's insane to trust a man I just met. But whatever danger stalked me tonight, it isn't with this man. With Nixon.

The forest is still around us now, but in the quiet hush of leaves and the rustling wind, safety wraps around me like a warm blanket, even if I don't yet understand why.

"Is there a doctor in town? A hospital?"

"I don't think you need a doctor for a simple sprain."

I raise a brow. "And you can tell that by looking at my foot? Through the sock?"

He exhales long and slow, like he's exercising monk-level patience. Or trying to. "If anything was broken, you'd be crying. You're not. It's swollen, yeah, but it needs ice and something for inflammation. Nothing serious."

"Well, thank you, Doctor Forrest-Gump, for your sage medical advice, but I think I'll get a scan done anyway, in case your backwoods x-ray vision has a glitch."

"Backwoods x-ray vision?" He blinks, then lets out a deep, rumbling laugh that rolls through his chest and vibrates into mine.

I don't laugh. I sit in his arms, stiff as a board, because the longer he holds me, the more I realize I'm completely at his mercy. I've been attacked, rescued, and now abducted all in the same night, and I still don't even know if I'm safe. It's too dark to see much of the path we're on, but he strides forward without hesitation, feet silent on the forest floor, as if he knows every bend and root by memory. I open my mouth to insist again that he put me down when the trees break open, and we emerge into a clearing.

Encircling a cabin.

A beautifully built one, with handcrafted joints, timber that looks older than Croesus, perfect angles and proportions. But the second realization comes with a cold rush.

This isn't the motel. We're not in town.

My stomach lurches as panic punches the air from my lungs. I struggle, but he clutches me tighter.

He didn't take me to help. He didn't take me toward people. He took me to a secluded house in the woods, and I still don't know who he is or what he wants.

I squirm in his arms, instinct kicking hard. "Let me go," I say, struggling against his hold.

His grip tightens, iron-hard and unyielding. His jaw clenches, and that calm mask cracks. "You're not walking anywhere on that ankle. You won't get far."

"I don't care," I snap. "Take me back to the motel. I'll crawl if I have to."

"You don't need to be scared of me."

But I am.

Because no woman should ever be carried away into the woods by a stranger, no matter how square his jaw or how perfect his beard or how impossibly chiseled his chest might be beneath that flannel. No matter how heroically he saved her. Nixon is a man who doesn't bend or break. That much is obvious.

"You can rest here," he says. "I'm going to take a look at that ankle and see what we can do to make it better."

"I don't want to go into your cabin," I hiss, my voice trembling. "Do you understand me? Take me back."

He keeps walking with determination, like a man so used to getting his way, he doesn't even register protest as resistance.

By the time we reach the porch, I've kicked and twisted enough to throw my balance, and when he finally sets me onto my feet, I stupidly try to stand. Pain explodes through my ankle, and I crumble with a sharp cry.

He catches me instantly, his hand closing around my elbow. It's hard to tell if it's support or restraint. Maybe both.

He's quick to unlock the door to the cabin, and when he throws it open and guides me through it, I forget my name.

Because inside... It's breathtaking.

The walls are paneled with slow-grown wood, rich and warm, polished smoothly. The furniture is handcrafted perfection with clean, classic lines that suggest obsession with symmetry and pride in detail. It's not rustic kitsch. It's art. Living, breathing, masculine art.

16

My mouth parts in a silent gasp of awe.

This isn't a cabin. It's a cathedral to craftsmanship.

My clients in Aspen would sell their souls to replicate this.

Nixon guides me into the center of the open-plan room and closes the door behind us. The sound of the latch clicks.

And just like that... I realize I'm trapped.

Not by a man with cruel eyes and yellow teeth...

But who is Nixon, and what does he want with me?

3

SCARLET

"Come and sit over here," Nixon says, guiding me gently by the arm toward the deep navy corduroy couch. I hop awkwardly on one foot until I reach it, then sink into the cushions with a relieved sigh.

I clutch my purse to my chest, acutely aware of the phone tucked inside. Knowing it's there provides a thread of control in a situation that's slipping through my fingers.

Nixon lowers himself onto the polished wood coffee table directly in front of me. His thighs spread slightly for balance, his body solid and broad, and before I can object, he lifts my injured foot into his lap and slowly peels away the sock.

"Don't," I say. "I can do it." I try to jerk it back, but he continues.

"Why don't you want me to help?" he asks. "You're so guarded."

"You're a stranger," I snap. "A stranger who carried me into his cabin in the woods. Forgive me if I'm not swooning

18

with gratitude while you try to undress me."

He shakes his head, eyes sparkling with amusement. "Undress you? It's a sock. A dirty, leaf-covered, damp sock. You think this is my idea of foreplay?"

I flush with embarrassment.

It isn't. Of course, it isn't.

But when his fingers slide beneath the fabric and ease it over my swollen ankle, it's not just pain that floods my nerves, but awareness. His touch is warm and sure, rough in the way that comes from working with his hands, but gentle, too. His focus doesn't waver, not even for a second.

And somehow, that makes it worse.

The sock peels away slowly, dragging leaves and forest debris with it. When he exposes my foot, he pauses.

"It's very swollen," he says quietly, setting the sock aside.

I glance down and wince. He's right. The bones of my ankle have all but vanished beneath red, puffy skin. It looks angry and injured.

But for some reason, what embarrasses me isn't the injury. It's my toes. Painted cherry red, neat and shiny.

Too bold. Too sexual. Too... obvious.

He notices. His eyes flick over the polish and then to mine. There's no teasing smirk on his face, just that cool, assessing calm again. His gaze is so deep, it seems to touch parts of me I don't show anyone.

I bite my lip at the intensity within their depths.

His silence is unnerving. His stillness is even more so.

I can't read him at all.

He's so damn sexy, from the straightness of his nose to the fullness of his lips, but it's his eyes that have me shivering. Cool and blue, they're as pretty as they are empty.

Nixon lifts my foot from his lap and settles it on a thick

cushion on the coffee table. Then he stands, walking with quiet purpose to the kitchen, pulling a tea towel from a drawer, and grabbing a plastic bag from the counter. I watch him fill it with ice, fold it in half, and wrap it. The whole motion is efficient and quiet, like he's done it before. Like he's used to people being hurt around him.

I reach into my purse and curl my fingers around my phone. It's there. Warm from my body heat. My lifeline.

But the moment of comfort is shattered when the front door swings open with a loud creak.

A man walks in.

And he's completely naked.

I freeze.

He's tall, lean, and broad-shouldered with the kind of body that could only be built in the woods or a weight room. His torso is marked with dark, intricate tattoos that spiral across his chest and arms, curling like ancient script. His hand goes to his cock, which he attempts to conceal but fails. It's so big that, even though his hand is enormous, there is still a whole lot on show.

My mouth drops open. He blinks.

"Reed," Nixon growls from behind me, his tone halfway between irritation and warning. "Clothes. Now."

The naked man, Reed, turns toward the door with a roll of his eyes. "We didn't know you had company," he mutters. "A sign might've been helpful."

But then a scratching sound attracts my attention. Heavy, like claws on wood.

Something massive moves just beyond the open door.

A moment later, a huge gray muzzle pushes through the frame. Not a dog. Not even close. The creature is enormous. Muscular. Predatory. Its eyes gleam with intelligence, ice blue, sharp, and utterly unnatural.

I press myself deeper into the couch cushions, heart thudding. "That's... a big dog."

Reed glances at the hand still cupping himself and smirks. "No one's ever called it that before. But I like it."

My cheeks go up in flames.

Nixon mutters a curse. "Get dressed."

I guess that Reed is Nixon's brother. Now I've had a moment to look him over. The strong family resemblance is obvious. There's something about his hard jaw, cheekbones, and eyes. Wow. Even the dog matches his owners in that regard.

"And take..." Nixon pauses, looking at the beast who seems so out of place in this crafted, clean environment.

Reed pats the wolf-dog on the head with his free hand. "Come," he says, heading off up the stairs, his perfect bare ass on display. I can't help but watch him striding away as heat floods between my legs.

Wow.

Two gorgeous men under one lonely and isolated roof. If I weren't desperate to return to civilization, a girl could find plenty to keep her occupied out here in the woods. Those reviews on TripAdvisor flash through my mind again. Maybe this cabin *has* seen its fair share of 'local hospitality.'

Nixon closes the front door and sits at the table before lifting my foot. "Sorry about that. My brother...well, we don't usually have visitors."

"So he walks around naked in the woods?"

Nixon shrugs, like it's the most natural thing in the world. "It's warm out. There's usually no one around."

"Isn't he worried the dog's gonna bite off his sausage?"

I mutter, as the icepack touches my skin. The cold shocks through me, and Nixon lets out a deep, rumbling laugh that vibrates my bones. Not a great combo when my ankle's throbbing like it's going to explode.

"Sorry." He places a warm hand on my knee, his touch sending a shiver down my spine. "I didn't mean to hurt you. That was an interesting mental image."

"Their whole entrance was a mental image," I say, trying not to laugh.

The ice soothes, and I take a deep breath, trying to relax.

A door slams upstairs, and footsteps descend. Reed returns wearing gray sweats and a worn blue T-shirt, like a model in an ad trying to convey casual cool. Another man follows behind him. Tall and broad, he's dressed in jeans and a plaid shirt. Classic lumberjack.

Three of them now. Brothers obviously. And no sign of a dog anywhere.

"So," Reed drawls, resting his elbow on the banister. "What do we have here?"

"This is Scarlet," Nixon replies. "I found her in the woods. She was running from some asshole."

I don't miss the intense look that passes between the men. It's quick, silent, and packed with some kind of understanding I'm not privy to.

"Not like you to play knight in shining armor," Reed snorts.

"You're lucky he didn't leave you there," the third one says, stepping closer. "I'm Finn." He holds out his hand, and I shake it. His grip is firm and dry; his palm callused from work. He holds on for a moment too long, his gaze lingering.

"Scarlet's ankle is pretty swollen," Nixon says, ignoring

the jibes. "She needs to ice it and keep it elevated. One of you want to get the spare room ready?"

"I'm not staying," I blurt. "I'd appreciate it if someone could drive me back to my motel."

"It's no trouble," Nixon says firmly. The others exchange glances, obviously confused by Nixon's refusal to take me back but not questioning him in front of me. "Better not to head out again until morning."

Right on cue, a long, low howl splits the night air. The sound is distant, but eerie, and the way the men react, the sudden stillness in their bodies, the quiet way they listen, makes the hair on my arms rise.

They're not scared. They're alert.

I try to tamp down the panic rising in my throat. "I want to go back." I sit straighter, shifting my painful ankle. "I don't know you, and I don't want to be rude, but I'm not comfortable staying here."

"Nothing's going to happen to you," Finn says gently. "That's not what we're about."

"You'll get some rest tonight, and we'll see how you are in the morning," Nixon says. Without another word, he gestures at Reed, who sighs dramatically and heads back upstairs. Even if there's a lock on that bedroom door, I already know I'm not going to sleep tonight. Not in a house with three strange men and a literal wolf.

"Can you grab some anti-inflammatories and water?" Nixon asks Finn. "And maybe something for her to eat."

"I'm fine," I say. "I already ate."

"Where?" Nixon's voice is full of disbelief.

"At the bar."

He lets out a short, incredulous laugh. "You like gambling with your life, don't you?"

23

"It was actually decent."

"Decent? Have you *seen* the chef?"

"Let's not talk about it." I raise a hand to draw a line under the conversation. "I've eaten it. No going back now."

Nixon smirks like he's enjoying this a little too much. "So, is the ankle any better?"

"A little."

Finn returns with two small pills and a glass of water. I eye them warily. They're not in a packet. No label. No branding. Just two anonymous white tablets.

"I can't take those," I say.

Nixon looks at me, head tilted slightly. "Why not?"

"I'm allergic," I say smoothly.

"They're over-the-counter painkillers," Finn adds. "Nothing strong."

"I get reactions," I lie, shaking my head. "Hives. Swollen throat. That kind of thing."

They don't argue, but Nixon doesn't look convinced. He readjusts the ice pack against my ankle, his hand lingering longer than it needs to.

"I think I should call the police," I say. "I don't know what happened to the guy in the woods, but if he's still out there, he could hurt someone else."

Nixon's hand adjusts the ice pack to curve around my ankle. "You can leave that to us," he says. "We know the sheriff in town. We'll let him know what happened."

"I should make a statement," I insist.

"We'll see what the sheriff says. Right now, you've had a shock. No need to stress more."

Finn sits across from me, his eyes searching mine. I don't think he fully understands why Nixon brought me here. I'm not sure *I* know. But it's clear he's not about to question

24

him in front of me.

Before I can press the issue further, Reed reappears at the top of the stairs, one hand sweeping out like an actor on stage.

"Your castle awaits," he says, voice rich with theatrical flair. "M'lady.

4

SCARLET

There's no way out.

The realization settles over me like a fog, creeping in without warning, curling around every thought. I've asked. I've argued. I've struggled. I've been reassured by three strangers with the kind of beauty that should come with a warning label. They insist they're only trying to help me.

But I don't know them. And I don't know what else to do.

"We'll help you up," Nixon says, his hand already reaching for me. I shuffle forward on the couch, clutching my purse like a lifeline. Before I can rise on my own, he tugs me upright and sweeps me off my feet again, effortless and unbothered.

"Showing off your manly strength," Finn calls out from the hallway.

"How do you think she got here in the first place?" Nixon's voice is flat, but there's something sharp beneath it.

Up the stairs we go to a room tucked at the back of the

cabin, and for a second, I forget everything.

It's beautiful.

The soft glow of a bedside lamp warms the wood-paneled walls, casting golden shadows on the hand-carved furniture. The bed is large, made from thick beams of polished walnut or oak, the headboard smooth and gleaming beneath my fingertips. Everything smells faintly of lavender and pine. If my motel room looked anything like this, I wouldn't have dreaded staying there for a night.

Well... I guess that's no longer a problem.

"I've left you a towel," Reed says, stepping into the doorway. "The sheets are clean, the bathroom is down the hall, and there's a crutch in the corner if you need it." He points to a gray metal contraption that stands waiting to assist me.

"Thanks," I say. "I need that."

"Not really," Finn says from behind me. "You have Nixon to carry you around. I'm sure he'd be happy to escort you to the bathroom, too."

"I'm sure he would," I reply, my tone dry. "But your hospitality can stop short of that."

Finn and Reed laugh, but Nixon remains straight-faced.

"Well, goodnight. And call us if you need anything." Reed lingers a little, but follows his brothers, closing the door softly behind him.

I exhale, finally alone. My gaze moves around the room, lingering on the details. The carved dresser. The ornate lamp base. The way the woodgrain gleams, as if polished by hand, not a machine. Every piece of furniture is a work of art—crafted, not bought. Someone loved the materials. Someone poured time and heart into shaping them. My fingers trail across the headboard again, admiring the lines of the grain,

27

the smoothness of the finish.

I shake myself. Focus.

This is not the time to swoon over furniture. I fumble in my purse and pull out my phone, exhaling in relief when the screen lights up. Low battery, but enough for a call.

I press my mom's number. Nothing happens. No ringing.

No signal.

Great. Perfect.

I'm stranded. Cut off. At least the room has a lock, though the idea of being locked *in* is almost as unsettling as being locked *out*. At least I won't have to lie awake worrying about Nixon, Reed, or Finn slipping in while I sleep. Or that giant wolf-dog slinking in and deciding I look like a midnight snack.

Where is it, anyway? It followed Reed upstairs, but I haven't heard a sound since.

Something catches my eye at the end of the bed. A soft heap of gray fabric. I unfold it and find a man's T-shirt, oversized and worn thin from dozens of washes. It smells like lavender, like the room. Thoughtful. I guess Reed left it for me.

It's a strange sort of kindness, and it makes my chest ache.

I push up from the mattress, using the edge of the dresser for balance, then grab the crutch. It's heavier than I expected, but it holds my weight. I make my slow, careful way to the bathroom. There's fresh soap and a brand-new toothbrush laid out by the sink.

These men don't usually have visitors?

Yeah, right.

They must have half the women in Braysville falling over

28

themselves to visit. Maybe these are the locals all the women on TripAdvisor were raving about. I wouldn't be surprised if this place had left more than one guest weak-kneed and breathless.

I freshen up with a washcloth, skipping the shower. I don't want to be that vulnerable. Not here. Not yet.

Back in the room, I tug the T-shirt over my head. It's soft and worn, and it smells like safety even though I know better. I slide beneath the crisp sheets and lie there, staring at the ceiling, trying to settle my thoughts.

As I drift into sleep, a long, sharp howl slices through the stillness.

It's close. Too close.

Painfully, I push myself upright and limp to the window. The sky is luminous with moonlight, casting silver across the clearing behind the cabin. Is it a full moon? I can't be sure. The trees sway softly in the breeze, shadows shifting in their arms.

And there they are.

Three wolves, lithe and gray, moving together through the brush, their bodies fluid and powerful as they disappear into the forest like ghosts.

I go cold. I can't look away.

There's no escaping this cabin. Not safely. I may not be miles from town, but between me and civilization lies a forest thick with shadows, secrets… and wolves.

So many wolves.

5

SCARLET

I don't sleep well. Not that I expected to. My nerves keep straddling that thin line between slumber and wakefulness all night long. My ankle throbs steadily beneath the covers, a dull drumbeat that won't let me forget it's there. And every creak of the old cabin, every rustle of wind through the trees, jolts my already-frayed senses.

Which is a shame because the bed is easily the most comfortable I've ever been in. I sink into the mattress like a fairy tale princess. There's even a hand-crocheted blanket folded at the foot of the bed, something that makes me smile at first, until the thought hits.

None of the men in this house looks like the type to make something soft and delicate. It's the kind of blanket a grandma would make.

Nixon, Reed, and Finn look like the kind who sleep under the stars, who fight, who live rough and thrive in it. Men made to survive. Soldiers, not homemakers. Wilderness types at home with wolves in the wilderness, not in curated cabins with throw pillows, quilts, and handcrafted furniture.

When sunlight finally slips through the gaps in the curtains, I give up pretending I'm going to get more rest. I ease into my jeans, careful with my ankle, and leave the oversized T-shirt on. It's softer and cleaner than my blouse.

I repack my things, loop the purse across my body so I can still use the crutch, and smooth the bed behind me. It's ridiculous, but I can't help it. I may be stranded in a stranger's cabin, but that doesn't mean I have to be a messy guest.

The cabin is too quiet, so I wait until a floorboard creaks somewhere down the hall, then I'm up and out of the room, heading for the stairs.

The crutch digs into my ribs as I make my slow descent from the room, each hop on the stairs harder than the last. Sweat beads along my spine by the time I'm halfway down, and that's when Nixon appears. He strides up to meet me, swooping me into his arms again before I can object.

"Seriously?" I huff. "You've got to stop doing that."

He doesn't answer, strides into the kitchen and deposits me gently onto a stool at the counter.

"I could've made it," I mutter, dragging the crutch closer.

"You were moving slower than a snail," he says over his shoulder, already opening cupboards. "You know, you have a problem letting anyone help you."

"Nothing wrong with being independent," I snap.

He stops and turns enough to raise an eyebrow. "Pretty sure the way I found you last night proves that theory wrong."

The air leaves my lungs like a punch.

Is he… blaming me? For walking? For needing dinner and trying to get back to my motel on my own two feet at a perfectly reasonable hour? That's not being independent. That's just being a human being who needs to eat and sleep. It's not my fault that a sexual predator was lurking around. Why do people always blame the victim instead of focusing on the perpetrator?

"Wow," I say, blinking at him. "I don't even know where to go with that caveman logic."

"Caveman?" He's amused now, leaning into the insult like it fits.

"Yeah, you know. The whole 'women should never leave the house without a male chaperone' attitude, instead of the more logical 'men should stop assaulting women'."

He shrugs, opening the fridge and pulling out a carton of milk and some orange juice. "Some men are assholes."

"That doesn't make it okay."

"No," he agrees, setting the cartons on the counter. "But some of us know how to make breakfast."

It's infuriating how quickly the scent of that brewing pot softens the edge of my irritation.

I'm still bristling, still wound too tight, but I can't help it. My stomach growls, loud and unapologetic.

With his back to me, Nixon is all hard lines and powerful muscles. Broad shoulders stretch his flannel shirt, and his jeans hug his hips and thighs like a second skin. I hate how attractive he is, especially when he's being a condescending jack ass.

"So, what can I get you?" he asks over his shoulder, catching me staring. "We usually start the day with something meaty."

The memory of the giant wolf-dog from last night

flashes in my mind. All muscle and fur and sharp, tearing teeth.

"I'll take toast," I say quickly. "Plain is fine."

He glances at me, one brow lifting.

"Toast," I repeat. "Safe. Familiar. Not likely to have once walked on four legs."

Nixon scoffs. "Actually, leave it to me. You don't seem capable of making a sensible decision about anything."

My jaw tics. Of course, he's ignoring me again, like my words are blood whistling through his ear. Maybe it's my 'weak girly voice' that fails to pierce his thick lumberjack skull.

"Toast," I say through clenched teeth, "is what I want."

He barely glances my way. "Wait until you've tried this bacon," he says, pulling a massive pack of streaky meat from the fridge like it's the Holy Grail. He grabs a skillet, sets it on the stove, and unwraps the plastic.

"But I said I want toast."

The back door creaks open. Finn strolls in, shirtless, his hair a tousled mess and his eyes still fogged from sleep. He looks like he's rolled out of bed and directly into a Calvin Klein ad.

"Well," he drawls, grinning. "This is a better view than I usually wake up to."

His voice is pure sunshine and mischief, and it only makes Nixon look more storm-cloud grumpy in comparison.

"Do you think you can explain to this stubborn man that I want toast? Not bacon. Not sausage. Not anything else he thinks I might want. Just two pieces of bread, charred and buttered."

Finn chuckles and shoots Nixon a look I can't quite

decipher. I suddenly feel foolish, like a guest who's overstayed her welcome and is now complaining about the color of the curtains.

"I'm not ungrateful," I add, softer this time. "I… I don't like being bulldozed."

Finn raises his hands, trying to smooth the tension. "How about coffee? That usually makes things better."

"Coffee would be amazing," I say with a sigh. "And then, a ride back into town."

Another look passes between the brothers, subtle but loaded. I catch it, even if I don't fully understand it. I decide not to push. One emotional outburst per breakfast is enough.

"So, what do you do?" Finn asks, filling a mug and handing it to me with a smile that's almost too genuine to be real.

"I make furniture," I say, taking a grateful sip. It's strong and hot, with the right bitterness. "I'm in town to source some premium wood for a client commission."

At that, Finn's brows rise, and he gives Nixon another quick glance.

"Well, if Braysville is good for anything, it's lumber," Finn says.

"And if Finn's good for anything," Nixon chimes in without looking up, "it's furniture."

"You make furniture, too?"

"Pretty much everything in this house has been crafted by my brother," Nixon says, sliding two slices of bread into the toaster at last. "The coffee table, the kitchen stools, the bed…"

"Really? You made the coffee table… and the bed that I slept in?"

He runs a hand through his hair, cheeks going adorably pink. "Yeah. It's kind of a hobby."

A hobby? That bed was a work of art.

"You're seriously talented," I say, leaning in despite myself. "Do you sell your work?"

"He does it for fun," Nixon says before Finn can answer. "We're too busy running our lumber business to start taking custom orders."

"You have a lumber business?" I ask, stunned. "Why didn't you say something?"

Nixon lifts an eyebrow. "You didn't exactly give me space to get a word in last night."

Fair. But also? Rude.

I ignore him and focus on Finn, who clearly wants to say more. "You should think about selling your stuff. I know a few clients who'd jump at the chance to own pieces like yours. And I could help with marketing, exposure, and selling online. I take a percentage, of course, but the profit would be all yours."

Finn's eyes meet mine, and they're practically sparkling. "You'd do that?"

"Absolutely. Quality work deserves to be seen."

I think back over all the people who've bought my furniture. It's what makes a home. It's what allows us to enjoy our surroundings. Quality pieces can provide a lifetime of service and enjoyment.

"Finn has a lot on his plate," Nixon cuts in, voice flat and firm. His palms rest on the edge of the counter like he's bracing himself for a storm.

I force myself to stay calm and not rise to the bait. The goal is to leave here with my dignity intact, and hopefully, Finn's contact info in my bag.

He might actually be interested in selling through me. I could help him build exposure, manage distribution, even take a percentage of each sale. My existing clients would *love* Finn's work; custom pieces with soul and history. I could open up new markets for both of us.

But maybe I'm going about this all wrong. Maybe instead of snapping at Nixon every time he opens his mouth, I should *butter him up*. My mother always warned me about my fierce approach. Said charm works better than fire, especially with men who think they're the apex of the food chain.

Maybe this detour wasn't such a disaster after all. Maybe being here is… fortuitous. I could walk away from Braysville with a new supplier, a new collaborator, and enough premium lumber to fulfill every order in my pipeline. Finn wouldn't get half the prices I could get him. I'd pay him fairly and still make a solid profit. Everyone wins.

Finn returns with cream and sugar, and as I finish my coffee, I practically melt into my seat.

"Mmmm…" I sigh. "That's… God, that's good. Where do you get your beans?"

Finn rolls his eyes. "Please don't get him started. Nixon's a total coffee nerd. If you so much as whisper praise, he'll give you the full TED talk on bean origins, roast profiles, and elevation."

"Thank you, dear brother, for your high praise," Nixon mutters, grabbing a plate. He sounds annoyed, but I catch the flicker of pride in his eyes. It's subtle, but it's there.

He slides a plate across the counter. "Here's your toast, Scarlet. And if you'd like to try some bacon, help yourself."

I take a slice of toast and butter it slowly, sensing Nixon's

36

gaze watching the bacon I insisted I didn't want. As much as I hate admitting defeat, I also know when it's smart to pick my battles. So I grab two pieces of the crispy, perfectly cooked strips and place them on my plate without comment.

He doesn't gloat but continues sipping his coffee like he didn't win that small, quiet war. I can respect that. Maybe he's a little less of a control freak than I thought.

"So... where's Reed?" I ask, biting into the toast.

"He had to handle some business," Nixon replies. "He'll be back later."

"Can you tell me more about the kinds of wood you supply?"

Nixon obliges, rattling off a list of lumber types and finishes. His knowledge is impressive—he knows his inventory inside out—and from the way he talks, their operation is larger than I expected. Not just a cabin-in-the-woods setup. A real business with real potential.

"This sounds like exactly what I've been looking for," I say. "Would you be able to show me some samples?"

Nixon's eyes flick to my hand as I help myself to a third strip of bacon. "We'll take you to the yard after breakfast," he says. "But only if you promise to stay off that ankle afterward."

"I can agree to that," I say, flexing my foot gently before wincing at the sharp stab of pain. "My room at the motel isn't exactly the Ritz, but it has a bed and a TV. I'll take it easy."

Nixon frowns. "That motel is a dump. No elevator, no room service. How are you supposed to rest when you'll have to hobble up and down stairs to feed yourself?"

I blink, taken aback. "I'll figure it out."

"I won't have it," he says firmly. His voice has a tone that leaves no room for negotiation. "You'll stay here. We'll make sure you've got what you need. You'll actually *rest*."

My pulse spikes. "I couldn't—"

"You can. And you will." He sets his cup onto the table, locking eyes with me. There's a flicker of challenge in them, and something else. Possessiveness, maybe? Or the unshakable confidence of a man used to being obeyed.

If I weren't still trying to sweeten him for the sake of a potential business deal, I'd be launching a full-scale protest.

"You can call the motel, cancel your room," Nixon continues. "We'll swing by and pick up your stuff. You'll have everything you need right here."

"I need to call my mom," I counter. "She'll worry if I go dark. She knows I'm traveling."

Nixon's hand pauses ever so slightly as he lifts his cup again. "Finn can go. No point in dragging your ankle all over town. I'll show you the yard. We'll kill two birds with one stone."

The glance Finn shoots him is cautious.

The family dynamic is taking shape. Nixon's clearly the alpha, the one who calls the shots. Finn, I'd bet, is the peacekeeper. The bridge. Reed's probably the wild card—funny, unpredictable, and chaotic enough to keep things interesting.

What do I do now?

I could push back. Demand to go into town myself. Insist on using my phone. Start swinging this crutch like a battle-axe. But that won't get me anywhere, especially with Nixon.

So I do what I rarely do: I pause. I play the long game.

Mom won't be worried yet. She knows I'm off the grid

for the day. And maybe, I can use Nixon's overprotective streak to my advantage. If I keep my cool, sweeten the tone, and play the part of the charming guest, I might not only get access to the lumber but get Finn on board, too.

I meet Nixon's gaze across the counter. His eyes are steely.

This man is going to be the most difficult deal of my life.

But he has no idea who he's up against.

He might win this round... but he's not ready for the full Scarlet.

Not even close.

6

SCARLET

The journey to the lumber yard is shorter than I expected. So short that if my ankle weren't swollen and pulsing like a second heartbeat, we could have walked. But Nixon, apparently done with watching me hobble around, scooped me up without ceremony and carried me to the truck.

Now, we're rumbling along a narrow dirt track that winds through the thick of the forest. Trees crowd close like silent sentinels. The cabin disappears behind us, and the canopy opens into a clearing alive with industry. Stacks of logs are piled into high towers, and heavy-duty machinery sits at attention, accompanied by the smell of fresh wood shavings.

A large metal shed anchors the place, all corrugated steel and shadowed mystery. It's clear this is a small operation, but it's clean, organized, and humming with purpose. If the furniture in the cabin is any indication, these men *really* know their wood.

When Nixon kills the engine and opens the truck door,

the sharp snarl of a mechanical saw grows louder. I glance around, uncertain where the sound is coming from. Do they employ a team, or is this a three-man show?

He moves to pick me up again, but I plant my hand on his chest before he can. "Seriously, Nixon. I want to walk. Please."

His jaw tenses, but then he grunts and steps back, his shrug betraying a quiet war inside him. He doesn't like being told no, but he'll accept it if I ask nicely. I file that away for later.

I follow him into the shed, where I find Reed, dressed in jeans and a plaid shirt, complete with a yellow hard hat and protective goggles. He's sliding wood through an automated saw, slicing it into narrower planks with practiced ease.

He notices us as we approach, finishes the cut, and hits the switch. The machine winds down, the ear-splitting screech of the saw giving way to a softer whir, then silence.

Reed lifts his goggles and grins. "Well, well. You're giving Scarlet the grand tour now? I thought she was supposed to be off that ankle."

"She wants to look at lumber," Nixon replies, clipped and businesslike.

Reed spreads his arms, motioning to the endless racks of timber. "We've got plenty of wood. Softwood, hardwood..." His smirk is shameless, his tone full of innuendo.

I arch a brow. "You rehearsed that line?"

He winks. "Only every day of my life."

"Ignore my brother," Nixon mutters, steering me toward a long row of neatly labeled boards. "Everything's categorized by species and cut. Take your time. Let me know if you have questions".

41

I run my hand over a slab of honey-colored maple, the grain smooth and cool beneath my fingers. The scent of sawdust fills the air—clean, sharp, grounding. I breathe it in like a tonic. Without realizing it, I sigh.

"You like the way it feels," Nixon says behind me.

I turn, caught in my reverie. His eyes are dark again, but there's a heat behind them this time. Something just shy of hungry.

"I like the story wood tells," I say, keeping my voice casual. "Every knot, every scar, every grain pattern... It's a memory."

Nixon steps closer. "You're the kind of woman who appreciates what most people miss."

I meet his gaze, unflinching. "And you're the kind of man who notices."

There's a beat of silence between us, thick with the tension that's been growing since last night. Then Reed's voice breaks it.

"Careful, brother," he calls from the far side of the stack. "Scarlet's going to have you writing poetry soon."

I laugh, grateful for the reprieve. "Now, that would be terrifying."

Reed steps into view, wiping sweat from his brow with the hem of his T-shirt, exposing a chiseled torso and a confidence that borders on indecent. He doesn't miss the way my eyes flick toward him and drink him in or hide his satisfaction. Instead, his smirk turns wicked. "You're not terrifying. You're a damn revelation."

He's shameless, but it works. His grin is disarming, and the way he looks at me like I'm something rare makes my stomach tighten in a way I'd nearly forgotten was possible.

Finn appears next, sleeves rolled to his elbows, sawdust

dusting his forearms and clinging to the waves of his hair. That same quiet warmth settles on his face. He gives me a casual once-over.

"Find anything you like?" he asks.

The question is innocent, but Nixon tenses beside me.

"I found a lot I like," I say, letting the double meaning linger in the air, tired of pretending I don't feel the pulse of wildness threading through this place.

Reed tilts his head. "You gonna stick around longer than a day?"

"Maybe," I admit. "If the product's right. And the company."

Finn's gaze flickers to Nixon, who, judging by the set of his jaw, isn't used to this kind of flirtation.

Reed gives a low whistle. "Well, damn. If you're angling for the deluxe tour, I could take you out back. Show you the log lift. Hell, the mill's got rhythm like you wouldn't believe."

"I bet it does."

"Reed," Nixon warns, voice low and blunt-edged.

But Reed grins and walks off, whistling.

Finn clears his throat, shooting me a glance that's half apology, half intrigue. "We've got some cherry wood in the back. You want to take a look?"

"I do."

As he leads me deeper into the yard, Nixon hangs back. Watching. Assessing.

And for the first time, I don't mind.

7

NIXON

Scarlet touches a walnut slab like it's capable of appreciating her gentle reverence. Her fingers trace the grain the way I've only ever seen Finn do, as if the wood is speaking to her and she's listening carefully for its secrets.

I lean against the beam out of reach, arms crossed, watching her. She doesn't notice. She's too lost in her work. I didn't expect to like that about her.

"You're good with your hands," I say before I can stop myself.

She glances at me over her shoulder, brows raised. "You wouldn't believe how often people assume I pick out colors and shapes and call myself a furniture designer."

I can believe it. A woman like her, who's fine-boned and feminine, but wrapped in lean muscle and strong opinion, must confuse people. They want to put her in a box, but she doesn't fit. I rub my beard, considering her.

Reed emerges from the side shed, wiping sawdust off his chest, looking far too pleased to see her. I grit my teeth. He's got that look again, the one that always precedes him doing or saying something idiotic.

"Careful, Red," he drawls. "Keep caressing that slab like that and it'll start groaning."

Scarlet laughs a short burst that's bright and real, and the sound hits me like a punch.

Reed is a pain in the ass, but he knows how to bring joy to people. I don't. That's not my job.

I lead. I protect. I carry the weight.

Laughter isn't part of what makes an alpha.

I wait until Reed disappears again before stepping forward.

"You like this one?" I point to the slab she's caressing. "We've got a few more from the same tree. Took it down last fall. An old black walnut. Finn cried when we milled it."

She smiles, tucking a strand of beautiful red hair behind her ear. "I might cry, too, when I run my hand across it one more time."

I'm not prepared for the image she creates of her hands moving over my chest, her lips parting. Fuck. I turn away.

"Cherry, walnut, oak. You name it, we've cut it," I say, trying to rein in the heat rising in my blood. "We can handle any size order. Even rush jobs if the client is worth the time."

Her gaze pins me. "Am I?"

I tip my head. "You tell me."

There's a pause. Tension coils between us, laced with unspoken intention.

Scarlet shifts her weight on her crutch, her jeans hugging long legs and curving hips that are not helping my self-control. She's not even trying to be sexy, and that's what makes it worse. Everything about her is unfiltered. Her irritation, her fascination, and her defiance. She holds nothing back and I don't know how to deal with such transparent, deeply felt emotions.

"You should get off that foot," I say finally. "You're pushing it."

"I'm not glass," she says, jaw lifting.

No, she's steel. And fire. And temptation in human form.

"Even steel bends," I mutter, stepping closer. "And I'd rather not carry you back again if you collapse in the damn dirt."

She laughs again. "You say it like it was a chore. You didn't seem that bothered when you had your arms wrapped around me."

I stare at her, silence stretching. She stares right back, defiant and amused. Daring me.

God, she makes me want to bite something. Her, mostly, in soft places like her ass, her breasts, and the inside of her thighs.

Her neck.

Claim her, my wolf growls in my mind, always impatient.

"I wasn't," I say quietly.

And that's the truth.

She doesn't know how close she's come to discovering what I am, what we all are, and the only thing more dangerous than that is how much I want her anyway.

I take a step toward her, caught in the soft part of her lips, and the curve of her palm still ghosting over the walnut slab.

And I *want*.

Fuck, I want her with a desperation that's almost violent.

Then I scent who's approaching before he comes into

46

view, as it cuts through the whiff of sawdust like a warning.

"Company," Reed calls from across the yard.

I turn toward the entrance, already knowing who it is.

"Stay here," I tell Scarlet. My hand lands firmly on her shoulder for a second. She tenses but doesn't ask why.

I step outside before she does.

Hunter's already halfway to me, wearing his usual scowl and smelling like fresh pine, irritation, and enemy, even though he isn't. The man's built like a semi-truck and has all the subtlety of one.

"We scented it," he says, no greeting.

"Last night?"

"Who was he?"

"Rival pack," I say, voice tight. "The same ones you chased off."

Hunter's brows lift as he scents the air. "She yours?"

Jesus. His bear senses are almost as good as my wolf ones. "Yes, but no."

He snorts. "I know how that is."

It took him a while to claim his mate, so I guess he understands that it isn't always a straightforward process.

I shoot him a look.

He lets it go, but barely. "I followed the trail halfway to the old creek. It ended too fast. It's like he vanished."

My gut tightens. Reed and Finn should have finished him and left his body outside territory lines, but he was fast, and the scent of our mate tore the rug from under us all.

"I don't like it any more than you do," I remind him. "They might be my kind, but that's where the similarities end."

"You still intend to keep them out of this area?"

He doesn't bother to conceal the hope in his voice, and

I don't think any less of him for it. He has two small boys and a mate to worry about. The last thing he wants right now is a battle between feral wolves and his family.

"I am." I glance toward the shed. Through the window, I can just make out Scarlet's silhouette. She's moving slowly, careful on her ankle, running her hand along another stack of timber like she's feeling for a pulse.

"Now more than ever." I run my fingers through my hair. "She doesn't know anything."

"She doesn't need to," Hunter says. "Yet. But you can't hide what you are forever, and she can't ignore what she is to you forever, either."

"You ever wonder why the fuck this works like this. Human women and shifters?"

"In the old days, it was easier. Raid a village. Carry off a bride. Wait until they stop hating you for claiming them and start loving being owned by an animal."

"I'm glad it doesn't work that way anymore," I say. "No way I want a reluctant mate in my bed."

"So, you're going to take your time to claim her? Even with a threat at your door?"

"I don't have a choice, Hunter."

He turns to stare into the depths of the forest that we both call home. "My brothers felt the same. They were right to have patience."

"I'll take care of it and her," I say. Then, remembering he's come out of his way to meet me today, I reach out my hand. "But I appreciate your eyes and ears, and your collaboration."

We shake, although it's alien to touch a man who should be my enemy, like our bodies were forged to repel each other, and our tentative truce is going against our natures.

"How is your family?" I ask, and before my eyes, his serious expression is transformed by wonder.

"I waited a long time for this happiness," he says. "Cubs and a mate have brought life and laughter to our dusty old house."

"That's good," I say. "Blessings to you all."

"And blessings to you. May your mate be fruitful."

Scarlet.

She's not claimed. She's not mine yet, but the thought of breeding her makes my wolf howl and my body flare.

"Thank you."

Hunter heads back toward the trees. His boots crunch over the gravel, then fade into silence as he disappears. In a few seconds, his bear scent intensifies. He's shifted and will now be bounding through the forest towards home.

And me? I'm already turning toward Scarlet again, knowing the only way to sate my wolf is to be in her orbit.

8

SCARLET

By late afternoon, I'm tired in a way I didn't expect. Not just physically, though my ankle still aches like hell, but mentally. Emotionally.

Spending time with these men is like standing in the center of a hurricane. There's tension in the air and a pull between us that I don't understand.

And yet, nothing bad has happened.

Unless you count Nixon carrying me around, whether I want him to or not. Or Finn smothering me with over-caring attentiveness. Or Reed making me laugh and threatening to take his clothes off again.

In fact, I've laughed more today than I have in weeks.

By the time I'm sitting in the soft chair in their living room, a mug of coffee in hand, I realize something strange.

I feel safe.

That should probably scare me more than it does.

"I should get my stuff from the motel," I say, mostly to the room.

Nixon's eyes flick to mine from where he's leaning against the doorframe. "I'll take you." I guess he changed his mind about Finn going alone.

"I can walk," I say automatically, even though I have no idea where I am or which way to walk. My independent streak is hard to bury when I've spent my whole life being told never to rely on anyone.

He raises a brow. "You hobbled across my lumberyard like a baby deer. You're not walking anywhere."

There's no bite in his voice this time. No smugness. Only… fact. He's watching me too closely again, like he's waiting for me to object. I don't.

"Okay," I say. "Let's go."

He blinks with surprise, then reaches out for the keys that rest on another beautifully crafted piece of furniture.

The drive into town is peaceful. The sun's slipping low in the sky, gilding the tops of the pines in yellow and orange. I roll the window open a crack and let the fresh air cool my face.

Nixon drives like he does everything else, with quiet intensity. He grips the wheel tightly, and he handles the truck like it's an extension of his body with strong, scarred hands that look like they were made to shape the world.

I pull out my phone, shocked to find service bars again, and type a quick message to my mom.

All okay. Working with a lumber yard. Doing business. Don't worry. Will call soon.

There. She won't freak out and report me missing. Not yet, anyway.

The motel is as depressing as I remember, with cracked paint, a faded sign, and the scent of stale air clinging to the breeze outside.

51

"I've got it from here," I say when Nixon pulls into a spot near my room.

"No, you don't," he says, already out of the truck.

Before I can argue, he's circling around to my side, opening the door, and offering a hand. I hesitate for a beat, then take it. His palm is warm and callused, steadying me as I ease onto my good foot.

We move slowly across the lot, Nixon hovering close but not crowding. When we reach my door, I unlock it and push it open.

"Let me make sure it's clear," he says.

I raise a brow. "You worried my underwear's going to attack me?"

He gives me a look and disappears inside before I can respond.

By the time I step in, leaning heavily on my crutch, he's already scanned the room like an elite bodyguard. Satisfied, he steps aside to let me pass.

I sit on the edge of the bed, gathering my things and mentally checking off what I brought with me for this trip: toiletries, sketchbook, phone charger.

"You rest," Nixon says, already moving toward the corner where my bag lies half-open. "I've got it."

I watch him kneel, this enormous, muscle-thick man, who methodically packs my things. He folds my T-shirt like valuable silk Kimonos, sets my hairbrush in a side pocket, then—

His hand pauses.

Panties. A lacy black pair.

He holds them for a second too long, frozen in place.

Our eyes meet.

My face flushes instantly. "I—I can get that—"

But he doesn't look away or make a joke. He sets them carefully in the bag, zips it shut, and stands.

My mouth is dry.

"There," he says, voice low and raspy. "All set."

I nod. "Thanks."

The air between us is thicker now. More charged like something has shifted, and we're both dancing around, pretending it hasn't.

When he takes my bag and holds the door open, I hobble out without another word.

As we pull out of the parking lot, a woman steps into the crosswalk ahead of us, guiding a wide stroller with two toddlers kicking and chattering in tandem. They're dressed in little fleece hoodies, one red and one yellow, and are deep in some toddler babble argument over a sippy cup.

The woman pushes the stroller with practiced ease, golden hair braided over one shoulder, a tote bag slung across her back. She moves like someone used to multitasking, taking motherhood in her stride. Beside her, a man walks close. Too close to be a friend or a helpful neighbor. He's tall and broad, with shoulders like a linebacker and a beard that gives me déjà vu. There's something in the way he watches the road, the stroller, and the world with an alertness that reminds me of Nixon. I turn to him and find him lifting his hand and giving the man a brief nod. The man returns it, but it doesn't seem open or friendly; instead, it appears a little wary.

The woman smiles at us as we pass, her wide mouth holding none of the man's guardedness. But behind that smile is curiosity. Her gaze catches mine like a hook. She doesn't look away.

It's like she's assessing me. Like I've walked into her

story uninvited, and she's trying to decide what role I'll play.

The truck clears the street, and I glance back once, watching as the twins wriggle and the woman crouches to fix a shoe that's half off one little foot. The man stands behind her like a sentry, solid and watchful.

And for one irrational second, something sharp twists beneath my breastbone.

The hollow ache of what I lost before it was ever had.

I swallow and look away.

"They're cute," I murmur, voice flat. "The kids."

Nixon doesn't respond.

"Who are they?" I ask a little louder. "Friends of yours?"

"Neighbors."

"Friendly ones?"

His jaw tightens. "Complicated."

Which, in Nixon-speak, says everything.

I turn back toward the window, pretending I'm watching the trees blur past.

But in my head is a different voice entirely. My doctor's soft, clinical, apologetic tone.

Low ovarian reserve... less than ten percent... pregnancy is unlikely without intervention.

I was twenty-six at the time.

Since then, every man I've told has looked away, or smiled and said it didn't matter, then slowly pulled away when they realized I wasn't going to be their fresh start. Their breeder. Their dream of a happy family.

Even the good ones couldn't help it. Biology shouts louder than love.

I grip the seatbelt tighter.

This isn't what I came here for. I didn't walk into these woods looking for a future. I came for lumber. For business.

For a break from the grind of everyday life.

So why does that woman's curious glance stay with me longer than it should?

9

REED

There's something deeply satisfying about feeding people. Watching shoulders loosen. Listening to plates clatter and drinks pour, and that one sound everyone makes when they take a bite of something that tastes better than they expected.

Tonight, that sound comes from Scarlet.

She makes it around the third bite of the venison stew I slow-cooked all afternoon. Finn baked the bread, I handled the meat, and Nixon? Well, he stood brooding like a thundercloud with his arms folded.

Scarlet's curled up on the couch now, one foot up, ankle wrapped and iced, cheeks pink from the firelight and the glass of wine she's halfway through swirling like a woman who knows her vintages, even though I'm ninety percent sure she selected it from the rack because of wolves on the label.

She's on her second glass now. Which means she's a little too relaxed to remember she popped painkillers after dinner.

Just enough to make her edges smudge.

I like her like this when the walls she keeps so neatly stacked show cracks. And what's behind them?

Interesting as hell.

"So," I say, refilling her glass with a grin that Nixon will growl at me for later, "Scarlet. Tell us something spicy."

Her laugh is bright and genuine, and she sets her glass onto the polished wood with dramatic care. "Why do I feel like this is a trap?"

"It's not a trap," I lie. "It's a bonding exercise. You share, we share. Next thing you know, we're best friends. Or better."

Nixon, who's nursing a beer in the corner like it personally insulted him, clears his throat and barks into my mind *you're pushing it, Reed.*

I ignore him. This is my lane.

"I don't have much spice to share," Scarlet says, her tone playful but with a thread of honesty woven through. "Unless disappointing sex and trust issues count as kinks."

I raise a brow. "Only in sad town."

She snorts. "Then I'm the queen of kinks."

Finn winces from the kitchen where he's cleaning up. "That sounds bleak."

Scarlet shrugs, swirling her wine again. "I dated a guy once who called himself an alpha in bed. Which basically meant he ordered me around, never made me come, and then told me I was lucky to have him."

"Sounds like a winner," I say.

"Oh yeah. Five stars. Would recommend to my worst enemy."

She's flushed now, tipsy and free talking, and Nixon's

practically radiating heat from the other side of the room. Not the sexy kind. The *I'm going to rip Reed's tongue out with my teeth* kind.

I meet his eyes and grin.

I top off Scarlet's glass again to keep the mood moving, and this time she lifts it like a toast, eyes sparkling with tipsy boldness.

"Careful," I say, settling beside her on the arm of the couch. "Keep looking at me like that and you're going to hurt my feelings when you don't climb into my lap."

"You have feelings?"

"Somewhere deep beneath the charm and perfectly sculpted biceps, yes."

She laughs, and her shoulders drop a little more, tension leaking out of her like heat from a wound. We're seeing what she's like when there's nothing to prove.

"Don't get too comfortable," she says, cocking a brow. "I still don't trust you."

"Fair," I say. "But do you *like* me?"

A pause. Then she bites her lip, trying not to smile. "Unfortunately."

Finn wanders in from the kitchen then, wiping his hands on a towel, and Nixon shifts in the corner. This is the moment.

Fuck it. This is how you get people to trust you. Not with rules and silence. With stories. By being *human*.

Or, in our case, pretending to be.

"You guys ever play Truth or Dare?" Finn asks, surprisingly casual for someone who usually speaks like he's rationing words.

Scarlet snorts. "What, like teenagers at a sleepover?"

"More like grown-ass adults with liquor and

questionable morals," I say. "Our version's better. Higher stakes. No dumb dares like licking doorknobs."

Nixon makes a noise in his throat, the sound of a man realizing this is spiraling, but it's too late to stop.

"Fine," Scarlet says. "Hit me. Truth."

I grin. "Most adventurous place you've had sex?"

She hesitates, then shrugs. "A dining table. In a showroom. With the lights on."

Finn raises a brow, clearly impressed. Nixon looks like he might combust.

"My turn," she says. "Finn. Truth or dare."

He considers, then answers, "Truth."

Scarlet grins. "Same question."

Finn leans one shoulder against the wall, relaxed. "Dining table. One I made. Six coats of hand-rubbed oil finish. Sturdy as hell."

I laugh. "He's humble."

Finn shrugs, eyes glinting. "I take pride in my work. All my work."

Scarlet's face is flushed now, whether from the wine or the imagery, I can't tell.

"Reed," she says, turning to me. "Truth or dare?"

"Truth, baby. Always."

"What's your thing? Like, in bed."

"Oh, we're going there." I wink. "Dirty talk. I like using my voice. Filthy things whispered in the dark. I like hearing a woman fall apart from the sound of it."

Scarlet shifts, her lips parting slightly.

"Your turn," I say, but before I can ask, Finn cuts in.

"Nixon."

Nixon lifts his eyes slowly, like he's only now acknowledging that he's part of this game.

"Truth," he growls.

"What's your thing?" Finn asks, even though he knows. He's caught onto my game, and he's playing it like a pro.

Nixon pauses enough to make me nervous, then he admits the truth. "Control."

Scarlet swallows.

Nixon adds, "Orders. Trust given little by little. I like surrender, not when it's forced but when it's given willingly."

Nobody says anything for a beat.

Then I lean closer to Scarlet with a grin. "And we all like to watch."

Her fingers tighten around the stem of her wine glass, and her lashes lower like she's trying to blink something away.

She doesn't speak right away.

And that pause?

That's golden.

Because she's not shocked or offended. She's thinking about it.

Her voice, when it comes, is quiet... *careful.*

"That's a lot of attention."

I tilt my head. "Only if you want it."

Finn folds his arms across his chest and leans against the wall, studying her with the same quiet attention he gives to his carving.

"Most people don't want to be watched," she adds, gaze flicking between us. "They want to pretend they're not being seen at all."

"Then they've never been looked at the right way." Nixon's voice commands without raising volume. "When a woman is really seen by someone who knows what they're doing… it changes things."

Scarlet shifts in her seat, wine glass trembling slightly as she sets it on the table.

"What if I'm not someone who likes being watched?" she asks.

Finn's the one who answers, his voice gentle but sure. "Have you tried it? I think you'll like it"

Scarlet stares at him and smiles. It's small and a little crooked, tinged with playful danger.

"You're confident."

I chuckle. "We're not offering theory, sweetheart."

Her laugh is a little shaky, her tongue's looser than usual, and her eyes are too shiny to lie.

"I can't believe I'm having this conversation with three men I barely know," she mutters.

"You'll know us better soon enough," Nixon says.

Scarlet arches a brow. "That a threat or a promise?"

"Whichever gets you to stay."

And *fuck*, the way she looks at him after that? Like her whole body listened before her brain caught up.

But then the moment shifts. The flicker of tension, the weight of the wine, maybe too much heat too fast. She sways slightly and stands, blinking as if surprised by the room's movement.

"I think I need a bathroom break," she says, more to herself than anyone.

Finn's already up. "End of the hall. Second door."

She nods, not quite meeting any of our eyes now, and makes her way down the hall, hobbling as she goes.

When she's out of earshot, Nixon shoots me a glare. "She's not ready."

"No shit," I say. "But she's *thinking about it.*"

Finn watches the hallway like he's already worried she won't come back out.

"She's never been with anyone who knew what the fuck to *do* with her," I add, quieter now. "You heard what she said."

Nixon says nothing.

But the look on his face tells me he did, and he plans to rectify it, soon.

10

SCARLET

I splash cool water on my face in the tiny bathroom, gripping the edge of the sink like it might steady more than my body.

It doesn't.

My pulse is everywhere. My mouth is too dry, and my core is too heavy with heat and want. I've been starved for too long.

Three years without a vacation.

Eighteen months without sex.

And now three men are watching me like I'm made of flame, and they know how to fan me into an inferno.

They don't hide what they want. They're not tempering their desire with polite disinterest or soft apologies. When they look at me, they feast.

I stare at myself in the mirror. My cheeks are flushed from the fire, pupils wide with attraction. My hair's a halo of red waves they could wrap around their fists. There's a part of me, the part raised by warnings and worst-case scenarios, that tells me I should get out while I still can.

But my body?

My body has already made up its mind.

When I return to the living room, Reed is still on the arm of the couch, Finn on a worn leather chair opposite, and Nixon standing with his arms crossed like he's barely holding himself together.

The air thickens as I step inside.

"Better?" Reed asks, voice lighter now, less teasing and more curious.

I nod, sinking slowly back onto the sofa cushion. "I needed a moment."

Nixon's eyes track me like a compass needle swinging north.

Reed passes me my wine. "Still with us?"

I take a sip, slower this time. "Yeah. I am."

Another pause. Then Finn, voice low: "You said you hadn't had much… spice. That you'd been with men who didn't know what you wanted."

I swallow. "Yeah. That's accurate."

"Want to tell us what *you* want?" Reed asks.

I hesitate.

I could say no. I could make a joke and blame the wine for my loose lips, but something raw is opening up inside me, and I'm too tired of being quiet to go back now. Chances like this don't come along often, and this trip was always about stepping out of life for a few days.

"I don't know if I can," I admit.

Nixon moves first.

He walks forward, stopping in front of me. Then he crouches to my level.

"We'd like to please you and watch you," Nixon says,

voice smokey and magnetic. "If you want it, all you have to do is say. Whatever you want, we'll give it to you."

My mouth opens, but no words come.

Nixon's fingers reach out and brush a strand of hair from my cheek. His touch is feather-light and surprisingly reverent.

Then he leans in and kisses me, and all breath and sense leave me in a rush.

His lips are soft, but the kiss is deep, commanding, and patient, all at once, a kiss that doesn't ask for permission so much as it offers a choice. Pull away, and everything we've talked about could become memories. Fall deeper, and they'll make all their promises come true. My hands find his shirt before I realize they've moved, gripping hard, pulling him closer.

I spin into his orbit, my mind drifting through the sky and stars, into the brightness of the full moon. My body is liquid, loosening and priming for everything I fear these men could deliver.

When he finally pulls back, I'm panting and dazed.

Reed and Finn have shifted. They're seated opposite me now on the other couch, drinks abandoned, eyes locked on my mouth.

I sit there between them, lips swollen, heart racing, wine forgotten, like prey that's been trapped in a snare.

11

NIXON

There are two ways to claim a mate.

The first is through force, the old way, hard and fast, rooted in dominance and instinct. It's primal, involving teeth, strength, and possession, and once done, it can't be undone. That permanence is both its power and its poison. A claim like that leaves marks that go deeper than skin; bruises of the spirit can be a bitterness that festers in the bond. I watched it happen to my mother. Her devotion to our father was rooted in tradition only. She submitted because she had to. He conquered because no one ever told him there was another way. His claim worked like fire, fiercely consuming without restraint, leaving the ash of their potential underfoot.

I never saw her look at him with softness in her eyes.

I won't have that with Scarlet.

She's bright and sharp and stubborn in ways that make my wolf rise and my hands ache. She's a challenge in all the ways that make all our spirits want to fly free, and if we do this right, if we take our time, it's my hope she'll bend to our will without breaking the potential for real love within our bond. She'll soften without losing any of that fire. She'll give herself over not because she's overpowered, but because she *wants* to submit.

The second way is through patience. Through care. Through pleasure. Through love.

It's a slower path, yes, but the result is unshakable. When a mate truly chooses you, she doesn't stay because she has to. She roots herself to you, her devotion climbing around her mates like ivy around a great oak. They become one with the earth and sky.

So, I begin with a gentle kiss. I kneel, lowering myself to her level, and press my mouth to hers with purpose. I'm alpha, and she will know it. She responds like a woman who's trying not to show how badly she wants to be touched. Her hands twist in my shirt, pulling me closer. Her mouth parts, lips yielding, tongue brushing mine, willing to taste what she didn't expect to want. She breathes me in and releases the tightly wound parts of her that she arrived clutching so close.

When I pull back, she's flushed and wide-eyed, her chest rising and falling. I watch her, cataloging every little shift: the tremble of her thighs, the heat blooming in her cheeks, the dazed hunger in her eyes.

I slide my hand to her knee, and she jumps slightly, gasping, her body reacting before her mind catches up. I look up, meeting her gaze, and ask, "Yes?"

She's as still as a deer in the moonlight, sensing danger but convincing herself that she's surrounded by nothing but the protection of the forest, ignoring her fear centers in the way that humans have convinced each other is a good thing.

I wait, inhaling her scent that makes my wolf arch under my skin. Human men prey on women like Scarlet, but not anymore.

When she gasps, "Yes," I move slowly. My hand glides up the inside of her thigh, her legs parting in a silent, instinctive response. She invites me. Even through her clothes, I can scent her hunger, and it's familiar in a bone-deep way that settles every longing I've ever had. I press the heel of my palm against her through the denim, and her hips roll.

She's ready.

With deliberate care, I unbutton her jeans, still tasting her mouth in gentle sips. She lifts her hips with barely any encouragement. That's trust. That's surrender, in its first form. I slip my hand beneath the waistband, under the lace, into heat, leaning over her, crowding her.

She's soaked, and I groan, pressing deep, coming home, knowing my brothers are watching it all. My fingers find a slow, even tempo, enough to keep her chasing. Enough to make her tremble. Her breath comes sharp, her thighs tense, and shake. Her hand clenches the cushion as her head tips back. I watch it all, like my brothers, my teeth itching to grip her nape and bite to make her ours. The first time I take her, I won't watch her face as she comes, rutting into her from behind the way us wolves prefer, but I'll feel it, though. She's tight, and we're big.

Then there's the knot.

Scarlet tries to hold back, but of course, she fails.

When she comes, it's with a soft, stunned cry, half-smothered by her hand. She shakes as waves of release crash through a foundation only just cracked open.

When she's done trembling do I withdraw my fingers,

sliding them over my tongue one after another while she watches.

Her taste is warm earth and summer sunshine, and I want to bury myself in it, mark me with her and her with me. Our eyes meet, and she blinks, stunned.

I lift her without asking, and without resistance. She folds into me, boneless and soft, the scent of her satisfaction clinging to everything.

I carry her to the bedroom and lay her gently on the bed.

I don't undress her. I won't stay. Not tonight. This is the beginning.

I tuck the blanket around her and smooth the hair from her temple. She blinks up at me, dazed, dreamy, and already drifting. I press one kiss to her forehead.

"You're safe," I murmur. "And this is the beginning."

Then I walk out even though I don't want to.

My wolf is a growling, ferocious beast who wants to claim what's his. But I'm a man, too, and this is how you build a bond that doesn't break.

The claiming will come.

But first, Scarlet has to *crave* it.

12

SCARLET

Morning arrives with a warm, decadent haze that softens my edges with the memory of Nixon's mouth. I blink until my eyes become accustomed to the soft light filtering through unfamiliar curtains. My skin tingles with awareness and my thighs are heavy and tender with a sweetness I haven't felt in far too long. I lie still, tucked under a thick blanket that smells like the forest, and replay the night in flashes.

Reed, Finn, and Nixon's voices, low and commanding, teasing out my secrets and revealing theirs. The heat of Nixon's mouth on mine and his hand sliding between my legs. The way they all watched me unravel, as if they'd planned it all along.

It doesn't feel real. More like something I imagined in a wine-drunk and lust-dazed state. A fantasy I coaxed out of my deepest, most shameful longings.

But it happened. The orgasm that's still blooming somewhere deep inside me, like a phantom echo pulsing in my core, and the way I opened myself, emotionally, confessing things I hadn't even admitted to myself. Things about my past, my loneliness, my hunger for more. I told them truths I've held locked behind my ribs like fragile glass, and they didn't laugh.

And God, the way Nixon touched with patience and devastating confidence, then walked away, leaving me aching for more. It undid something in me. It shifted the axis of whatever I thought I wanted, replacing it with desire for more.

I swing my legs over the edge of the bed and pause, stretching, still half-expecting my body to ache from too much tension or not enough sleep. But I'm loose like my bones melted eight hours ago and haven't yet knitted themselves back together.

When I open the bedroom door, the warm, homey scent of bacon and brewed coffee curls through the air, but what makes my breath catch isn't breakfast. It's the single red rose lying on the floor outside my door.

A perfect bloom, the color of unripe cherries, wrapped at the base in rustic twine. And a note. *Something scarlet for Scarlet.*

My throat tightens with emotion, and I stoop slowly to pick it up, brushing my fingers along the velvety petals, the scent heady and lush. It's a gift more intimate than any I've received before, this small gesture, thoughtful and precise.

I hobble down to find Reed and Nixon in the kitchen, dressed in jeans and rumpled shirts, casual and maddeningly handsome in the way only men who don't try to be handsome can be. Reed leans against the counter, sipping coffee, while Nixon stands at the stove flipping bacon with determined precision.

They both glance up when I enter.

Reed grins and crosses the room in two strides, pressing a kiss to my cheek like it's the most natural thing in the world. Nixon, who's less overt but no less present, brushes a hand along my spine as I pass, and then kisses my lips so softly, I find myself leaning in for more when he pulls away. His palm warms through the fabric of my shirt.

They're affectionate, but it's like they're deliberately pulling back, giving me space to think. But Reed's gaze lingers, and Nixon's fingers graze mine as he passes me a cup of coffee, and need inside me coils tighter.

"Sleep okay?" Reed asks, voice thick with insinuation, one brow raised as he watches me from across the kitchen island. "You look... relaxed."

I arch an eyebrow, already reaching for the creamer. "Better than expected, considering I slept in a stranger's bed."

"That bed's not a stranger anymore," he says with a wink. "And neither are we... especially Nixon."

Nixon makes a low sound that's probably meant to be disapproving, but there's a ghost of a smile tugging at his mouth, like he's remembering the way I taste, as he sets a plate of eggs and toast in front of me.

"This is too much," I say, overwhelmed by the portion.

"You need to keep your strength up... give your body a chance to heal."

"And..." Reed grins, "for energy."

Energy? Jesus.

"You have a good appetite?" he asks, more seriously. "You'll need it."

"We're heading out to the lumberyard today. You're welcome to come if you want to finalize your order. But tonight—" Nixon glances toward the window, where the trees sway like dark sentinels in the morning breeze. "—we thought we'd grill. Eat outside if the weather holds."

"Outside?" I sip my coffee. "Is that safe? Aren't there... wild things in these woods?"

Reed leans in, voice low. "Only if you wander off the path."

Finn appears at the back door, smiling. "Or if you invite them in."

I blink. The way they exchange subtle and unreadable glances sets something twisting low in my gut.

"Speaking of wild things," I say slowly, "what happened to that giant dog?"

There's a pause. One breath too long. The kind that reveals secrets lurking beneath.

Finn clears his throat. "He's tame. You don't have to worry about him. He goes where he wants."

Nixon follows with a nod. Reed grins into his coffee like a man remembering a joke.

Right. That's not suspicious at all.

I let it drop for now, even as questions needle at me.

"What can I contribute tonight?" I ask instead. "I guess your grilling expertise doesn't extend to dessert."

Reed perks up. "Dessert?"

I shrug. "I make a mean muffin. Blueberry. Sometimes apple-cinnamon if I'm in an ambitious mood."

"Apple," Finn says quietly.

Reed tilts his head. "We'll need to supervise that. Thoroughly. Taste-test the batter. Maybe twice."

"You're our guest," Nixon says. "You don't have to cook."

"Maybe not," I reply, "but I don't want to lie around looking pretty while you do all the work."

Reed leans forward, grin sharpening. "Lying around looking pretty is *exactly* what I want you to do."

"Don't mind him," Finn murmurs. "He was raised by wolves."

I snort. Nixon's mouth twitches.

Outside, the sun is climbing past the treetops, and everything feels normal. A woman and three men in a cabin in the woods, drinking coffee and making plans, as if the tension isn't palpable and the world outside these walls doesn't thrum with danger.

This could be a life for another woman who didn't know the danger of strangers and wasn't sure that her brokenness would fracture anything good.

As Nixon and Reed leave for the lumberyard, Reed throws a wink over his shoulder and says, "Try not to seduce Finn while we're gone."

"I'll do my best," I murmur, but the smile that pulls at my mouth contains more than humor. Even though I'd never admit it, the idea of kissing Finn, and discovering if he kisses like his stern brother, is what I'm thinking about as they leave.

Finn stays behind. He's quieter and more restrained than the others, but there's a magnetism in his calm and silence that draws me in. He's a kindred spirit with his creativity, and I find that artistic part of him intriguing.

"I want to show you something," he says after a moment.

"Sure." I grab my crutch in readiness.

Finn walks out back to a workshop nestled between the trees. I'm still hobbling, but my mobility has improved overnight. His place of work is a rustic outbuilding with sunlight pouring through sawdust-clouded windows onto rows of tools, carved wood, and unfinished projects that hum with potential. The space is warm and smells like pine and varnish, scents that are familiar and relaxing.

"This is where I work," he says simply, watching as I take it all in.

I run my fingers over a narrow table, the scrollwork delicate and elegant, the craftsmanship so fine. "You made this?"

"Yeah. From ash. Good for detail. Strong."

"It's beautiful," I whisper, and I mean it. Not just the table but the whole space that exudes the same calm energy as Finn.

"You should sell them," I say. "I could list them on my website. I know people who would love these."

He hesitates. "I don't think—"

"Let me try a few pieces. You can decide the prices. I won't take a cut until I prove there's demand."

He looks at me for a long moment, then gives a reluctant nod. "It's not about the money, Scarlet, but okay."

His pause tightens my belly. We're standing too close. There's something carved into the lines of his face, and his dark eyes hold mine, staring like he sees into places I usually keep locked. His forearms flex with quiet strength, veins and tendons shifting beneath sun-kissed skin, and his hands... God, those hands. Rough from his works, but elegance in motion. Beautiful, not because of what they look like but for what they can craft. I wonder what they'd feel like on my waist and in my hair, maybe between my thighs. His hand brushes mine, and the air tightens between us. His gaze drops to my mouth, and my heart trips in my chest.

For a second, I think he's going to kiss me.

I *want* him to kiss me.

Would it burn with the same heat as Nixon's, or would it be softer and quieter, like Finn?

He steps back instead, clears his throat, and turns away, and the loss of his attention is so sharp it surprises me.

"How about this?" he says, waving toward a small table. "And this?" The chair is intricately carved and mirror-polished.

"Definitely. What about this?"

I trail my fingers over a shelving unit with flared legs that seem to emerge from the ground like they're anchored to roots.

"Okay."

"I can do it now, if you price them."

He pulls out a worn, yellowed notebook that curls at the edges. His pen, in contrast, is a beautiful, gold-tipped fountain pen, and his writing is an elegant cursive that fills me with envy for its neatness.

I lean my crutch against the wall and shuffle into position to photograph the items. I can crop them and adjust the backgrounds to better match my website theme. In a matter of minutes, I have the images completed. Finn passes me his costs and the price he'd like to charge for each piece, which are way below what I'd have suggested. Taking the pen from his hand, I write the prices I'm going to list next to his.

"Seriously?"

"Trust me," I say. "Rich people don't value anything cheap."

He shakes his head. "You have people who pay that much."

"For craftsmanship like this? Of course. These are unique pieces with an origin story. Can I take a picture of you to feature? People love to see the creator responsible."

He seems reluctant, but I hold up my phone.

"I'm not smiling," he says, through gritted teeth.

"Even better. Nothing appeals more than a handsome, tortured artist."

"Three descriptors that have never been applied to me."

I stare at him through the screen, wondering how that could be true. His features are artful and beautiful in a way that hurts to look at for too long. There's a wildness to him that makes me want to discover more.

"What about a bio?"

"Whatever you think?" He shakes his head. "Nixon won't like this."

"Why?"

"He's a private person."

"So, don't tell him. If nothing sells, no harm, no foul."

Finn hesitates, rubbing between his eyes.

Jeez. He's really stressed about his brother's reaction in a way that doesn't seem rational. Why does Nixon have so much power over what Finn does, and why the desire for privacy?

I sit on a low workbench, working on the images as Finn sweeps the floor and collects the wood dust in a dustpan and brush. When I've completed Finn's page and added the chair, I notice that I have service. Messages from my mom and friends spill into my inbox, but I'm driven to complete this task while I can. I finish my edits and pull up the live webpage. He takes my phone, squinting at his photo and the edited image of his masterpiece in wood.

"You did all this now?"

He meets my eyes, and my heart stutters.

"Yeah. Is it good? I can get the others up now."

"It's…" He shakes his head. "You're really something, Scarlet."

I'm not a woman who blushes easily, but I do now. To distract from my raging flush, I take my phone and add the small table, but it rings in my hand before I get a chance. Finn startles, then leans back against his workbench, folding his muscular arms across his broad chest.

"Hello?"

"Scarlet, Hi! It's Amber Sinclair. I saw the chair you listed, and I want it. Tell me it hasn't sold yet."

"No. Not yet."

Finn tips his head to one side.

"He's a new furniture designer, right?" she asks.

"He's well established in his small town," I tell her. "I was lucky to get some pieces from his current collection."

"Could he make another one?" she asks. "A matching set?"

"Well, it won't be a perfect match," I say. "That's the beauty of what he makes. It showcases the wood, and each piece will have unique aspects."

"That's perfect," Amber says. "I'll transfer the money for both now."

I mouth to Finn, "When can you finish another chair?"

He's startled, straightening and uncrossing his arms. "Two weeks?"

"Delivery will be in five weeks," I say. "Does that work for you?"

"Perfect." She sighs. "I can't believe how perfect they'll be for the hallway in our cabin."

"I'm so happy you like Finn's work."

We say our goodbyes, and I smile as Amber's payment lands in my account immediately. That woman is the perfect customer.

"One down," I say. "I hope you're ready to get to work. I suspect you're going to be rushed off your feet."

Finn shakes his head, the corners of his lips lifting. "If Nixon doesn't have anything to say about it."

13

REED

When Finn and Scarlet pull up at the lumberyard, Finn guides her out of the car with the careful gentleness he reserves for things he treasures. I'm a tough guy but seeing my brother stare at our future mate with wide, open eyes and a heart to match, puts a fucking lump in my throat.

Nixon pulled me aside earlier, instructing me to stall Scarlet from making a final order. Once that's done, she has no more reason to stay. But knowing Finn, he'll want to meet all her needs. He has trouble saying no.

It's delicate, this dance we're doing. She wants to finalize and go home, and Nixon intends to give her time to develop feelings for us and be certain of her choice before we claim her and make her ours forever.

Hope is a tricky thing. It slips in as soft as sawdust, and before you know it, you're building castles in your head.

I never thought I'd want something this badly, but Scarlet is hot as a wildfire, and I'm ready to burn.

So, I set the plan in motion, sweeping my gaze over the

stacked beams as I say, "We've got a special delivery of reclaimed cherry, oak, and maple due in tomorrow or the day after. It's worth waiting for, right? We can draft your list now, from the stock we have, and do a final walk-through when the new stock arrives."

Scarlet looks at her list and the yard piled high with lumber and seems torn. When her eyes return to me, they're slightly narrowed, assessing. Is it a stalling tactic, she's thinking? Or could she be missing out on some excellent wood?

I grin at the innuendo. Between Nixon, Reed, and me, we'd show her the kind of wood she's only dreamed about experiencing. Mate bonding sex is like nothing else. I wish I could tell her without terrifying her. Right now, any kind of confession would send her running from the big bad wolves who want to eat her up.

"A draft list... we can do that."

Relief washes through me. That was easier than I thought.

We head to the big shed, her heels crunching softly on the gravel. She unfolds her notebook, and I lean in close, watching as she writes dimensions, finishes, and grain details. Nixon stands nearby, arms folded, tense from the sweet scent of our mate that lingers. I watch Scarlet relax into the process, her brow smoothing and appetite sharpening.

She discusses furniture with Finn, and I smile as they bond over carving and varnish techniques, and passion swells between them. As we finish the draft list, our hands brush as she flips a page, lingering long enough to make me smile some more.

***

81

The drive home is quietly comfortable. We crawl through the narrow road as trees arch above us like sentries. Scarlet spends the time looking at her phone with an adorable V between her brows.

As we pull into the cabin's clearing, Nixon halts, lifts his head, nostrils flaring in an animal silence. "Finn." Without a word, Finn opens the door and walks into the forest, leaving Scarlet staring after him. I step out of the vehicle and open her door, using my body to block her view of Finn, who is shifting to investigate the stench of an unfamiliar wolf that's woven around our home.

My eyes meet Nixon's over the truck, as he turns to smile at Scarlet. "I've been dreaming about those muffins all day."

She glances over her shoulder, then back at Nixon. Her lips part, but she must decide against asking the question that lingers on her tongue because she follows us inside.

In the kitchen, I slide onto a stool as Scarlet unpacks ingredients from our well-stocked pantry: flour, sugar, and baking soda. She finds butter and eggs in the fridge, apples on the counter. Finally, she turns in my direction. "Vanilla? Cinnamon?"

"We have both."

"I'm impressed."

"We may be bachelors, but that doesn't mean we're incompetent heathens."

"Who bakes when I'm not around?"

"Finn mostly," I admit. "He has a sweet tooth."

"It's a disgrace," Nixon says, with an armful of meat. I know he wants to follow up with *what kind of wolf prefers brownies to steak*, but he can't.

Scarlet snorts and sets to preparing muffins from a recipe in her pretty head and fills the cabin with sweetness.

Nixon and I prepare the fire pit, positioning the grill and cleaning vegetables. We tease about where we learned to cook: me, on weekend camping trips with my cousins; him, perfectionism taught by our mother. We laugh about how men always seem to gravitate to meat. "It's savage," Scarlet says, but her eyes tell a different story, lingering as I turn a steak slowly to get the char just right. Wine flows, deep red and heavy in our glasses, like foreplay.

Midway through muffin baking and steak sizzling, the front door clicks, and Finn slips back in, his wolf fur sleek and black, gold wolf eyes softening when he looks at Scarlet. She gasps, stepping back, heart thudding, until I step forward to pat Finn's broad, damp shoulders. Scarlet straightens as though she's winning an internal battle to be brave. When Finn pads toward her and nuzzles her hand, the transformation in Scarlet is beautiful. Fear shifts to wonder, and strength sparks in her stance. She leans over, brushing his muzzle, and his tail flicks with gratitude. Nixon watches with the intensity of an alpha in wait.

"Where did it come from?" Scarlet asks. "Does it live outside? Does it belong to someone else?"

"Looks like it wants to belong to you," I laugh.

She smiles almost shyly. "My apartment's barely big enough for me, let alone a giant animal. I think my super would have something to say about it. Pretty sure giant wolf-dogs are excluded from my rental agreement."

I don't want to think about her in a tiny apartment, far away from us.

Wolf-Finn whines, making Scarlet jump, then he pads back out of the cabin. When she attempts to follow, I gently grip her elbow. "Let him go," I say. "He likes to roam free."

"Don't we all," she whispers.

83

***

When Finn returns in human form, complete with rumpled clothing that is damp from the forest floor and warm pink cheeks, we gather outside, easing the door closed so Scarlet can't overhear. We can communicate using our mental channel but it's harder to debate and discuss that way.

"What did you find out?" Nixon says, focusing all his attention on Finn.

"Gregory's pack. It wasn't only one. The scent of them spread through our territory like they were hunting for something."

"Scarlet?" I ask.

Finn shrugs and takes a long tug of beer from the cool bottle he grabbed from the table. "They wanted her, but we don't know if that was planned or if she was in the wrong place at the wrong time."

"If not Scarlet, who?" Nixon barks.

"I don't know. There was a human scent there, too. Female. I tried to follow it, but I lost it at the stream."

Nixon growls, scraping his hands through his hair. "We can't leave Scarlet alone, but we need to investigate this further. I want to know who was in the forest, and what Gregory's pack is planning."

"You think they'll attack?"

He stares into the tree line, his brows drawn low like he's hoping to look into the future. Gregory is the most unhinged alpha in the state. He tried to start a war with Hunter and his brothers. I wouldn't put anything past him.

The door behind us slides open.

"Is the food ready?" Scarlet asks, bearing a plate of finished muffins.

"It sure is, sweetheart," I lick my lips hungrily.

We gather around the outside table. The muffins are warm, and they scent the air with the sweetness of vanilla, cinnamon, and apple. The plates are piled high with grilled vegetables and thick-sliced steak. The woodsmoke curls through twilight, whipped away by a burst of fall-scented breeze.

Wine glasses wait to be refilled.

"Where did you go?" Scarlet asks Finn. "Leaving the hard work to the rest of us and turning up when it's ready for eating."

"Last-minute meeting about lumber," he says, using his fork to stab the top steak. It drips juice, and my mouth waters.

"In the forest?"

"Is there a better place to talk about wood?"

She blinks. "I guess not." But her gaze trails him, cataloging all the signs that might contradict his far-fetched tale. The leaf poking from the neck of his undershirt catches my eye, and I snort, but I don't brush it away. No point in drawing attention to it.

Nixon reaches for Scarlet's hand across the table, his thumb dragging along her pulse point; he kisses her temple when she smiles back, soft as a promise. Finn and I exchange a look, tension humming. Memories of last night and her release flood my mind, and I'm so eager to get through this part of the evening that I almost knock over my wine in my haste to assemble a plate of food.

The flush in Scarlet's cheeks intensifies as she eats and drinks, and a light sheen forms on her skin. Is she as excited as we are? Her scent intensifies, and Nixon's nostrils flare. When he closes his eyes, tension bunching his shoulders, I clap him on the back to jolt him from his lust-soaked fantasies.

Scarlet washes down the last of her wine with a slow grace and then glances between us. I lean forward and inhale her sweet, aroused scent, then ask her in a voice that's as low as the embers in the firepit. "You okay?"

She nods, breathing deeper. Alcohol, heat, and lust swirl inside her, releasing a steadily increasing heady perfume that tantalizes us all. The forest around us seems to draw closer. We've built this moment carefully, and there's no turning back.

This is a ritual as old as time.

We will claim her, but will it be tonight?

14

SCARLET

Even as my hands slip into the sudsy warmth of dishwater, scrubbing away sauce and char from our plates, my thoughts are far from the kitchen sink. They're focused on the subtle brush of Nixon's fingertips along my collar last night, and in the way the evening's wine has made me soft and pliable. They're anchored in the quiet masculinity these men carry so naturally and the way it makes me want to be soft enough to bend to their desires.

Reed's casual confidence hums in my chest, and Finn's earlier shy pride makes my skin prickle from the inside out. Nixon's solid, calm presence and the way he took me apart like he knew my body already, vibrates inside me.

I breathe evenly, despite my heart pounding like I've sprinted through the forest. Even when I feel so small between them, the thought of being lost in their arms is one of safety, like I've always belonged here.

My mom's voice echoes in my head. *Men know how to get women to spread their legs. They know how to take from you, especially when they're handsome.* She has a warning for everything, but strangers and men are at the top of her hit list.

Nixon, Reed, and Finn aren't strangers anymore. I know what books they like; Reed is partial to comedic sci-fi, Nixon to history, and Finn to artists' biographies. I know that they're new to the area and don't have any family living nearby. I know that Finn likes country music, and Reed prefers seventies Rock. Nixon is more of a classical man because he finds lyrics distracting.

Slowly but surely, I'm creating a layered picture of them that tells me it's safe to lower my guard.

I push aside questions about the huge wolf-dog and the strangeness of Finn's sudden disappearance into the woods.

They move around me as we finish the dishes, and my head spins with a torrent of fantasies. Three strong, handsome men, their hands working over my body with those rough, callused palms, sliding up my thighs, cupping me, and teasing me. Their pretty eyes are watching everything. I can almost taste the heat and salt of their skin, hear Reed's soft chuckle, Finn's reassurances, and Nixon's orders. I pinch my wrist to jar me back to reality, but the hum of arousal doesn't leave me. I keep scrubbing, but my mind is already counting to what comes next.

Reed settles beside me at the countertop, his arm brushing mine, and the sudden warmth sends a flood of yearning through me. He pours another glass of wine without a word, sliding it into my hand, his lids heavy, and I brace, wanting him to touch me. The wine is cold on my lips, sweet on my tongue, and the muscular press of his thigh against mine subtly shifts us from friendliness to intimacy.

Across the room, Nixon leans against the far wall, arms

crossed, watching us. Finn stands near the sink, running a dish towel through his hands, his expression gentler, but no less attentive. They're both quiet, but their eyes are on us like heat on my skin. It should make me self-conscious. Instead, it sharpens everything.

They like to watch.

I take a long gulp, and as I set the glass on the counter, Reed reaches for my hand, his fingertips grazing my skin with a careful boldness that sends a tremor up my arm. "You okay?"

I nod, but words refuse to come. My throat tightens, my mouth suddenly bone-dry. He watches me with that slow, knowing smile, that peels back layers I didn't know I was hiding behind. Then, without breaking eye contact, he lifts my hand to his lips and kisses each knuckle, one by one, warming them with his mouth.

A tremor shivers down my spine. My skin tingles, tightening with heat. My stomach coils, low and deep, and my thighs clench of their own accord. I'm not thinking anymore, just *feeling*. Every nerve ending sparks to life, drawn to him like he's gravity, and I'm already falling.

Nixon's gaze sharpens and Finn's breath catches, but I don't stop. I don't want to.

All of this is reckless, but how can it be wrong when it feels so right?

A holiday fling, they'd probably call it. What's there to lose when there's so much pleasure to be gained? The idea of forgetting my real life for one night, of setting down the weight of tomorrow and all the ways I don't know how to shape it, is like a drug I can't resist.

Reed leads me from the kitchen and onto the sofa. Nixon and Finn follow, sitting in positions around us where they have a clear view.

A shiver runs over my scalp and tickles my clit.

Reed plays with my hair first, twirling a red tendril around his finger like he's discovered fire and can't decide whether to tame it or let it burn. His eyes dance with that teasing glint I'm coming to recognize as all spark and mischief, but there's fascination there, too. His lips twitch, curving into the kind of smile that shouldn't be legal on a man this beautiful. The black ink that coils over his shoulder peeks from beneath his shirt.

My breath is sawing out of me, but he doesn't rush. He just watches me, patiently letting tension build so that when he finally leans in, his mouth hovers above mine, and the air shudders between us. And when our lips meet, slowly and deliberately, I can taste his warm, wicked smile in the kiss, full of promise.

When he brings a hand to the hem of my blouse, there's a thrill in knowing it's him; that voice that teased me is now undoing the buttons on my shirt. I tense on a wave of arousal that's been building all night.

His fingers slip inside, over lace that's suddenly too tight and too formal, and he snaps my bra open with the sort of light, expert flick that leaves me gasping. His other hand presses firmly against my lower back, pulling me into him until his heart beats against me. My knees tremble, and I clutch the sofa while the other hand drifts to his shoulders, relishing the shift of hardened muscle under his shirt. He's strong, and every brush of his skin against mine charges the air.

Somewhere behind us, a soft groan weaves through the air as Nixon or Finn loses a little of their quiet control.

They're watching.

I don't know which thought excites me more. That all three of them want me, or that they'd watch me when one of them claims me. I slide both hands up under Reed's shirt and anchor them at the small of his back, tangling my fingers in the waistband of his jeans, able and ready to tug him closer.

His mouth descends to my collarbone, then, along the smooth curve of my neck, and I arch into it, panting as his fingers brush over my waist. There's an ardor in his mouth that's slow, hot, and intense, and I let myself sink deeper into him, emptying myself into the moment.

Reed's hand finds the edge of my blouse again, slipping beneath to cup the curve of my breast. His thumb brushes lightly over my nipple, a teasing, feather-soft circle that sends a pulse straight to my core. I gasp, barely, and lift my gaze, finding Nixon in the low light. He's watching from across the room, wine glass forgotten in his hand, his eyes locked on mine like a tether. Just... waiting. Like a wolf on the edge of the clearing, patient and sure that the prey will come to him.

If he asked, I would give it all to them.

And tonight, I think maybe I will.

15

REED

I've dreamed about this.

Not only the way she tastes, though fuck me, that's already written into the back of my throat, but the way she moves. The way she surrenders, like she's been waiting for someone to give her permission to fall apart her whole life. And now she's in my hands, red hair like lava and breath soft as prayer, and I know I'd burn to ash to give her what she needs.

Scarlet's scent rolls through me like a fever, rich and warm and dizzying, and my wolf claws against my chest, hungry to take over. But I don't let it. Not yet. Not when I have her open and gasping. Not when I still have control, and my alpha is watching, not objecting as I taste the treat of our mate before we claim her.

She arches when I tease her nipples again, that sweet little moan punching straight through my gut. I circle one with my thumb until it's a tight little peak, then duck to take it into my mouth, sucking gently. She writhes, her fingers twisted in my hair, and when I glance up, her eyes are half-lidded, and her pupils are blown to dark pools of want.

I should be careful. Nixon's plan was patience, the long game, a slow seduction to draw her in with control. But maybe Nixon didn't kiss her like this or has more restraint than I do.

He's watching now, and I know he's seething in that quiet way of his, because I'm off-script.

I don't care.

Scarlet isn't scared. She isn't second-guessing. Her body's telling me everything I need to know, reeling me in with tendrils of scent that wrap around me, stealing my free will.

I unfasten her jeans and ease them slowly over her hips, giving her time to change her mind, but she doesn't. She lifts her butt instead, her hands sliding to help me, thighs inviting. My wolf growls below the surface, demanding the claim.

She's wearing lace. It's pale pink and already damp, the scent of her slickness hitting me like a brick wall at seventy miles per hour. I groan, low and guttural, as my mouth waters like a slathering dog. If I were less of a man, more of a wolf, I'd rip the damn fabric off with my teeth and bury my face between her thighs, lapping with my rasping tongue until she comes undone.

Instead, I leash that wild thing in me and lay my palm against the heat of her as she grinds into my touch like it's instinct.

"You're soaked," I murmur, half reverent, half wrecked. "Fuck, baby. You're perfect."

She whimpers, hips rocking, and I press a kiss above the lace, then another. She jerks when my tongue traces a stripe over the fabric, and I hold her steady with a hand on her hip. Then I pull the panties aside and finally taste her, slow and deep and thorough, until her thighs shake and her nails bite my shoulders.

Behind me, I hear movement.

A footstep. A breath caught.

It's Finn who steps forward, kneeling behind her, brushing her hair off her face, and whispering something so quietly, I can't make it out. Whatever he says makes her tremble.

He kisses her jaw, her cheek, her temple with gentle, anchoring kisses that give her something to hold onto while I drag her closer to the edge. His fingers tease her nipples, as she pants and writhes as two of us work her over.

Scarlet clutches at Finn, moaning louder now, helpless against the rhythm of my tongue and the weight of his presence behind her. Her body undulates, mouth opening on a soundless gasp, and when I slip two thick fingers inside her and curl them, she comes undone like we planned it that way all along.

Her cries echo through the cabin, raw and full of need as she pulses around me, every tremor lighting me up from the inside.

I lift my head, mouth slick with her pleasure, and meet Nixon's eyes.

He's still sitting, still watching, but his jaw is tight and the heat behind his stare is feral. He wants to be next, even though that wasn't his plan.

I stand to defer to my alpha, but before I can say anything, Scarlet surprises me. She shifts forward, slipping from Finn's arms, breathing ragged and eyes glazed, and then she reaches for me.

Her fingers find the buckle of my jeans.

And suddenly, this night changes shape entirely.

Her eyes stay locked on mine, wide and golden, dazed and burning.

My shoulders tense, body bracing for what's to come.

Scarlet's kneeling at my feet, fingers brushing along the waistband of my jeans because she wants to. Because she's choosing *me*. The rough, laughing mess of a man who never thought this kind of softness would belong to him.

I brace one hand on the back of the couch and reach out with the other to cup her jaw, my thumb brushing along her cheekbone as she leans in and presses a kiss above my zipper. The heat of her mouth bleeds through denim, and I can't hold back the groan that rips out of me. She unfastens my jeans slowly, her movements unhurried. The reverence undoes me.

I've never been worshiped like this.

Her mouth finds me, and the world stops spinning.

Every thought is wiped clean from my mind except the shape of her lips and the velvet slide of her tongue. I watch her take her time, eyes fluttering closed, like the act itself gives her pleasure, too, and everything primal in me *howls* with gratitude.

She's made for us.

The scent of her still clings to my skin, mingling with my own, and I swear I can feel the goddess herself smiling down, blessing this.

The gift of a mate is holy and sacred, whispered through bloodlines and carried by magic and moonlight, and somehow, she's here, in our cabin and in our lives.

With every kiss, I get closer to unraveling. My hand fists in her hair, not to force control, just to hold on and ground myself in this miracle.

My brothers watch silently, and their bond pulls tight around us. Scarlet's not only mine, she's ours, and she's showing us how ready she is to let go.

I grit out her name, panting, body taut, and it's spiritual, rooted in the forest, calling our wolves forth.

But will Nixon believe she's ready for what must happen next?

16

SCARLET

I'm doing this.

I'm on my knees, on their rug, in their cabin, while Reed towers above me, his eyes as deep as midnight, his muscles tight as a bowstring drawn to the edge. A giant among men. A powerful presence letting me take him apart. My palms press to his thighs for balance, but it's more than that. I want him to know this is a choice I'm making, and something I want, rather than a reflection of his expectation.

His eyes burn into mine, daring me to break the connection as I lean forward and let my lips brush the base of him. A soft hiss escapes him, pleasure laced with disbelief, and the sound drives me further.

I drag my tongue upward, slow and sure, teasing him with the lightest flick at the tip. His hips jerk, his fingers twitch, and his expression is devastated in the best way.

I'm in control of this moment, yet somehow I'm still out of control, wilder and more confident than I've been before. That dichotomy thrills me. I've never felt more powerful or more exposed. Never felt more wanted or more owned.

From the edge of my vision, I sense movement. Finn, somewhere behind me, is still quiet. Nixon's presence burns like a torch in the corner of the room. Their restraint is a quiet inferno, and their hunger is palpable, fueling me.

I take more of Reed into my mouth as a shudder rolls through him and he braces against the back of the sofa, his other hand threading tightly into my hair. Not to push. Just to hold. His body trembles under my touch, every tiny quake a surrender I lap up.

His head tips back, a low moan rising from his chest as I take him deeper, sliding my tongue along the underside, lips sealed tight, matching the rhythm he's fighting to maintain.

He's losing.

His breathing rasps through gritted teeth as he fights to keep control of his hips that twitch to thrust deeper. His voice breaks the silence, hoarse and cracking. "Scarlet—Jesus. Baby, I—fuck—"

His body tenses, a full-body tremor rippling through him as he groans and releases. I take it all because I want to taste the storm of his surrender as I tame him with nothing but my mouth.

And it's there again. The echo of the impossible, that somehow, this moment was written by an outside power. Braysville wasn't the only town where I could find lumber, and Doug's wasn't the only restaurant where I could find food. If I'd left home an hour later or bought a sandwich at the last rest stop, I would never have met these men. What pulled me here to this cabin in the woods? It's like I've followed a breadcrumb trail into the woods and been let in on a secret I wasn't supposed to overhear.

Reed slumps back onto the couch, spent and stunned, his hand dragging over his face before cupping himself with a sigh. His chest heaves, and when his eyes meet mine, they're glassy and awed.

I sit on my heels, wiping my lips with the back of my hand, my pulse still galloping in my throat. When I dropped to my knees, I knew what I wanted, but now?

Behind me, the others are still watching. I'm in uncharted territory and have no idea what they'll want or expect to happen next.

Behind me, the couch creaks again.

Finn slowly slides down beside Reed, moving with a fluidity that marks him from his brothers. I don't look up, but the hush of intention is behind the subtle shift of the air. The sound of denim buttons parting one by one, and the exhale that tells me he's not just watching anymore, sends a rush of arousal through me.

My gaze flicks up. His intense eyes meet mine, warm and steady. One hand rests on the waistband of his jeans, the other brushes through my hair in a gentle sweep, the way he might caress the highest quality wood or a piece of his beloved furniture.

My pulse roars, and then I shift.

Still on my knees, I slide to face him, and he's already there, waiting. Hard, thick, flushed, his erection stands bold against the open cradle of denim. He's quietly offering himself in a way that shakes something loose inside me.

I bend, and he groans as my palms press into his muscular thighs. His fingers twitch where they rest at his sides. I take him slow with a soft kiss at first, my lips brushing the head, and then a slow, teasing lick. His groan turns strangled as I wrap my mouth around him, and his

99

taste floods my senses: salt, heat, the unique tang of wild, creative Finn.

It's different than with Reed. He's quieter, his body taut with restraint, and yet he leans into me like he's desperate to drown in the pleasure I offer.

And I give it freely.

I want this.

I want *them*.

As dangerous as it is to succumb to their rugged, handsome charms, I can't regret a thing.

A footstep and the vibration of a presence close to my spine alert me to Nixon's approach.

My heart skitters, but my mouth doesn't stop. My lips glide, my tongue curves, and Finn's thighs tremble beneath my hands. But my awareness has split. Nixon is close, and my thighs clench. I'm still wearing my panties, but my whole ass is on display for his pleasure.

One is watching as I take another into my mouth, and the third stalks closer, his intentions unknown.

I lose myself to the heavy fog of lust and the danger of surrender that curls in my veins. It's the kind of feeling that cracks you open from the inside and spills all your hidden longings.

I'm falling.

Into them, and into this moment.

I'm facing up to desires I didn't dare to admit, even to myself.

And as I sink deeper into Finn's lap, his restraint frays with every stroke of my tongue. My awareness sharpens around Nixon's heat at my back. He hasn't touched me yet. But he will.

And when he does, I know I won't survive it unchanged.

17

NIXON

Scarlet is moving between my brothers, worshipping at their feet the way a mate would. Reed is flushed and spent, slumped into the couch, chest heaving and eyes wide. He holds her hand gently, maintaining contact even as she touches his brother. Finn is quiet and taut beside him, chest rising in slow, steady hums as she bobs her head in his lap, taking his cock deep into her throat.

And I'm behind her, my gut tightening with every clench of her thighs. She's so wet that the lace is clinging to the cleft of her pussy, outlining what I've touched but not seen, what I've tasted from my fingers but not directly.

She's the driving force behind this, not my plan or my schedule. But that's what makes it impossible to resist.

Her scent curls into my senses like incense, and I can't think of anything but the sweet taste of her. My cock throbs, heavy and impatient, a lesson in restraint I've practiced all my life because I know how easily this can end in premature ravishment and loss, something none of us wants.

My wolf howls at me to throw caution to the wind, but my human self holds the reins tightly because she hasn't invited me yet. She hasn't locked her consent in place with her eyes or voice. But still, she chose this path the moment she went from accepting pleasure to giving. Finn would have walked away like I did last night, to handle his business in the quiet of his room, but she wanted more.

It's a silent dance: her lips wrapped around Finn, her lashes half-closed, and my own gaze riveted to the small space between her thighs, the part of her that belongs to me and my brothers but is still a threshold she bars or allows entry at her will.

She turns her head to look over her shoulder, and her eyes meet mine, wide, lust-soaked, feral even, and my hand moves of its own volition. I bring my fingertips up to brush her center, and I groan at the gentle give, the dampness, and the tremor of her muscles under my palm.

Her look says it all. *You can, if you want. Try to see what I say.*

My cock presses into my palm inside the confines of my jeans. It would take nothing to free myself and slip inside her, to mark her with my scent. I'd write myself so deep, I'd leave no doubt as to where this woman belongs and to whom. But if I do it now, can I hold back my wolf instinct, or will the scent of her nape call to my fangs? Will I go all the way and claim her, and what then?

It's too soon.

She doesn't know what we are. She doesn't know what she is to us, and what it means to be claimed.

The claim can be terrifying, the pain overwhelming if the pleasure is resisted.

I won't lose her. Not for a moment of need that could

extinguish more than it fulfills.

So my hand stills. I lean into the quiet of the moment and the tension that hums too loudly. She shifts her hips back, spreading her thighs wider, granting more of herself to me without a word, and the walls inside me crack. I trace her slick skin with a single fingertip, slow and coaxing, and she leans back into the touch. She gasps.

She can say no. I'd let her pull back in a heartbeat if she did. But instead, she moans. I lean forward and whisper her name against her shoulder, her sweet nape already calling to me. My fangs bud, but it's my tongue I allow to explore. She exudes warmth and invitation, her scent as sweet as summer blooms.

I taste her desire on her skin. It rises from her like steam in the cold. My mouth brushes the slope of her shoulder, as my hands splay along her hips. Her panties slide the rest of the way over her thighs and fall to the floor in a whisper. I'm curved over her the way it would be, the way it should be, so close to taking what my wolf viscerally aches for, my hands tremble as they grip the sofa on either side of her. I lick her sweet skin, and my fangs press deeper into the flesh of my cheeks, but I can't let them out. I'm drugged, but still I hold onto the last vestiges of my self-control. This desire I have for the right kind of love bond has been with me for so long, I can't toss it aside at the first temptation.

I have to draw back.

But I can't resist looking at the space between her legs, and when I find it slick and open, glistening in the low light, I am overcome with awe. The gravity of knowing that this is what we've waited for, she is what we've waited for, weighing heavily.

My fingers fumble with buttons, and my hand wraps

around my length, already hard and beaded with precum. I stroke once, twice, dragging the head of my cock through the heat of her, testing her wetness, testing myself, lost in desire and the need to let go, relishing marking her with my scent in this small way.

Her thighs tremble.

Her lips part.

Her hips nudge back enough to tell me yes.

Scarlet arches her back, and in that moment, I lose every wall I thought I could hold.

I press into her slowly, not because I'm unsure but because I have to relish every second of her taking me in: the tightness, the pull, the warmth.

She's *home*.

Being inside her is everything I imagined and everything I feared and everything I never dared believe I'd find. She gasps, tilting her hips, her hands braced against the edge of the couch, and I go deeper, groaning low against her skin as I fill her, stretching her wide around me.

The world goes quiet.

My thoughts are obliterated beneath the weight of this moment, the rightness of her, and the deep satisfaction I derive from the tight squeeze of her around me. This beautiful body was made for our pleasure, but also to bear our children. One day, after we've claimed her, we'll fill her with our seed and watch her bloom with the future of our family.

The rhythm of her breath and the wild beat of my heart as I move inside her punctuate each thrust. I grip her hips and she pushes back into me, greedy and glorious, and I match her, every stroke deliberate.

I don't pound into her. There's no rush. I give her what

I know she needs, and I *take* from her the bliss of our deepening connection. Her moans mix with the soft encouragement of my brothers, who remain silent no longer. Reed curses. Finn groans long and deep as he comes into her mouth, gripping her head to him for as long as it takes him to spill every drop.

And then she's looking at me over her shoulder, eyes wide, lids half-lowered, her pretty pink lips parted as she groans with pleasure.

Even as her body writhes and her back bows and her nails dig into the couch, it's *me* she looks for, and I know this isn't only lust for her.

It's everything we've been promised and so much more. She has to feel it, too.

She cries out, hips jerking beneath mine as my hand slides between her thighs. Two fingers, slick and sure, pressing where she needs them. She bucks, crying out, as I drive deeper, my hips rocking into her with a pace that's almost too measured because if I let go now, I won't stop.

Her body tightens around me, muscles fluttering as she spirals, and her voice breaks like glass. Her orgasm crests fast, wild and unrestrained, pulsing against my cock in waves so fierce I almost lose control.

My knot flares and swells, but I resist the biting urge to shove it into her and fuse us together.

I growl, deep, low, and broken, and thrust harder, once, to feel her almost clasp around the bulb at the root of my cock that she'll only take when she's been claimed.

I'm shaking.

My hands find hers, fingers laced as I pin them to the couch, my chest curved over her trembling spine.

How did I live without this? How did I go each day

without her scent to breathe, and her laughter to hear, and her body to taste, and her pussy to fuck? How did we wait so long?

"Oh. Fuck. Yeah," I growl, beast rising. "Fucking take it like a good. Fucking. Girl."

Scarlet whimpers and her pussy clamps rhythmically.

And then *instinct hits.*

Fangs.

They drop without warning. My mouth finds the nape of her neck, her soft, exposed skin, the sacred place where the claim is made. I pant into it, trembling. She doesn't flinch away but moans and leans into me like she wants it. More than that. Like she craves to be marked with every atom of her being.

My wolf is frenzied.

I could do it. Right now. Bite. Knot. Fill her with pups and fate and *forever.* She'd be mine. Ours. No doubt. No distance.

Across the room, Reed sits forward. His face open and awestruck, it tightens into something sharper.

He *knows.*

I meet his eyes, teeth grazing her skin, and he *shakes his head.*

Not like this.

I breathe harder, my jaw aching. My whole body's trembling with the strain of holding back what my wolf has wanted from the moment I scented her and our eyes met.

But Reed's right.

We said there could be another way.

I said there could be another way.

My fangs retract slowly, aching with the loss, and instead of biting, I press a kiss to the spot I almost scarred. A kiss full of promise, loaded with everything I will give her when she begs me for it.

And then I come.

Pleasure swells through me, and I jerk inside her with a cry I can't swallow. My forehead drops to her shoulder again as my body convulses. My cock pulses as I jerk back, releasing over the rug and the panties still loose around her knees, clutching my knot in case she turns her head.

Curved over her sweet, spent body, I'm huge and dangerous, but I have reins on my feral side that most other wolves would never think to cultivate.

"I'll wait," I mouth against her skin. "Until you *want* it."

Because I could claim her now.

I could make her ours forever.

But what I really want is for her to beg for us.

18

SCARLET

I'm floating, completely undone, almost naked on the rug where my world dissolved into theirs, and nothing's quite real anymore.

Nixon's lips trace lazy kisses along the curve of my spine, lingering at my waist before drifting lower. He presses his mouth to the place where we were joined, lapping at the slickness, marking me as his animalistically. His scent of winter breeze, earth, and forest surrounds me like a protective shield. It fills my lungs.

Finn's fingers drift across my shoulder, sliding slowly and teasing until they find my nipples, one then the other, coaxing them into tight peaks that bloom under his touch. His fingertips are soft but confident, like he's inside my mind and knows exactly what will make me stir.

Reed, ever the smiler, is enthralled by my hair, threading his fingers through the red strands over and over, like he's memorizing its texture.

It's quiet, except for the hum of our breathing and the

faint creak of shifting weight. The silence is a weighted blanket pressing gently against my skin.

I need them to speak. I need words.

I need to know who I am now that I'm with them.

My mother's voice rises in my mind: *What would people say? Who are you, letting three men touch you, taste you, fuck you... Watch you?* It finishes with the huff of disapproval. *You should know better.*

I almost pull away, but their touches anchor me now rather than unravel me. I sink into the pleasure and the gravity of their bodies around me, and I let them *pet* me.

Nixon's hand curls around my waist, lifting me gently, his intention clear. I don't even need to stand. I follow the gentle current of his strength until I'm boneless and wrapped in his arms, flanked by his brothers. We bypass my bedroom and end up in a grand room across the hall, which is large and quiet, with a bed big enough for all of us.

He sets me at the center of the mattress as if laying out the world at his feet, eyes never leaving mine. Finn and Reed settle on either side of me, creating a cradle of warm flesh and the promise of comfort. Each one presses kisses to my shoulders, my hips, the crease of my thighs.

Nixon lies behind me, tracing the line of my collarbone. "You're ours."

It's a statement of fact, not a question. No one has ever staked a claim on me with such confidence.

"For tonight," I whisper back because, of course, he means temporarily. He knows I'm leaving. I'm pretty sure they'll want me out of their hair tomorrow, when the sex-haze has left us all, and the new light of the morning reminds us who we are and where we belong in the world.

He doesn't disagree, but then again, he doesn't agree. He

keeps stroking me until Finn climbs between my legs to slide his tongue through my folds and over my sensitized clit. Reed sucks my nipple, connecting streams of pleasure I didn't know were possible. Then Nixon is next to me, kissing my mouth like he's sipping dessert wine, until three brothers beckon another orgasm from me, and I drown in the deep water of pleasure, drifting into the coma of sleep.

***

I wake up to the soft scent of roses and the quiet absence of bodies around me. The bed beneath my bare skin is cool, the linens tangled from a night I still can't quite believe happened. Beside me, a single red rose lies on the pillow, dewy, unblemished, and beautiful. I draw it close, inhale deeply, and let the sweetness fill my lungs.

When I glance down, the marks that reveal the heat of what we did last night are the first thing I notice. My nipples are still tender, peaked from the memory of mouths and hands. Hickeys bloom across my hips and belly in scattered clusters. I haven't worn marks like these since high school. Rather than juvenile, there's a possessive, territorial quality to them.

I trace a bruise with careful fingers and the echo ripples through me. Their touch, their voices, the pleasure they gave me again and again until I drifted, not drowning, but flying. Soaring.

I stretch slowly, testing my ankle. It pulses with stiffness, but not enough to stop me. With a little help from the painkillers in my bag, I could probably drive today.

And I should.

I can't stay forever.

A note sits on the nightstand, scribbled on a napkin:

At the yard. Finn will return for you at 11 AM.

I glance at the clock: 10:30. I slept three hours past my usual alarm, and I didn't even stir. My body must've needed it.

I shower quickly, sorry to reluctantly wash away our night of passion, and dress in jeans, a loose tee, and boots.

Even though they're everyday actions, I'm dazed, as if I'm still in the rhythm of last night's surrender. As I move through the cabin, every step stirs memories. The way Nixon kissed my spine. The bubble of Reed's laughter against my thigh. Finn's fingers, reverent and patient.

The place is empty now. But it's not cold. The cabin still carries their energy that surrounds me with warmth.

At exactly 11:00, Finn opens the door, freshly shaven, dressed in a soft gray shirt and well-worn jeans. He looks like morning should: crisp and calm, except for the warmth in his eyes when he sees me, and the passion that stirs in his lips when he kisses me, pulling me close with a possessive arm around my hips.

"You ready?" he asks, like it's any other day, and he didn't watch me come apart beneath his brothers and then take me to pieces himself. Like I'm not a random woman his brother rescued in the woods and brought home like a lost orphan.

"I think I am." I push my purse strap onto my shoulder, shift my crutch, and follow him to the truck.

"You guys started early," I say as we pull onto the road winding through arching trees that seem to be leaning in to listen.

"We had a delivery," he says, opening the window.

Dappled light paints the hood of the truck, and I draw in the scent of the woods, and the crisp, clean air clears the last of sleep from my head. When we're a minute away from the cabin, he lifts his head and scans both sides of the road and then slows, pulling the truck over at an unmarked patch of shoulder.

"What is it?" I ask, watching the way he lifts his chin.

"I need to go into the forest." His hand is already on the door.

"What for?"

"Stay here."

He's out of the car before I can object, taking his keys with him and striding toward the tree line. I glance around, remembering the man who attacked me and how comfortable he was in the forest, and make a quick decision to follow Finn. I'm a sitting duck in a truck with the windows open.

I trot after Finn, crutch and feet crunching over the fallen leaves, adrenaline driving me, even though my ankle protests. "Finn—wait!" I call, voice echoing between the trees. He is already quite far ahead, but he halts abruptly, a glaze in his eyes that I've never seen before. Is he angry that I ignored him?

"I'm sorry. I was scared to wait in the car." He steps out of the shade, and we make our way to a point between us. I'm about to apologize again when a soft whimper cuts through the air. It's so pitiful that I stop mid-step.

"What's that?" I ask, already stepping in the direction. Finn puts his arm out as if to stop me, but I'm close enough to see a small writhing shape under a looming, wide-trunked tree.

It's furry and gray with a pointed muzzle. A lot like the wolf creature that came into the cabin last night. Does this baby belong to him?

"Is it a wolf?" I ask, as Finn moves level with me.

"Yes."

When I glance at him, his jaw tightens in a way that's more like Nixon than I've seen.

He kneels, and the creature looks up, its nose rising, scenting the air. Finn places a hand gently beside it, but he doesn't touch it, and I don't understand why.

My chest constricts. I limp forward, crutch abandoned, compelled by instinct. I bend and scoop it into my arms. It's tiny, trembling, its body is cool, and its fur is matted and wet. It's clearly in distress. Why is it alone?

"Finn—please," I whisper, pressing it tight against my chest, feeling the chill through its damp coat. Its whining breaks my heart.

He stares at me, his face pale and stunned. "Scarlet... don't... You shouldn't have..."

But I'm already holding it like a newborn, rocking it gently. "It's so cold."

The whimper becomes a twitch, then a shudder, and under my fingers, something shifts. Fur ripples into soft skin, paws shrink into tiny fists. A gasp escapes me as the cub arches its back, and suddenly, it's not a cub. It's a baby.

A human, pink-cheeked, red-haired, tiny and bewildered, putting a thumb to her sweet pink lips, blinking up at me with eyes that search my face.

Finn stands, arms flaring out like he's ready to catch but also ready to recoil.

I press the girl closer, wrapping her in the folds of my shirt. Her hair is damp and scented with a powdery baby smell that ripples through me like an ache I can't explain.

"What..."

Finn shakes his head, as disbelieving as I am.

"What the hell is going on?" I continue, voice shaking.

Around us, forest sounds press in, but all I can hear is the baby's quiet inhale, and the sharp intake of breath from the man who seems as shocked as I am at the transformation that happened before our eyes.

Or is he?

19

FINN

My breath catches somewhere between disbelief and wonder as Scarlet cradles the trembling bundle against her chest, revealing the delicate curve of a baby's cheek and a mop of red hair matted against damp skin.

A girl. A female shifter.

A miracle no one in our pack has ever seen. So rare, I stare, unable to comprehend.

For a long moment, the entire forest seems to hush around us, the air tightening as though nature is drawing itself taller.

The child smells like clean earth, milk, and the first wild bloom of spring. She smells like Aura, Gregory's mate and an unfamiliar wolf scent. Over a year ago, Gregory's mate from the neighboring territory was brutally attacked, her body broken and her spirit shattered. Sharp-edged whispers ran through the pack like wildfire. Gregory did nothing to avenge the attack, and Aura was kept out of sight.

The cub is her child. It makes sense, but it also rips my

throat out.

To leave the cub behind in such circumstances isn't unusual. The wounds, the danger, the shame... the cruelty of pack politics demand it. This miracle child was left behind, tucked away in the woods, a sin too unbearable to claim.

But all I can do is stare.

Scarlet presses her lips to the baby's temple, her face pale with a kind of awe that hooks into my heart. She holds the child not like a stranger, but like a mother, like someone who has already decided the shape of love and wrapped it around this baby like armor.

"We have to take her to the police," she says, and though her voice trembles, there's quiet steel through every syllable. "We can't leave a baby out here. Not alone."

"Scarlet, she—" My voice falters under the weight of that single syllable. *She.* It feels foreign on my tongue, almost sacrilegious. I've never said it in this context. Never had to.

She looks at me with wide eyes, waiting for me to make sense of the world that's upended itself in her arms.

"She's not human," I manage to say, though the words taste like ash. "She's... a wolf baby."

Scarlet's gaze flares. "Then why's she human now?"

The baby lets out a soft sigh, a contented little sound that guts me clean through.

I don't answer, because there *is* no answer. Scarlet knows nothing of our kind, of the shifting and the bloodlines and the rules older than memory. But she's seen what she's seen. She held a wolf cub in her hands and watched it become a child. And that kind of truth has carved something new into her understanding of what's possible.

And maybe mine, too.

I have to say something. But the words lodge in my throat.

"There... there are rules," I manage. "This isn't our problem."

Scarlet fixes me with a narrowed stare. "Rules don't apply to a baby."

Her tiny limbs moving like sapling branches in the wind, her breath quick and fragile. The sheer vulnerability of her scent threads into the space between us. She belongs nowhere and everywhere.

And goddess help me, she looks *right* in Scarlet's arms. There's something uncanny about the resemblance in the matching shade of their hair, the delicate tilt of their eyes, the softness of their mouths. It's as if fate, or whatever force governs these cruel turns of life, has decided that Scarlet should find her.

Behind us, the forest rustles, alive. I inhale sharply, scenting the air for a friend or foe. Are we being watched? The only wolf scent belongs to the tiny cub in Scarlet's arms.

No one else is here.

I glance at Scarlet as she brushes the baby's hair back from her face, her fingers trembling only slightly. Her expression is one I'll never forget; open and fierce, like she's already made a promise to this child, whether or not the rest of us will help her keep it.

I should call Nixon. I should let him decide. But out here in the silence, there's no signal. No voice of reason to anchor me. No one to tell me what the hell I'm supposed to do.

As I observe Scarlet swaying with the baby in her arms, I realize I don't have a choice.

"We need to bring her somewhere safe. To the yard.

Nixon will figure out what to do."

My chest tightens. Protecting her means angering him. But this baby is human now, and Scarlet won't leave her.

"Okay." Her voice is quiet, but it matches mine: resolute and unwavering. "To the yard."

The baby coos in response, as if agreeing. Heat blooms in my chest.

I reach out to take her, to give Scarlet a chance to steady herself and grab her crutch, but she tightens her hold and shakes her head. She's not letting go.

So I retrieve the crutch, tuck it beneath her arm, and together we begin the slow, uneven walk back through the trees toward the truck.

This may be the biggest mistake I've ever made.

Only time will tell.

20

NIXON

I'm in the yard, sweeping up after unpacking the morning delivery, when I catch sight of the truck creeping up the drive. Finn's behind the wheel, and Scarlet is perched beside him with her wild red hair forming a luminous halo against the washed-out sky.

My heart thuds at the sight of her, relief pouring through me. I hadn't even realized how tightly I'd been wound until now. Leaving her in bed this morning was the hardest thing I've had to do in a long time, and being separated from her is a torture I couldn't have endured for much longer. She's the fire I've been craving, and the missing piece I can no longer do without.

Then a scent hits me, sharp and foreign. A wolf, not of our pack. My shoulders lock, every nerve ending razor-edged with instinct. My wolf surges beneath my skin, furious and territorial. Has someone touched her? Claimed her? Brought her back marked with another pack's scent like a brand?

The shift claws at me, hot and wild, begging to surface. I shut my eyes, grip my rage by the throat, and force it down into bone. Now is not the time.

The truck stops. Finn climbs out, rounds the vehicle, and opens Scarlet's door. She swings her legs out slowly, cradling something in her arms. My gaze drops, and the rest of the world vanishes.

A baby.

A tiny naked baby, vulnerable, skin damp and flushed. It's a little girl with red hair and a Cupid's bow mouth, so perfect she looks like a cherub in an oil painting.

But it reeks of wolf.

Not our pack.

The animal in me stills.

I step forward as Finn guides Scarlet toward me. She meets my gaze, those green-gold eyes bright with fierce determination. This is not the shaken woman we pulled from the woods days ago. This is my mate. My strong, vibrant, beautiful mate.

Reed steps through the warehouse door behind me, his entire body going taut, senses lashing like whip cords in the direction of that scent. He smells it, too.

Where has this baby come from, and why does it smell like it's been curled up with a wolf?

Finn straightens. "Let's go inside. We need to talk."

Scarlet shifts the baby in her arms. She looks at me like she's already made a choice and is daring me to have something to say about it.

I step aside, gesturing toward the office. Reed follows, his brow tight, his fists balled, his wolf ready. We move in silence that pulses with questions.

The baby sleeps, belly rising with every tiny inhale.

My gaze locks with Scarlet's. "Where did you find her?" My voice is quiet, but the edges are sharp as wolf claws. *Tell me the truth.*

Scarlet tugs the baby closer and meets my eyes. My brothers are watching, waiting, but right now, it's me who needs answers.

"She was in the woods," Finn says, his voice low. "Alone. Whimpering. But she didn't look like this when we found her."

I straighten, bracing for more. "What do you mean?"

Finn shifts uncomfortably, his hand scrubbing the back of his neck. "It was a wolf. Small. It shifted."

The air cools around us. Even the dust motes seem to pause, suspended in light. Reed swears. I don't move.

He said it.

Out loud.

In front of Scarlet.

The secret we've kept buried. The truth we've shielded Scarlet from since the first moment she stumbled into our world.

I stare at him, eyes wide, waiting for an explanation, but instead, he meets my gaze with grim finality.

My mind spins. Not because he spoke freely, though that's a problem all on its own, but because what he's saying is impossible.

Female.

My eyes drop back to the sleeping child, her fingers curled, her lips parted, totally at peace.

Females don't shift.

Except sometimes… they do.

Rare cases. Freak occurrences. The kind of stories whispered at firesides, about one in a generation. Myths and legends. Worshipped and feared. Because a female shifter, if she lives, is a miracle.

"She smells of Aura," Finn says. "The scent is weak, but it's there."

The name slices like a blade to the gut. "Aura? Gregory's mate?"

"Yes."

"No. She was——" I trail off. Everyone knows what happened to Aura. Gregory took her violently and claimed her before she was ready, binding her by force. She survived the bite, but not the aftermath. A rival pack attacked. She was violated and left for dead. At least, that was the version of the story that drifted from wolf to wolf. Then again, wolf whispers are notoriously unreliable.

I swallow the bile rising in my throat.

"She had a child?"

"She must have," Finn says. "And left her here."

My stomach knots.

"Abandoned her? This miracle child was left to die in the woods."

Reed shifts closer, brows drawn low. "And Scarlet found her."

I close my eyes. This isn't our business. This isn't our war. Gregory is a tyrant, but he's an alpha with allies. Interfere with his pack, and we invite a blood feud. We've worked too hard to keep peace in Blackwood.

"This isn't our business," I say, because I *have* to say it. I have to be the one who sees the whole board, even if it means sacrificing the piece everyone else wants to protect.

Scarlet stands taller, the baby tucked to her chest like she'd fight to the death for her already.

"It's my business now," she says. Her tone is soft, but

every syllable lands with determination.

"You don't know what you're asking," I tell her, stepping back. "Wait here."

I nod toward the door, and Reed and Finn follow, silent and tense. Scarlet's voice trails behind us, low but firm enough to echo against the glass walls:

"We have to take her to the authorities. They'll know what to do…"

I pull the door closed, filling the narrow hallway with our quiet tension.

Outside, the morning sun warms the dew from the leaves and grass. Reed shifts on his feet. Finn turns to me, anguish twisting his expression.

"We have four options," I say, voice even but tense. "First, we take the cub back to the woods. Let nature decide her fate."

Finn looks away. No one speaks.

"Second, we let Scarlet take her to the authorities," I continue. "And risk exposing everything."

"Third, we find the mother and return the child," Reed says quietly. "But we risk getting involved with a volatile pack."

I swallow hard and press on. "Fourth, we tell Scarlet the truth. About who we are. About what she's seen. And pray she chooses to stay."

Reed exhales sharply. "You're seriously considering that?"

Finn's voice is quiet. "We crossed a line with her last night. Made her trust us. Took things further than we should have. She gave herself to us. We showed her what life could be if she were our mate."

"And we gave ourselves to her," I say. "It's already done.

Now we owe her the truth."

"But that doesn't affect the child," Reed says. "That child... It's a miracle."

"It is."

I rub my stubbled jaw.

"What are we choosing here?" Reed asks. "The baby? Or the woman?"

I meet his eyes.

I close my eyes. My wolf claws at me from the inside, roaring to claim my mate and only protect what's mine. But my heart, the human part, pushes back.

I open my eyes and square my shoulders. "We're choosing both. You remember what Mom used to say about the goddess... that she had her ways and that questioning them was a sure way to turn fate away from your favor."

"And Dad used to say that the goddess was wily and liked to test us, and it was up to us to use our free will to decide our own paths," Reed reminds me.

I sigh and rub the bridge of my nose. "Aura knows that Blackwood Forest is our territory. She ventured into rival territory, risking herself to leave the baby where we'd find it. She didn't want it to die. She wanted us to find it."

Finn sighs. "That's exactly what I thought."

"So what?" Reed's usual humor is replaced by stress and tension. "She thinks we'll be great daddies? Gregory can't want that child... the way it was created..." He shakes his head, lines bracketing his mouth. "So, we're supposed to raise it alone. Scarlet's leaving unless we can convince her otherwise. This baby isn't guaranteed a new momma with its three daddies."

Finn snorts. "I'm trying to imagine Nixon changing diapers."

"You think I can't?"

He shrugs. "This morning started out spectacularly, but it's taken a weird turn."

"You think the goddess wants us to raise this baby... this female?"

"I don't know. But what I do know is the woman in there is waiting for us to tell her what this is all about. Whether it's the right time or not, we have to tell her about the world she's stumbled into. Then, we work out what to do next together."

I inhale deeply. The weight of legacy, of pack politics, and all the complexities of being a shifter in a human world sits heavily on my shoulders. But so does the need to protect what we're building with our mate and find a way to handle a child that is a gift to the world, even if it isn't ours.

Scarlet's already claimed more of my heart than I thought any mate ever could. And, from the way she's looking at that cub, I think she's lost her heart, too.

"Let's go."

I lead the way back inside, ready to face whatever comes next.

Everything we've been hoping and dreaming about is now at stake. I don't know what Scarlet will choose when she learns the truth of who and what we are, but I know this: the goddess is watching us now, and whatever she wants will come to pass.

21

SCARLET

I sit in the office surrounded by the familiar scent of fresh lumber laced with the faint tang of sawdust like my studio at home.

The baby sleeps in my arms, a perfect little angel with red curls and cheeks so soft, they seem too fragile to be real. My fingers trace the curve of her tiny cheek, marveling at how peaceful she looks nestled against me.

I'm a stranger, but she doesn't seem to care.

But why was she alone in the forest? My mind lurches back to that moment when she was a wolf cub, her fur slick as she trembled and whimpered and then, impossibly, shifting into this perfect human shape in the span of a heartbeat.

Did I imagine it? Was it a hallucination brought on by exhaustion and adrenaline?

My breath catches. It can't be a werewolf, can it?

I snort quietly, embarrassed by the thought, recalling teenage fantasy novels about high school werewolves, tales

I wrote off years ago as nonsense.

But then I think of Finn wandering off into the trees, drawn by an unknown, and the dog-wolf returning in his place.

More wolf than dog, although I didn't want to admit it at the time.

Something's going on here.

Muffled voices filter in from outside: Nixon's controlled baritone, Finn's low rumble, and Reed's sharper edge. They all sound tense as they debate what will happen next. My grip on the helpless baby tightens.

Any normal person would have dialed the police the moment they suspected an abandoned infant, waiting for them to dispatch a worried social worker to swoop in and declare the child safe. But this? This is far from normal.

I shift the baby so she nestles closer. Her tiny fist unfurls and curls around my finger, and my heart splits open, like a ripe fruit fallen to the ground.

No. She's not just an abandoned child. She's... something else. An abandoned changeling. A miracle clothed in flesh and unanswered questions.

But how did Finn know she was out there?

"Scarlet?" Finn's voice at the door interrupts my thoughts.

I look up, adjusting the child as he fills the doorframe. His expression flickers from hope to fear and finally to wary tenderness. He's such a soft-hearted man.

I swallow. "She's not human?" I whisper, more to myself than to him.

"Not entirely."

Behind him, Nixon's shadow looms, and then Reed's. They fill the office with their tall, muscular frames and their intensity.

I close my eyes, cradle the baby close, and steel myself for whatever comes next. Because whatever they decide, I know one thing for sure: she's safe in my arms, and I don't want to let her go.

Nixon's shoulders are curved like he's carrying the burden of centuries of worry. His eyes find mine, intense, but not unkind. The baby stirs against my chest, her cheek nuzzling my collarbone, and I tighten my hold without even thinking.

"There are things you don't know about the world, Scarlet. Things we haven't been ready to tell you, but this... this discovery has brought forward an inevitable discussion."

"Inevitable?"

He shoves his hands into his pockets. "Listen through to the end, okay." He sighs and looks at the ceiling, searching for inspiration. "There was a time when the goddess, our goddess, grew tired of humankind, destroying her forests, slaughtering animals without thought, poisoning the rivers. So she gave a few humans something new. Animal aspects. Wolf forms. Bear forms. A reminder of the beauty of the wild. It was supposed to be a lesson in humility and connection."

I stare, not blinking, holding my body tight.

"She thought it would teach compassion. If your brother could turn into a bear, maybe you wouldn't hunt bears for sport. If your lover could become a hawk, maybe you'd leave the skies alone. Your lover could tell you of the freedom of the hawk and the beauty of the skies, and you'd think before you acted in a way to destroy either."

My arms tighten instinctively around the child. "This

sounds like a myth."

"Mythology is often rooted in distant truth. We make stories from the parts of history that seem too distant to be real."

My lips part, but no words come. It's too much. Too strange. My mind reels, trying to fold this wild tale into something logical, something grounded. Shifters? A goddess punishing mankind with animal blood? It's the kind of thing you read in dusty old books or hear in half-remembered folklore, not something whispered in a quiet room, by men you know to be serious. Not something that makes your skin prickle because some part of you knows... saw the truth of it. I shake my head, more to clear it than in denial. "So it's not just a story?"

He shakes his head. "It's real."

"So, what happened?"

He looks at me then, and the raw and haunted depth of his gaze spears me. "The shifters were hunted. Rejected. Feared. Packs scattered. Many died. Those who survived learned to hide in plain sight."

My voice is barely a whisper. "So, you're saying that this baby is a shifter. A wolf-human. A werewolf."

"Yes."

I blink, heart thudding, glancing between the three men who have been my rescuers and my company, my friends and my lovers, dread swelling until it almost chokes me.

"How do you know this story, Nixon?"

"We're not what you think, Scarlet." he says softly. "We're the same as this child."

The night of the attack rushes back: the snarling wolves, Nixon's inhuman strength, the wolf in the house. This can't be right. It's stories. Old folklore. The kind of thing my

129

mom would drag out to warn me of the dangers of the world.

"You're saying you're... shifters."

"Yes...men... and wolves."

The breath I take rattles through me. "And the night I was attacked?"

"Finn and Reed found you," he says gently. "They fought off your attacker. Protected you. And the wolf you saw in the cabin?"

"Finn," I murmur, heart twisting. "It was him."

"Yes. When he changed back, you saw him in his human form."

Everything inside me feels like it's turning inside out. Fear and fascination war for dominance, but I have a million questions, and the most pressing ones involve this child. "So, this baby..." I glance down, brushing a thumb across her tiny cheek. "She's a shifter, too?"

"Yes," he says. "Born to a woman named Aura. Mate to a neighboring alpha, Gregory. He claimed her as his mate before she was ready. Then she was attacked by a rival. Left for dead. Gregory cast her aside because she was carrying a bastard child."

I can barely breathe. "She's a baby... an innocent."

"She's a miracle," he says. "And a warning. Shifters are almost always men. In all our years amongst our own kind, this is the first female shifter any of us have seen."

I stare at the child, so small and precious against my skin, and warmth blooms in my chest.

Then I look at Reed. "Show me," I say, voice steady.

He flinches. "Scarlet..."

"I need to see it," I insist. "I need you to show me it's real."

He meets my eyes, holding them captive. The air shift before it happens with a release of invisible pressure, laced with electricity, like a storm on the horizon. His body quivers, muscles tightening, spine curving. In seconds, he's gone and, in his place, stands a wolf, huge, sleek, golden-eyed, and silent.

My breath leaves me in a rush, overwhelmed.

It's not a costume. It can't be. And it's not a trick. Reed's clothes are in a pool at the wolf's feet.

It's a real wolf… a wolf housing the heart and mind of a man.

Reed lowers his head to me like he's bowing.

I reach out my hand, filled with awe and wonder, and when he nuzzles into my palm, gently licking my skin, I want to laugh out loud and cry, too.

There's something so tragic about this; men forced to live with half their natures concealed. They're beautiful, rare, and special, and yet they hide themselves in the mundane, fearful of rejection or persecution.

How many years have they lived like this, building furniture with calloused hands, managing lumber shipments, all while something primal simmers beneath their skin? I see it now, the way their silence was never emptiness but restraint. The way Nixon's eyes held storms he didn't dare let break. The way Reed wore laughter like armor. The way Finn softened everything, even his secrets, like he was trying to apologize for what he was before I ever asked the question.

And I never would have asked, not before today.

But now I know.

Now I've held the evidence in my arms: a baby girl who shifted forms as naturally as a sigh, and did it in the safety of my hands, as if trusting me with her truth before I even knew how to hold it.

They've been carrying this alone.

The weight of their own inheritance.

And it hits me sharply that everything I've felt —the pull between us, the connection that defied logic —might not be some random twist of chemistry. The bond between us is stronger than it should be after so little time, and the desire I have for them is instinctual.

They're not just men. They're wolves.

And they've been letting me come close without knowing if I would run screaming the second I glimpsed what lay beneath their skin.

God. The strength that must be taken.

It makes me ache, not with fear but with fury. That the world has told them they must hide. That being this powerful, this magical, this other, is something they should apologize for.

But they don't need to hide from me.

Not anymore.

I might not have known this truth when I first arrived in this town, but I know it now, and it doesn't scare me. What terrifies me is how much I already care. How much I want to protect the miracle child sleeping in my arms. I want to fight for these men, not because they need saving, but because they deserve to be seen.

Wholly.

Truthfully.

Unconditionally.

Even the wild parts.

Especially the wild parts. Even if only by me.

When Reed shifts back, it's quick, accompanied by a

rustle and gust of air, and one form merges into another. There's no spilled blood, no cracking of bones. An arched back, a gasp, and he's standing there again, naked but unashamed, his chest rising and falling with effort.

I can't take my eyes off him. The stunning carved lines of the firm muscle that shifts beneath his human skin, the huge black tribal tattoo over one pec and shoulder, and the wolf's head inked on his arm. A slight sheen of sweat has formed across his chest, and when my eyes drift lower, I stare at the dark curls around his impressive cock and the scar that mars his thick thigh.

I cradle the baby tighter, stunned. "I believe you," I whisper.

Nixon steps closer, placing a steadying hand on my shoulder as Reed dresses. His touch is warm and grounding. "I know this is a lot to take in," he says. "We wanted to tell you, but we didn't want to frighten you away."

"Why would you tell me? Why would you want to trust me with this?"

Nixon's jaw tics, and he doesn't reply.

I could have left, and I would have been none the wiser. Their secret would have been safe. Immersed in my ordinary life, I never would have learned about the hidden world that exists behind the curtain of normality. I could have spent the rest of my life believing that fairy tales were merely far-fetched stories concocted by the minds of darkly creative imaginations.

Instead, I'm here, with my eyes open to the wonders of the world, with a sweet girl in my arms, an impossibility made flesh, and three men around me who've treated me like a princess they snatched away from imminent danger.

I'm living my own fairy story.

I glance up at Nixon, at Finn, and at Reed.

"I'm not leaving," I say. "Not while she needs me."

Not while my heart is swelling with feelings I'm not ready to voice.

Nixon lets out a long sigh that sounds like relief.

Their secret is out now; our world has shifted, and none of us can pretend otherwise.

"I think we should go home," he says.

Home?

Funny how their cabin in the woods is already starting to feel that way to me.

22

REED

On the journey back to the cabin, the baby wakes, and her soft whimpers grow into a full cry that rattles through my chest. I wince at the unfamiliar sound, as Scarlet tries and fails to calm the infant with nothing but her arms and her voice.

"Nixon, we have nothing to care for this baby. None of us has experience with children."

"We should call Hunter," Finn suggests. "Ask Goldie to help?"

"Who's Goldie?" Scarlet asks as the baby cries even harder, and panic tugs at her cheeks. She grips the baby tighter.

That's a whole other conversation. Until a year ago, the idea of calling on a rival shifter species would have been laughable. But now?

Nixon scrunches his jaw but nods. He fishes his phone from his pocket and dials as the world blurs past the window, leaving the life we knew far behind.

***

When we arrive home, Scarlet's in full mama mode, asking for old shirts and towels and a pair of scissors. In a few minutes, she's fashioned a chunky diaper and a soft garment for the baby to wear until help arrives. I watch with fascination at her resourcefulness.

"You have experience with kids?" I ask.

She shakes her head. "No, but they're little humans, right? They need the same things as we do."

Despite having some creature comforts, the baby's still whining, most likely for food.

When there's a brisk bang on the front door, Nixon practically sprints to open it.

The cabin door swings open, and Hunter steps in with Robert and Evan, their bearish frames filling the doorway as they pass through. Hunter's carrying a large bag, Robert, a small boy, Evan, another small boy, and Goldie follows with a stack of blankets.

Hunter lowers the bag. "Formula, diapers, bottles. Some neutral baby clothes... hand-me-downs, if that works."

"It works," Scarlet says, already rummaging. "Thank you so much."

Robert, Evan, and Hunter all stare at Scarlet, then at us, their brains working. Is she our mate? Unlike wolves, bear shifters can't tell, and we're not about to have that conversation in front of her, so I hope to the goddess they don't ask.

Robert glances at the baby as Scarlet switches the cloth diaper for a disposable one, and his eyes bug out of his head. "Is that a...?"

"Girl," Nixon says. "Yeah."

"But how?"

"It's rare, but not unheard of."

"Where did you find her?"

Finn, who's pulling bottles from the bag and studying them, looks up at Robert. "In the forest near here. She was abandoned."

"That's so sad," Goldie says. She approaches the baby, her eyes wide and almost wary. Then she smiles at Scarlet. "I'm Goldie, by the way. Six men, and no one can manage an introduction."

Scarlet snorts. "I'm Scarlet. Thank you so much for rushing over to the rescue."

"It's not every day we get a baby-related SOS." Goldie runs her hands over her jeans and reaches into the bag for a packet of wipes. "We should wash her face and hands and then give her a bottle."

"I'm on it," Evan says. He hands his little boy to Robert so he can tip formula into a bottle. "Need to stand this in some hot water."

"I can help you with that," Finn says.

I lean against the counter, feeling like a spare part in my own home.

"I'm so far out of my comfort zone, it's a dot on the horizon!" Scarlet says. I know exactly how she feels.

"Whose baby is it?" Hunter asks, his serious gaze watching everything. As the bear alpha, he understands the pack politics of a discovery like this.

"It's complicated," Nixon says. "An alpha's mate was violated. This is the resulting offspring, cast out from the pack."

"They left her to die?" Goldie asks, horrified.

"Yeah," I say. "No alpha would want a cuckoo in their nest."

"She's not a bird," Scarlet blurts, her fingers intertwined with the baby's. "She's a perfect child."

"She's a reminder of something horrific," Nixon reminds her gently. "For her mother and her mate. We believe Aura was cast out, yes. But she wasn't forced to abandon the child. Word on the grapevine is that Gregory has already taken another bride."

"He's a fucking asshole," Scarlet hisses. "What kind of man deserts his woman after she's been violated?"

"A territorial beast," I say, because that's precisely what Gregory is. The truth is, I don't know what Nixon would do in the same situation. Our eyes meet as though we're having the same thought, and he shakes his head. He might have a similar initial reaction, but I know my brother. He always wants to do what's right, and the way he looks at Scarlet… I know the lengths he'd go to keep her safe and avenge her if she was wronged.

"So, what are you going to do?" Hunter asks. "You can't keep it, obviously."

Scarlet stiffens, her hands gripping the edge of the table until her knuckles turn white. The air around her seems to harden.

"Turning her over to the authorities isn't an option," Goldie says, voice steady. "Not if she's shifting."

Goldie reaches across the silence, resting a gentle hand on Scarlet's shoulder. Their eyes meet in a quiet exchange thick with understanding.

Goldie's hand stays on Scarlet's shoulder a moment longer, steadying her like an anchor against the storm of everything we've laid out. I can see in Scarlet's eyes the clash of maternal instinct with the reality of what we are, and what this world is, and I admire her for standing amongst

138

strangers and not running.

Evan presents Scarlet with a bottle, and she gathers the baby into her arms hovering the milk over its lips. It latches onto the teat gratefully, and gulps away, while Scarlet's eyes soften and her lips part in wonder.

Hunter exhales slowly. He shifts his weight like he's grounding himself, then asks again, "So… what are you going to do?"

It's a fair question. One we haven't answered.

The room falls into silence, broken only by the soft gurgling of the infant in Scarlet's arms.

Nixon's jaw ticks. Finn paces near the window, hands clenched at his sides like he's bracing for an argument.

Scarlet doesn't speak right away. She stares at the baby, her thumb gently stroking the soft curve of her tiny shoulder.

Finally, she looks up. Her voice is quieter than I expect, but firmer than anything I've ever heard. "What are we going to do, Nixon?"

Nixon turns to her, slowly. His expression softens a little, his heart showing through his tough outer shell.

"We'll figure it out," he says. "Together."

Together. Is he ready to claim Scarlet? Is he prepared to tell her everything?

Goldie eyes us all, interest gathering in her curious eyes. "We're close. If you need anything… supplies, help, advice, say the word."

Hunter grunts his agreement, lifting one of the twins from Robert's arms. The toddler lets out a soft yawn, tiny fists curled against his father's chest.

"So, you're keeping her," he says, understanding something we haven't faced up to ourselves.

Nixon rubs his stubbled chin. "For now."

Hunter heads for the door.

"Good luck," Robert adds, following them out with Evan not far behind.

Goldie lingers, eyes scanning Scarlet one last time. "It's tough, but totally worth it," she says with a gentle smile.

Scarlet offers her a worried smile in return. Goldie grins and leaves, and then it's us: me, my brothers, Scarlet, and the miracle child who has landed at the center of our lives like a bomb.

Scarlet sits back in a chair and exhales.

I don't know what'll happen next, but what I do know is that nothing has ever looked as right in our kitchen as Scarlet does right now.

23

SCARLET

I settle on the couch with the baby curled against me. In sleep, her breath stirs in a soft rhythm, her tiny chest rising and falling against my heart. The scent of supper drifts from the kitchen, where Finn is chopping and seasoning.

Nixon and Reed slipped out a while ago, shifting outside the door with the intention to track Aura and discover more about her abandoned child. I don't know where they've gone, but I've been anxious since they left. Their absence is a gaping hole, the cabin too big and too empty. This world is so foreign that it's hard for me to accept, but the real danger they might be in hangs like black drapes over my heart.

I shift slightly to cradle the baby more comfortably. Her little fingers curl into my shirt. I stare at her perfect form; her tiny red curls have tightened, her rosebud mouth moves as though she's dreaming about milk, and her tiny fingernails seem too thin to be real. She's a warm weight, and my heart is like a gently inflating balloon, the part of me that cracked open when the doctor told me my dreams of motherhood were unlikely to ever be made real, sealing inch by inch.

It's dangerous to want and to hope, but I'm helpless to resist. The hole in my heart craves to be filled.

From the corner of the room, Finn's voice drifts over: "She's asleep? Dinner's almost ready."

I turn to rest the sleeping baby on the couch beside me, tucking pillows around her in case she rolls.

Standing, I approach Finn as questions tumble through my mind. "So… what is it like?" I ask. "Being a shifter."

He pauses at the door, wiping his hands on a towel. "Do you mean the shifting?" He holds the knife above the zucchini. "Or being part-wolf?"

"Both."

He rubs the back of his neck with his free hand. "I don't know any different, Scarlet. When you're born as something, it's all you ever know."

"But you know the difference. The way you are when you're a man, and the way you are when you're a wolf."

"I'm the same person inside, but a simpler version of me when I have fur." His gaze slides to the sleeping child and back to me, thoughtfully. "When I'm a wolf, I can run free. The world is closer, the smells are more intense. My nature is… different."

"Different?"

"As a wolf, I'd kill on instinct. As a man, I'd have to be pushed to the end of reason to do the same."

He pauses, then his voice lowers. "The *feeling* of it, Scarlet. Being a wolf… It's as if your body becomes the focus, and your mind goes quiet. There's no doubt or overthinking, just pure clarity and instinct. It's intoxicating.

And terrifying. Because the part of you that's human doesn't get to steer. You have to trust the beast in you. And if you don't..." He lifts his eyes, their golden flecks catching the light. "The wolf will eat the man."

A shiver runs up my spine, and I take a step back, forcing my hands into my jeans so he doesn't see them shake.

"And your family... don't wolves live in big groups... packs?"

"We used to, but there can be friction and sometimes, it's easier to split off and start a pack of your own." Finn's eyes trail away, and his voice, too. I wait as he seems to brace himself to continue, straightening his spine. "It's what Hunter did."

"Hunter's a wolf?" I ask. I suspected but didn't want to assume.

"Hunter, Robert, and Evan are all bear shifters."

"Bears?" It makes sense. They're so big and burly, with dark brown curly hair and serious chocolate brown eyes.

"And Goldie?" She's tiny and not bearlike.

"She's human." He resumes chopping the zucchini into thin slices. "Their mate."

"Mate?"

"Fated for each other," Finn says.

I snort and then realize my stupidity. That's the part I find unbelievable? Not the men changing into ferocious apex predators, or the babies that are furry one minute and wrapped in human skin the next. It's the fated love that I have trouble comprehending.

"You don't believe that people can be fated to meet?" he asks.

"I guess I never thought about it. I haven't seen a lot of true love in my life. Most couples I know have a begrudging tolerance of each other."

"That isn't how it works with shifters."

"So, where's your mate?" I ask. "You'll need one, won't you. If you want to create a pack of your own."

"We will," he says, staring at me with soft dark brown eyes. I don't know why, but his attention and words make me flush hot. Our night together seems like a hundred years ago, but it was only a matter of hours.

I pull my phone from my pocket and scan my emails. "I've sold all your furniture, Finn."

He shakes his head, but smiles.

"And they're desperate for more. I've got five inquiries here for the first sight of anything else produced by my handsome new furniture designer."

Finn's cheeks turn a pretty shade of pink. "I don't think I'll be able to keep up with that kind of demand. I'm not a mass producer."

"You don't have to be. The longer it takes you to deliver, the more in demand you'll seem and the more people will want what you create."

"That doesn't make any sense," he says.

I approach the sink to wash the baby's dirty bottle, but glance over my shoulder at the closed front door. "I'm worried about Nixon and Reed. Why are they taking so long?"

"Our territory is large. There's a lot to search, and they won't want to return unless they've found something that's going to guide our decision."

"Maybe I can take the baby home with me," I blurt, before I've had a chance to think about what I'm saying.

Finn frowns. "You can't raise a wolf shifter in the city, Scarlet. She'll shift at any time. How are you going to explain the appearance of a wolf cub in your shopping cart when you're at the store?"

That's a good point. My heart sinks, and he must see my expression fall.

"Do you want kids?" he asks.

"More than anything," I admit, then go further. "But it isn't on the cards for me."

"Why not?" He tips his head, studying me.

"I have a physical problem. The doctors told me it's not going to happen."

His brow furrows. "I'm sorry."

I shrug, my throat tightening with emotion I haven't needed to expel for months. I've gotten good at not thinking about the things that tear out my insides. I swallow it back, forcing a bright smile. "You guys are cheffy."

"We like nice food, so we had to learn to cook it," he says. His eyes are so watchful, like they can see through my protective masks to the kernel of truth and sadness at my core.

I turn to stare at the bundle of sleeping baby still curled peacefully, in human form, on the sofa. Who knows what Nixon's going to say on his return? Maybe they'll take the baby back to her mother, and I'll never see her again. The thought brings metallic-tasting tears to the back of my throat. I drift back to the couch and lift her into my arms, smelling her soft head, and close my eyes at her weight and warmth. I'm not going to let a moment of it pass me by.

If it's possible, I already love her, and I don't even know her name.

24

NIXON

My legs burn and lungs roar as I sprint through the forest with Reed on my right. The wind sails past us, and leaves crunch beneath our paws. Our voices are silent, but our hearts pound in matching beats.

This is freedom, this wild flight that only a wolf can crave. It's the pull of muscle against earth, the bite of air in your chest, the thunderous rhythm of paws hammering the ground like war drums, and the scent of the world exploding all around you.

It's instinct and wonder, a pull so strong that sometimes, it's hard to find the desire to shift back into our slower two-legged form.

We leap fallen logs, dodge sharp boughs, and weave between trees worn smooth by time and weather. The forest is alive around us; flowers blinking in the underbrush, birds lifting into the canopy with scolding cries. Everything sharpens. The smells. The sounds. The pulse of life all around.

This is the part I wish I could share with Scarlet. Not for the first time, I find myself wondering how much easier things would be if our mates were female shifters instead of humans. To run like this as a pack with Scarlet between us, her beautiful red hair turned to russet fur, would be a dream come true. To mate in our wolf form is an experience I'll only ever be able to imagine.

Scent in the wind forces us to change direction. The faint traces of Aura's scent linger on everything she touched. It's an ache in the back of my throat. Her scent is weaker than it should be, worn thin by fear, fading like condensation against a mirror.

But it's there. Enough that we can follow.

And follow it we do, through thickets that tear at our sides, across narrow streams, up ridges slick with pine needles. I push harder. My body doesn't tire. Instead of aging, it seems to get stronger with each year that passes. The wolf in me hungers for the end of this search, for the moment we find her and finally understand why she left the baby and vanished without a trace. The animal part of me can't comprehend a mother leaving a child.

Beside me, Reed runs like he's being chased, his shoulders fluid, his nose skimming the air for confirmation.

We don't need to speak. The bond between us hums as clear as any howl.

Then the trees thin, and an undercurrent of vibration intensifies. We're close.

When the forest opens to a small clearing, I slow, signaling Reed with a sharp bark. A dilapidated shack crouches between trees, built by hands that cared about sheltering from cold and storms but didn't seek luxury.

We creep forward. I sniff, then listen to the sharp intake

of a fearful breath.

Aura's inside, and she must have seen us.

I shift quickly, the soles of my human feet sinking into the soft earth. Reed does the same, his tattooed chest emerging through the fur.

"Aura," I call. "It's Nixon. You're safe. We're here to talk."

A soft rustle answers as she moves inside the shack.

My throat tightens. I nudge Reed, and he slides to my side, a silent guard as we approach.

Inside, bathed in dim light, she huddles beneath a ragged blanket, wrapped tight around herself. A handful of possessions—books, a few packets of food, another blanket—lie scattered at her side. She doesn't look well. Her red hair is dull, her eyes hollow and haunted. She's so small. So fragile and pale.

She freezes at the sight of me, naked and looming.

I drop to my knees, heart pounding, and cup myself. This is the problem with shifting and having no clothes to wear. "Aura. It's Nixon. You remember me."

Her frightened eyes flit between me and Reed, and she cowers as though she's expecting violence. Gregory and her attacker did a job on her.

"We found your baby."

She shakes her head. "I don't have a baby."

"We know it's yours. It smells like you."

She grimaces, out of guilt or disgust at our wolf senses. Humans are often dismissive of the fact that our differences can offer certain advantages, yet still manage to look down on us.

"Leave it, and leave me," she croaks.

"You don't look good," I say. "You need some medical

help?"

"I need you to leave me alone."

I glance at Reed, who shakes his head. This is pitiful and uncomfortable. "We can't do that, Aura. The baby needs you. We can help you get set up somewhere so you can take care of her."

"I don't want her," she says. "You think I could even look at that thing... see their faces... remember every day what they did to me. I have nothing. You people... you creatures have taken everything from me."

Faces? Whose faces?

"Not us," Reed says firmly. "We're nothing like them."

"You're all the same. Beasts beneath your pretty human shells. You make us believe we can live in your world, but you use us to birth your legacy because you have no women of your own." She laughs, and it's a hollow, exhausted sound that tears at my heart. "Except, look what I produced! A female shifter. A freak."

"A miracle," I say.

"I needed a miracle before Gregory tore out half my neck. I needed a miracle before they... they..." Tears streak her cheeks. "I needed a miracle before I had to grow a child in my womb... their child."

I flinch. The baby is sweet and innocent.

"She needs her mother." I try one last time, even though it's clear that Aura is traumatized past any kind of empathy for her child.

"She needs to be put out of her misery before she comes of age and is ruined like me."

Reed shakes his head, turning to scan our surroundings while I think on what to say next. "Does Gregory know about the child?"

She laughs, her eyes wide and her head tipped back.

She seems unhinged.

Wolves are supposed to worship our mates and protect them. Gregory's done nothing for poor Aura.

"Can we bring you anything? Food. Clothes. If you come with us, we can get you settled into the motel in town. Get you back on your feet."

Aura shakes her head, her lank hair dropping around her face as she pulls the blanket higher. "Just leave me in peace," she says.

Peace. She doesn't have enough food to last more than a day or so. Her clothes are filthy. Is she intending to hide in this shack until she dies? I shiver as the breeze whips around us, already craving the protection of my wolf coat.

"We should go," Reed says.

I sniff the air, wondering if he's scented something. We're close to the border with Gregory's territory here. We can't stay too long and risk him crossing over to investigate our presence.

"Peace isn't something you find alone," I tell Aura as I rise. "Peace is something you find in friendships and family and love. You've lost a lot, but while you have air in your lungs and beats in your heart, there's always a way out of the darkness. Don't waste it. If you want us to help, come to the cabin."

She looks away from me, as though my words disgust her.

In a blink, Reed is back in his wolf form, already bounding toward home.

Scarlet is waiting for us. Our mate.

We don't have a solution to this baby issue, but as I bound after my brother, eventually taking the lead, I know we're going to need to explain the truth about our bound destinies, whether it's the right time or not.

25

REED

By the time we arrive home, Scarlet is asleep on the sofa with her head resting in Finn's lap. The baby is, like Moses, sleeping in a laundry basket. Finn is reading a book, his glasses perched on the end of his nose, and he looks up when we enter the house wearing our boxers and clutching our clothes. The pretense is over. Scarlet knows what we are.

She doesn't know what she is yet, though.

"Did you find her?" he asks, placing the book on the arm of the couch.

"We did." Nixon runs his hands over his sweat-damp hair, staring at Scarlet... our very own sleeping beauty. "But it isn't good news."

"She doesn't want the baby?"

"Nope." I lean over the little bundle, wondering how anyone could bear to leave her alone in the woods. But unless you've lived through hell, it's hard to judge the ones it scorches.

"She's in a state of distress. I tried my best to encourage her to let us help her, but she's adamant we leave the baby to die."

"We're not doing that," Finn blurts. "Are we?"

Nixon sighs. "Of course not."

"So, we're daddies now?"

"I guess we are." Nixon drops his clothes and kneels next to the baby, staring at it. All of us are staring at it.

"You ever think you'd see a female shifter?" I ask.

They whisper no, the wonder of it still aching in our hearts. "She's a blessing born from tragedy," I murmur.

"She's a miracle."

"Scarlet loves her already," Finn says. "She talked about taking her home with her, but I pointed out that wolves don't belong in the city."

We both stare at him, and then at her beautiful face, so peaceful.

He touches her hair gently, reverently. "She told me she can't have children."

Nixon's head jerks back, his shock reverberating through me, too.

"Why?"

Finn shrugs. "Doctors told her."

We all look at the baby again; her tiny fingers curled, lashes brushing her cheeks. The goddess has blessed us with this child, and she will continue to bless us with others. Our mate is made for us alone, and that thought sends a ripple of satisfaction through me.

"She isn't ours," I say, as my brothers stare at me. "But she will be in all the ways that count."

Finn bites his lip. "What if Gregory finds out who she is? We're not going to be able to keep her scent concealed forever."

"We'll find a way," Nixon growls. "That asshole isn't going to hurt another female, if I have anything to say about it."

"So, we claim Scarlet now. Tell her what she is to us. Tell her what her role will be."

"Steal her from her life and her family," Finn says, still stroking her hair. "You didn't see her when she talked about leaving. Her whole face lit up. She loves her life and her business. She's so passionate."

"She can be passionate here," Nixon says.

"Let's take her to bed," I tell my brothers. "While the baby sleeps, let's remind her why staying is her only option."

"You think good sex is a cure-all?" Finn asks.

"I think good sex is the glue that will bond her to us. Until the claim, that is."

"Maybe."

Nixon rises and gathers Scarlet into his arms. I pick up the basket with the child, an action so foreign that I marvel for a moment at how quickly our lives have changed and how quickly we're adapting.

When Scarlet stirs, murmuring, "You're back," Nixon leans in close to tell her, "The baby's staying with us," and her face goes from drowsy to elated in a second.

We climb the stairs as a family.

But right now, the only ones who are bonded are me and my brothers, and we're running out of time to change that.

Her eyes drift to the bedroom door. "Let us show you what you mean to us... What you are to us." Nixon bends to kiss her tenderly.

We can't control how Scarlet feels about us, but we can give her all the best reasons to want to stay.

154

26

FINN

When the baby cries, Scarlet is off the bed in seconds. She grabs my shirt and pulls it over her head. I snag a pair of sleep shorts from the chair, tug them on, and follow her, my feet thudding against the wood floor.

Nixon and Reed are out cold, sprawled in the tangle of sheets, dead to the world after their long night of pursuing Aura and pleasuring Scarlet. They don't stir as we slip out, and I don't blame them.

The baby is squirming in her makeshift basket crib. Scarlet scoops her up, holding her against her chest, her lips already whispering soft shushing noises.

"I think she's hungry again," she murmurs, not quite looking at me, but rocking gently.

I peer at the squirming bundle, who kicks with surprising strength for someone so small. "Probably needs a diaper change, too."

"Yeah. Of course." Scarlet's voice is low and a little unsure, but there's a calmness about her that I appreciate. If she were panicking, this whole situation would probably implode. We share a wide-eyed, amused, overwhelmed glance. Neither of us knows what the hell we're doing. But there's no panic. Just this strange, sweet willingness to try together.

"Let's take her downstairs," I say, tipping my chin toward the hall. "Leave the others to sleep. We'll figure it out."

Scarlet exhales, a puff of relief that makes me want to kiss her. Instead, I open the door and gesture for her to go first. She gives me a grateful look and pads barefoot down the stairs, cradling the baby like she's made of spun sugar.

***

The kitchen is dim and quiet, the navy blue of the midnight sky pressing in through the windows. I flick on a small lamp above the stove while Scarlet settles onto the couch with the baby. I grab the emergency bag Goldie left behind, digging for supplies before I prepare a bottle.

"You're getting good at that," Scarlet says.

I glance over and smirk. "I'm a fast learner. Especially with a vocal teacher."

She chuckles, and it cuts through the quiet. I want to hear that laugh again. And again. And the sighs she makes after she comes, when her body is as relaxed as it can be.

By the time I hand Scarlet the warm bottle, the baby's fussing, but it quickly turns to eager sucking. Her cheeks puff and deflate with each determined pull, and Scarlet watches her like she's witnessing a miracle.

"I thought about names earlier," she says after a moment. "Before I fell asleep. I thought... maybe we should give her one."

I settle beside her, shoulder to shoulder. "Yeah? Got one

in mind?"

She watches the baby, who is going at the bottle like it's her last meal. "Ahya," she says softly. "It means miracle."

Ahya.

It isn't a name I've ever heard before, but it's beautiful. I swallow the lump rising in my throat and nod slowly. "It fits."

Scarlet's smile is small, but radiant. "She survived the woods. Whatever that pack did to Aura... And whatever fate tried to do to her. She's still here, alive and strong." She pauses, stroking Ahya's cheek.

I rest a hand on her thigh. "Doesn't matter how she got here, or how little we know. She's safe now. That's what counts."

The baby finishes the bottle with a triumphant gasp, then goes utterly still until a rumble rolls through her tiny body. The sound is both hilarious and horrifying.

Scarlet's eyes go wide. "Oh god."

I crack up. "That's a code brown!"

"How does something that small make that much noise?" She's laughing, but she's already standing, shifting Ahya into the crook of one arm and grabbing a clean diaper with the other.

"Miracle or not, Ahya's gonna test our capabilities."

We spread out the supplies on the couch. I help peel off the onesie while Scarlet wrangles the wipes. It's clumsy, awkward, and wildly endearing. The smell hits us both at once, and we recoil, then burst into shared laughter.

"Is this our life now?" she says, barely containing her giggle.

"It sure looks that way."

Scarlet glances at me, eyes shining, and my heart aches

157

at the hope that's so clear in her pretty eyes.

Once Ahya's fresh and clean, we tuck her back into the basket. Scarlet curls up next to me, and I sling my arm around her, pulling her close.

"She's so perfect."

"You both are." I kiss her temple, inhaling her scent that relaxes me to the core.

She turns her face to me, forehead resting against mine. "Do you think it's weird?" she asks. "That I'm already this bonded to Ahya?"

"No," I say. "I think it's fate."

She presses a soft kiss to my lips, then lets her head rest on my chest, melting against me as the baby settles nearby. The house is still again, full of possibility and growing love. Full of questions, truths, and complications, too.

"We need to talk tomorrow," I say gently. "All of us. My brothers should be there."

She looks up, searching my face.

I cup her head and pull her to my lips, pressing another kiss to her temple, unable to get enough of the sweet scent of her hair. "Don't worry. It's good. The best. I promise."

She rests against my chest, wrapping her arm across me. "You ever think about what you *really* want out of life?"

"You mean like... hopes and dreams."

"Yeah."

"All the time," I admit. "There are things I want, and things I know I need. They don't always fit together."

"So what do you do when they don't?"

I exhale slowly. "You make a choice. Sometimes you give up what you want to keep what you can't live without."

I think about the furniture I'd build if Nixon didn't need me at the lumberyard. The places I'd travel if my wolf weren't a liability in unknown territory. The family I lost, whom I'd trade every dream to see again.

She sighs. "I think our generation believes we can have it all. And in chasing everything, we let the important things pass us by."

"What do you want, Scarlet?"

She doesn't answer right away. When she does, her voice is too practiced. "I love my life."

But then her mask cracks.

"The truth is… I want to be a momma." Her words are a whisper.

Maybe she fears that admitting the truth too loudly might shatter something inside her. "Maybe it's because I can't have children. Maybe if the choice hadn't been taken from me, the need wouldn't burn as much as it does."

I gather her into my arms, holding her as tightly as I dare, as if I could shield her from the ache, as if my touch could rewrite the years of heartbreak and grief she's buried beneath that quiet strength.

My gut twists, my chest hollowing with the weight of what she's been denied.

And beneath that pain, my wolf awakens, howling to give her what she craves. To fill her with my seed. To claim her. To heal her. To breed her.

This desire to plant our legacy deep in the woman fate carved for us is primal.

She's ours.

The doctors were wrong. Her body was waiting for the right mate. She was meant to be ours all along.

And we can give her everything she thinks she can't have.

This may be the key to making Scarlet our willing mate.

27

SCARLET

The morning unfolds in a cascade of new roles. Ahya's cry carries through the silence, a tiny whimper that crescendos, and in a heartbeat, I'm awake. She needs a bath, but Nixon suggests we use the shower. The water is tepid on his skin and mine as we gently soap Ahya's fragile frame together. Her surprise is endearing as the water trails through her red curls, slicking them to the gentle curve of her head. She blinks wide-eyed, then relaxes, lulled by the warmth. Gentle laughter drifts between us, me at how startled she is and Nixon at how perfect she looks with her hair teased into a mohawk. She's so tiny that, clutched against Nixon's broad chest, cradled by his huge hands, she seems impossibly small.

Reed dresses her in a powder blue onesie and Finn mixes her formula to her liking. They head out soon after, Nixon and Reed to the lumberyard, and Finn to his workshop, leaving me cradling our little miracle. I'm more complete than ever.

Ahya is the sweetest little thing. She listens, entranced, when I softly sing the lullabies I remember from childhood. When I lay her on the rug with a tiny plush toy Goldie packed for us, she kicks with delight. When her eyes flutter shut, she fusses only briefly before curling into me and slipping into a deep, peaceful sleep.

Before I realize it, lunchtime arrives, punctuated by the rumble of the truck and footsteps through the front door. Nixon and Reed enter, bags of tacos and sodas in hand. Finn is right behind them, carrying more.

"I could have made sandwiches," I say, fishing a taco from a bag and letting the aroma flirt with my senses.

"You're taking care of Ahya," Reed says, his gaze drifting to her sleeping form. "That's full-time work on its own."

"She's no trouble," I admit. "I thought babies were supposed to be exhausting, but she's so easy."

"Wait until she shifts," Reed teases. "Then you'll be chasing her around the house."

I freeze at the reminder of that part of her nature. "Do you think she will?"

"It's hard to predict," Nixon says, between giant bites of his taco. "Sometimes the shift comes later. But in Ahya's case, maybe being left alone triggered it early. A human baby wouldn't survive the woods, but a wolf cub might."

"Poor baby," I whisper. Fear climbs in my chest as I think how close she came to freezing.

Nixon wipes his hands. "We have something to talk about."

My heart skips. "Finn mentioned."

All three men fix their eyes on me. My stomach flips.

"You're making me nervous," I laugh, but it comes out like a squeak.

161

"It's not bad," Reed says, offering a crooked smile. "One more truth bomb, amidst everything you've already learned."

Nixon's pale blue eyes are so serious, my mouth is suddenly dry.

"You came here and found us."

"You found me," I remind him.

"Whatever." He waves his hand as though the specifics are unimportant. "You're here with us, not because of a set of random circumstances but because fate brought you to us... You're our mate."

Finn adjusts his weight beside me, his expression solemn and steady. Reed nods with silent support in his gaze.

I laugh and it bursts out of me unexpectedly loud, making Finn jump.

"Scarlet, we're serious." Nixon leans forward, crowding.

Outside, the forest crowds in, the trees bending in the wind that rattles the windows in their frames, reminding me that everything about this palace is unfamiliar.

"Our mate bond," Nixon continues, "it's not like a human relationship. It's deeper. When we claim you... when you choose to be ours... it's forever." He reaches across the table, takes my hand, and his touch is warm, grounding me. "You'll feel it? The bond. I think you already do."

Reed stands behind him, arms crossed over his broad chest, his brows furrowed in concentration. "It's not only about love," he adds. "It's total devotion. It's waking up every day knowing we belong to each other and this place."

My heart pounds like a drumbeat because he's right. The pull he's talking about is like roots springing from my feet to anchor me, waking old and powerful sensations inside me.

But I shake my head.

"No," I whisper. "I don't... I don't belong here. I have a home, a life, and family."

"Your home is here. Your life is here. We're your family, Scarlet. And you'll bear our children to make a new pack."

I shake my head, knowing for certain now that they're wrong about all of this. "I can't have children, Nixon. I'm barren." I wince at the archaic word but it's the only way I can make him hear the truth. "You need to find another mate."

"There is no other mate," he says. "It's you. You're the one marked for us. Born on the wolf moon. You're ours, and there's no changing it."

"I can't have children, Nixon. You're not listening." Frustration curls my fists in my lap. "There must be a way for you to find another mate. What if I died."

"No," Finn says, surprising me with this firmness. "There is no other way."

"This is..." I look around, trying to find words that wouldn't be insulting. I want to say it's primitive, crazy, ridiculous. It's a fantasy, an illusion, like the magicians on TV that wow with sleight of hand tricks. But none of those is right. "I'm an ordinary woman," I say. "Not even that. I can't give you what you need. I'm broken. I'm not what you want."

Nixon's fist thuds so hard against the table that I flinch.

"You are exactly what we want, Scarlet. Do you hear me? You're not broken. You need to be with us to fulfil your destiny."

"I don't have a destiny, Nixon," I yell. "This isn't a fairy tale. You want to claim me, to bond me to you, but I'm human. I don't belong in this world of yours."

Finn is slumped forward, sunlight catching the dark threads of his hair and turning them bronze. His eyes are soft with understanding, his voice low and rich as the earth that cradled Ahya. "Goldie's human. She didn't think she belonged with Hunter, Robert, and Evan, either. She fought it for a long time, but the bond changed her. The forest changed her. But we can't do this if you don't want it."

"We can," Reed says. "We can do what Gregory did and force the claim, but we don't want that. We've never wanted that. This only happens if it's what you want, Scarlet."

He stands and crosses to me, laying a hand firmly on my shoulder. "Scarlet, you're not just a woman. Not anymore. The forest called to you. The goddess handed you a miracle child, the chance of a mate-bond, and a place in this pack. It's fate."

I glance at my hands, relishing the strength of Reed's reassuring grip, Nixon's firm words and Finn's gentle explanations. These men... these wolf-men have done nothing but look out for me. Since I arrived at their cabin, they've been gentle and considerate, passionate and kind. They've given me space to develop feelings and waited to explain their world to me. Now they're promising me a forever commitment and the family I thought could never be mine. "You said... you could give me children?"

Nixon nods. "Our seed is meant for you. If you choose us, if you ask for the claim, and let the bond settle into your body, it will heal what was broken. You were told you couldn't have children in the human world. But here, with us... anything is possible. We will breed you, Scarlet. We will fill you with babies, and this house with our pack."

The cabin seems to brace with my hesitation. Outside, a

bird trills and I close my eyes, fighting the sting there. I came on a quick trip to do business, but instead, I found men who want to promise me forever, a baby I've bonded with, and a world that doesn't want to let me go.

"I thought I knew who I was," I whisper. "I thought I had a path."

Nixon reaches for my hand, and his fingers tighten around mine. "You did. And it led you here."

"This place," Finn murmurs, "You're part of it now, Scarlet."

I look from one to the other, these men who carry the wild in their eyes and speak like prophecy.

"I need time," I say, my voice trembling.

"Take it," Nixon murmurs. "We'll wait. But know this, Scarlet. Your place is here. Not because we want you to stay. Not because you're a part of us already. But because the forest, the goddess, the bond... you were chosen for us to love."

And in my heart, something soft cracks open.

Because they're not willing to overwhelm my choice and claim what's rightfully theirs. They're waiting for me to choose them, too.

28

NIXON

A part of me understands why generations of wolf-shifters have taken their mates by force. The patience required to convince a reluctant human woman to give up her ordinary life to join a wolf-pack and bear wolf children is enough to try the patience of even the most patient man, and I am not a patient man.

But when Scarlet falls asleep in my arms, her red hair cascading around her, and her pretty pink lips parted, my wolf is quiet. She's everything I hoped our mate would be. Beautiful, of course, but not only on the outside. Her heart is sweet and open enough to love a child who isn't her own. She works with us, finding a role in whatever task we need to tackle. She's down to earth, not pretentious, and as in love with the forest and the craftsmanship that shapes its trees as we are. She challenges us, and holds her own, even against the strength of my will, with its alpha stubbornness.

Finn told me about how she helped sell some of his furniture. It warmed my heart to know that when we claim her, she'll be able to continue the life she loves. The goddess is wise to send us a mate who could find happiness and contentment in our lives.

She's bright and clever, challenging us and bringing new light to our world.

And in bed, she's fire, accepting her place between the three of us, bringing us more pleasure than we could have hoped for.

All we have to do now is convince her that this life is better than what she could have if she returns home. No human man could give her what we can.

"Nixon," Reed whispers, interrupting my thoughts. His arm is around Scarlet's waist, and he was breathing so evenly, I was convinced he was asleep.

"Yeah."

"You think she's going to choose us?" he asks.

"Of course." It's my role, as alpha, to be strong and sure. My brothers are relying on me for confidence and guidance.

"I'm not so sure," he says. "There's still doubt in her mind. She's holding back. Isn't she?"

She is, but I was hoping he would be too overwhelmed by her to notice.

"I think you should give her your knot."

I flinch at his suggestion, and Scarlet stirs, burrowing closer to my chest, arching her back in the process, and Reed groans as her naked ass grinds against his dick.

"She's not ready," I say. "That's only for after the claim."

"There's no rule against it," Reed counters. "Nothing to say you can't breed her before the claim. Maybe, if you prove to her that the doctors were wrong, she'll believe that this is where she belongs."

His words reverberate in my mind. The thought of tying

her to us irrevocably is potent and dangerous. But also… beautiful.

The image of Scarlet swollen with our pups is what fills my mind as Reed finally drifts off to sleep, and I'm left to keep watch over my pack.

***

In the morning, we load ourselves and sweet Ahya into the truck. Scarlet cradles the baby in her arms as I close the door. Her red curls peek from under a wool cap, and her cheeks are rosy and eyes bright with wonder at the trees rustling overhead. Everything in me stills to watch them together; two strangers, but so bonded, there's no longer an inch of space between them.

As we drive toward town, the cab is quiet. Finn and Reed seem as lost in thought as I am, our wolves' desire for the claim almost overwhelming. I picture a future filled with mornings like this, of quiet roads, family contentment, and anticipation of a day spent happily.

But that will only happen if Scarlet can see that this future is her destiny.

At the baby store, the light is stark with bright overhead panels illuminating cribs, colorful toys, and walls lined with pastel clothing. Reed positions himself near the exit, alert, while I stay close to Scarlet and Ahya. Braysville Town isn't strictly our territory, and there is always a chance we can come across other shifters, wolves, or otherwise, while we're surrounded by humans.

We move through the aisles following Scarlet, who lifts tiny socks from the rack, her eyes soft. She smiles when she finds a onesie printed with woodland creatures and a forest scene. She picks up organic formula packs, passing them to Finn.

I imagine returning to this store again when she's swollen with our cubs. I guide her gently from rack to rack, pointing out items I know Ahya will grow into, and boys' clothing I like, too. *For our sons*, I think. I wonder if she understands.

At the register, I pay and am presented with the purchases in two large bags. Finn carries the box containing the stroller and another containing a car seat, and we flank Scarlet and Ahya as we approach Reed to leave the store.

Glancing left and right, I observe the townsfolk going about their days. A couple passes us, and the woman smiles as Ahya waves her arms up and down, clearly excited to see so many people. I stick close, my wolf senses on high alert.

Protect.

Mate.

Mine.

The words buzz through me, bunching my muscles against an invisible threat.

Invisible until the breeze fills my nostrils with the scent of a rogue wolf.

A tall figure pauses fifteen feet ahead, his face tipped. He's scented us, too. He's lean and angular and his scent freezes me. One of Gregory's pack has crawled out of the woodwork at the worst possible time.

Reed braces as Finn becomes aware. I position myself between the man and Scarlet, hoping it will be enough to mask Ahya's scent. The stranger stares, not threatening but interested.

My wolf snarl is silent, but I bare the tips of my fangs beneath my mask of calm, enough to glint in the morning sunshine. His stare flicks to me and then to my brothers. Scarlet, unaware of the danger, moves slightly to the side to avoid bumping into my back, and I throw my arm up to prevent her. A flicker passes across his expression at the sight of her and our defensive stance. He knows she's someone special now. Not our mate because she carries no wolf marking, but enough to warrant our protection. Then his eyes drift to the baby in her arms.

"Don't move," I grit out to Scarlet, who flinches with sudden awareness.

If he approaches, we'll be forced to take action, and none of us wants a snarling battle of fangs and claws on Main Street.

"Nixon."

A gravelly voice calls my name from the coffee shop to our right. Hunter is there with his family, holding a tray. My stillness alerts him, and Robert and Evan respond immediately, stepping forward and guiding Scarlet to where Goldie is sitting with their sons.

Like ice in the spring sun, the threat melts into the crowd.

"Take care of her," I order Finn, striding after the enemy wolf to confirm he's leaving town. Reed follows a little behind, and we both pause when we observe him climbing into a black truck.

Reed growls low and possessively. "It was going to happen sometime, but not when she's unclaimed, Nixon. We can't leave her unprotected."

He's right, of course.

I'm not a patient man, and now my hand has been forced.

"She's ours," I say. "They're both ours. The claim happens tonight."

***

"Thank you," I say to Hunter, Robert, and Evan, shaking each man's hand in turn.

"Trouble?" Hunter asks.

"Pack politics," I say. Our truce with the bears of Blackwood Forest is new, and I'd rather not drag them any further into wolf business.

"It's something we avoid." Hunter rubs his thick brown beard, his frown deep enough to tell me he suffers with similar complications among his own kind.

We have made similar choices to set ourselves apart from our packs to find peace for our families. I'm unsure how Hunter avoids getting dragged into issues with the wider bear group, and I'm not in a position to ask for that kind of advice.

What I'm sure of is that wolf will report back to his alpha, and what happens next could impact everything we're striving for.

Goldie is watchful, her attention only half on Scarlet, who's holding Ahya close as she fusses. Can she sense the tension that's vibrating through us all?

"We should go," I say.

Hunter's eyes scan the section of road outside the coffee shop. "Do you have others to call upon if necessary?"

I grit my teeth at the thought of being forced to call on the family we left and the memory of the blame they threw in our direction. It's too bitter a pill to swallow, but if Gregory decides to make a claim for Ahya, I will humble myself and do whatever needs to be done, no matter the cost.

"We do," I tell Hunter. "Reed. Finn. Get the truck and bring it outside."

To Scarlet, I say. "Be ready to leave. It's time."

171

"Okay." Lines bracket her mouth. I'm impressed with how calm she's remained, and the way she's avoided asking questions as though she can sense that it isn't the time to reveal anything about our situation.

***

We leave the boundaries of Braysville before Scarlet asks, "Who was that man?"

"One of Gregory's pack," I tell her. "We have to assume he knows about Ahya."

Her expression falls. "Will he come for her?"

I reach out to cup her cheek. "I don't know, Scarlet. Gregory is unpredictable, but we can assume he'll be interested in her existence. Not necessarily because she's Aura's child, but because she's a she." I reach over to touch Scarlet's wild hair. "Don't worry. We'll keep her safe. We'll keep you both safe."

"I believe you." Her hazel eyes are soft as they gaze at me, giving me the confidence that now is the time.

"But while you're unclaimed, Scarlet, your life is at greater risk."

She blinks, the softness morphing into something immediately more suspicious. I touch her lips before she replies. "I know you're unsure and you have questions, but sometimes in life, our hands are forced. Sometimes we can't wait for the perfect moment, and we have to jump in feet-first, regardless of the dangers ahead. This is one of those times."

She shakes her head, but I lean in to kiss her, showing her with the softness of my lips all the emotions that I hold in my heart for her. Ahya gurgles, and I pull back to look at the sweet little girl whose existence is still a mystery.

"Sometimes we have to trust that the goddess's plan for

us is greater than the plan we made for ourselves."

"The goddess?" Her eyebrow arches in question.

"She was wise enough to send you to us, and Ahya to you."

I steel myself against a shiver. The world we live in is shifting, and "ours" means more than shared love. It's a promise to protect. To defend to the death. It's ownership and territory. It's fate solidifying beneath my skin.

Scarlet might not be ready, but it's time to do what is required. It's time to claim our mate.

29

SCARLET

The tension in the cabin is palpable. The threat to me and Ahya looms over the men in this house in a way that I'm struggling to comprehend. I'm not from this dark corner of the world, and trying to understand the relationships and the customs of wolf culture is complex and baffling. All I know is I haven't wanted to put Ahya down all day. Keeping her close is a fierce instinct. I'm not her mother. I've never spent time around young babies, and yet, I seem to know what she needs as though she's my own.

I love her.

And watching stoic Nixon, rugged Reed, and gentle Finn fight for her smiles, try to anticipate her needs, and hover around her like silent guardians has me melting over them, too. There's something about a man showing kindness to children, especially when they're not blood, that reveals an essential inner trait that ticks all my female boxes.

They've even started to override my fears about this strange world I find myself in.

174

They think I'm their mate. A woman fated to join their pack. But I'm just Scarlet, an ordinary human woman with a splintered past and a sharp tongue. I came to Braysville for lumber, and now? Now, I find myself aching when one of them leaves the room, caring for a child, and at the center of a poly relationship with men who are also wolves. My mind is blown at how fast my life has changed.

My mother warned me about strangers.

But how can I be afraid of men who treat a foundling child with such tender care? How can I run from protectors who see me, all of me, and never once ask me to be less?

Still, I ask myself quietly, *Is this really what I want?*

After we returned home from town, Reed disappeared into the woods. Nixon and Finn engaged in much low, angry conversation. Then Nixon disappeared, and Finn encouraged me and Ahya to join him in his workshop. It was so calming to watch him take tools to wood, smoothing surfaces and engraving marks. Ahya watched calmly from my arms, clutching a miniature wooden horse Finn had whittled for her. Outside, birds called, and the trees rustled their secrets, and the scent of an unfamiliar world seeped into my consciousness. I realized that I'm settled in a way I never had in my life back home.

My mom's warning voice that's always there whenever I'm thinking about making changes or decisions, interrupts my calm.

Beware of strangers, Scarlet. They're wolves in sheep's clothing. You never know what they want from you until it's too late.

But I know what these men want from me. They want to love me, claim me, bind us together forever in a way no paper or ring ever could, and that should terrify me. It should make me want to run for the hills, but I've seen the

175

way Hunter, Robert, and Evan look at Goldie like she hung the stars for them. I've seen the gentle way they touch her, and the softness in their eyes when she speaks. They've shown me the mate bond, and from the outside, it looks beautiful.

***

After dinner, when Ahya is clean, fed, and asleep, I slip into the bathroom for a shower, hoping the water will wash away the confusion clinging to my thoughts. The steam is thick, and I lean my head against the tile, overwhelmed by the weight of it all.

I'm only alone for two minutes, then the door opens, revealing Nixon, Reed, and Finn naked and glorious, powerful and intense. They climb in around me, and I glance up at each of them, overwhelmed by their size and proximity, finding softness in their expressions, but hunger, too. Their eyes rove over my body, lingering on my pale skin and the red curls between my thighs, slick with water. Nixon cups my cheek, his voice a rasp of reverence.

"You're shaking," he murmurs. "Let us hold you."

Then, with a smooth strength that overwhelms me, he lifts me against his chest. My legs wrap around his waist. My arms circle his shoulders. My lips find his without hesitation.

Reed's hands are at my back, fingers tracing the ridges of my spine. Finn's body presses into mine, solid and warm. He kisses the curve of my shoulder, his lips reverent.

"Let us show you what it means to be ours," Finn says softly.

They kiss me all over, their tongues tracing softness beneath each breast, sliding over the curve of my belly, planting tiny claims on my skin. Every action is deliberate and reverent. I'm slick with water, but also with want.

When Reed cups my breast, his thumb circling my peaked nipple, I tilt my head, swamped by sensation. My skin comes alive with every caress. I'm open for this. For whatever they want.

Finn's lips trail from the bend of my neck to the outside of my thigh as Nixon's cock presses hard and insistent along the length of my sex. The glass fogs behind us, until nothing exists but the weight of them, the need in their eyes, the truth in their mouths.

I sense the shift in atmosphere as the tension between us turns electric. This is the moment before the claim. My rational mind whispers I'm not ready, but at the same time, every fractured piece of my heart is pounding, wanting so fiercely that fear dissolves into longing.

I want the love and devotion these men are willing to give and the softness of Ahya's little body to always be close.

I want the security of a life surrounded by love and protection, where I no longer have to hope for a fairytale ending or fear the danger at the door.

I find them in the steam; three faces, three promises, three wolves determined that I belong to them.

I'm uncertain about this world, but I'm already entwined.

I move with them, turning, responding, tasting each one. My resistance softens with every kiss.

Finally, Nixon brushes a towel over my shoulders. I shiver, though I'm burning, and he nudges me forward, hands resting gently as a promise on my hips.

I know this is the path to the claim. I'm not ready, but I can't step away, either.

Their breath, their heartbeats, and their wild devotion coils around me. Their pack has become my sanctuary, and more importantly, the only safety Ahya has ever known. And while fear claws at my thoughts, I lean into that promise.

In this moment, my world shifts beneath my skin.

And part of me welcomes it.

Because running back to a world without them now?

I don't know how to do that anymore.

30

NIXON

For every wolf, the knowledge that there will be a mate in their future is a part of life. One of my earliest memories is of my father telling us about the deep, abiding connection between him and my mother. That connection seemed holy for a long time, until I was older and could see the tiny flaws in their relationship. They never considered parting. That isn't how the mate bond works, but there was always a lingering sense of resentment at my mother's lack of choice. I wanted real love, and to be a choice for my mate, rather than a fated inevitability.

Now, here we are, walking Scarlet into our bedroom, and I'm still not sure how she feels. She's attracted to us, sure. No woman comes as hard as she does if her mind isn't connected to the men she's with. Attraction is important, but it isn't enough.

She sits on the edge of the bed, skin still dewy from the shower, hair tumbling in damp waves over her shoulders. She's the picture of raw beauty, bared and vulnerable, yet holding herself like a warrior who doesn't quite trust the battlefield.

Her knuckles are white against the mattress.

I crouch before her, bringing my face close to hers. I lift my hand and cup her cheek. She closes her eyes at the contact, leaning into it like she needs it more than air.

"We don't want to force you," I say, trying to leash the wild edge clawing its way into my throat. "But we can't leave you unclaimed, not with the danger that's coming. If you want to stay… this is the only way."

She trembles. Her eyes open, and she looks at each of us like we might hold the answer she can't find inside herself.

"What do you think, Scarlet?" Reed asks. "About everything we've told you. About us… this life… what we're asking of you?"

"I…" Her voice cracks. Tears well in her eyes, and my heart lurches in my chest. Goddess, I can't claim her like this.

Reed kneels in front of her, brushing his fingers along her thigh. She doesn't pull away. We flank her, surrounding her, but not boxing her in.

"We're not here to take," Reed says. "This isn't about marking territory or sealing fate. It's about choosing you because you've already changed us. You've crawled under our skin, Scarlet. You've settled into the empty spaces we didn't even know we had."

"You're what we want," I add, my hand still on her face. "What we need. But you have to want us, too. All of us."

She swallows hard. Her fingers tremble as she reaches for Reed's. "I don't know how it happened," she murmurs, "but I feel you all. Here." She touches her chest. "And here." Her temple.

I lean closer. "Do you want us to claim you?"

Her frustration sparks like a match. "How am I supposed to know? Your world isn't mine."

"It can be," Finn says quietly. "Our world exists within yours. The claim isn't an ending. It's a beginning. A new skin you grow into."

"And danger," she says, eyes flashing.

"Danger exists everywhere," I say. "But at least with us, you'll never face it alone."

"You're asking me to commit to you... like marriage?"

"More than marriage," I say proudly. "This is a lifelong bond. You will never want to leave us... never have reason to be dissatisfied. We will give you everything you need. You will become part of us as we will become a part of you."

My wolf paces inside me. The moment is close. Scarlet's scent is thick with uncertainty... but it's laced with want, too.

Finn steps closer. "We wanted to wait for you to come to us. To ask. But we can't wait any longer. Our wolves are tearing us apart. Every second we don't claim you is another where we're craving what we can't survive without."

Her legs shake a little, and not from the cold.

I lift her chin, so she looks up at me. "If you say no, we'll take you back to your car. We'll let you drive away. But if you want us, then lie back. Give yourself to us, and we will take you... completely."

My wolf growls at the mental image of her leaving, fury making my fingertips ache as my claws strain.

There's silence. Her hands relax and she looks at each of us like she's searching for proof that we mean what we say.

Then slowly she lets go of the bed and leans back first onto her elbows, pausing for a second, her body trembling, and then she reclines fully. I exhale in a rush. With her hair spread around her and her pale white skin reflecting the full moon, she looks like an altar sacrifice.

That's all it takes.

I move first. Climbing behind her, I pull her into my lap, into my chest, into my heart. I kiss her like I've waited lifetimes. Finn groans like a starving man. Reed brushes his lips over her throat.

I find the place.

The spot where wolf meets mate. Where the bite will take.

"This is how it starts," I murmur. "This is how we claim you."

She shivers in my arms.

"Will it hurt?"

Reed's voice is low and sure. "Only for a second. Then... only pleasure."

She pants softly, her body vibrating with anticipation. Reed's hand finds hers, and he squeezes it gently, grounding her in the moment, tethering her to us.

My hands roam her body, palming her breasts until she arches, letting her legs fall open. The scent of her intensifies as I run two rough fingers between her pussy lips, grazing her clit with enough pressure to make her gasp. My cock finds her entrance almost instinctively and her gasp turns into a scream when I thrust into her, hard and deeply, over and over.

She's so tight around me, already rippling with barely restrained pleasure. I push deeper, until my knot nudges her opening, my wolf shuddering with excitement.

I lick her nape before my fangs bud, marking her with my scent, soothing the place I will wound her. Shivers run down my spine and coil around my knot. Then I bite, and my head spins. Images of her flash through my mind; the first time I saw her alone and wounded, in our kitchen, proudly presenting muffins, cradling and singing to Ahya, coming apart beneath me in this very bed. She cries out again, a sharp, gasping moan that lances through me like lightning. Her whole body arches, caught between pain and the essence of the soul-bond that already slides through her veins. I wrap my arms tighter, my growl becoming lower and more possessive as my saliva seals the bite and ancient magic rushes into her bloodstream like wildfire.

Her fingers grip mine, nails digging into my skin. But when she lifts her face, she's glowing.

"You're ours now," I whisper against her skin, my voice dark and reverent.

Scarlet moans, her back bowing as I drive into her again and again, the slap of skin and the desperate sounds of our bodies colliding filling the room. My knees nearly buckle with the force of it. I fuck her harder, driven by the primal pulse in my blood, by the need to make her feel everything.

She's sobbing now, caught in it, breaking open around my body.

"Nixon…" Her voice shakes. "I'm going to—" She tightens, and my knot pulses.

I lean forward, covering her back with my chest, my thrusts growing erratic.

"Scarlet," Reed warns, brushing her temple. "His knot's coming. You'll feel it swell. It'll lock him inside you. Don't fight it. Breathe through it."

"What?" she gasps, but it's too late to explain further. I snarl, driving deep one last time. My knot inflates, and she cries out, hips grinding, locked to me, her climax ripping through her like a storm. I release like a cannon firing, filling her with pulse upon pulse of my seed, marking her as ours as deeply as I can.

Her skin is flushed and sweat slick when Reed presses his lips to the hollow of her neck, but the moment his tongue grazes that sensitive spot beneath her ear, her breath catches. His wolf claws at the surface, ready to bite, to *mark*. When he bites, I know it's the most primal sensual moment of his life as his mate's skin breaks against his fangs, and she moans as her body begins to change for us.

Finn is last, claiming the other side of her throat, his eyes closed in rapture.

Scarlet doesn't even know it yet, but her body is *responding* like a wolf's would. Her thighs tense, scent spiking sweet and sharp, and I groan because she's changing. She smells like us now, heat and musk and the wisp of our magic.

I hold her steady, whispering words of praise and encouragement against her shoulder. Finn's hand slides slowly up her thigh, teasing her with more pleasure. Reed flattens his hand over her belly, feeling the tremble of her nerves, and the shape of my cock buried deep inside her.

She's still human in so many ways, but the bond? The bond is crawling under her skin like wildfire.

The claim is complete.

And goddess, she's never looked more beautiful.

Scarlet is still panting softly when Reed presses a kiss to her temple. I'm still locked inside her, our bodies fused, moving in synch like two chords of the same song finally played together.

Reed crouches beside her, brushing damp hair from her brow, scanning the dazed shimmer in her half-lidded eyes.

"How do you feel?" he asks, voice low. "Tell us, Scarlet."

She blinks slowly, like it takes effort to return to herself. She lifts her head. "Like I've been struck by lightning," she says hoarsely. "But instead of breaking me... it lit something up that I didn't know was dark."

My grip tightens at her waist. Finn slides his fingers gently along the inside of her thigh. But I stay there, grounded inside her, absorbing the moment of *rightness*.

She lets out a long breath. "I feel... like I've been rewritten. Like something inside me snapped into place after a lifetime of sitting crooked."

She's ours.

And I don't let go.

Not when her body softens around me, still trembling from the aftershocks. Not when she cries out as I finally slip free, our mingled release seeping onto the sheets. Not when her soul curls around mine with the surety of a vine finding its tree.

I hold her tight for as long as it takes for her to find herself again, truly content for the first time in my life.

31

REED

Scarlet is still locked around Nixon, her body limp and trembling, her breath coming in soft, stunned pants. Her skin is flushed, shining with sweat, and there's this raw, dazed look in her eyes like she's been pulled from one world and dropped into another.

Because she has.

I kneel beside her, brushing her hair back from her face. Her cheek leans instinctively into my palm, and the tiny, unthinking gesture makes my throat tighten. The bond is beginning to pulse between us, even if she doesn't realize it yet.

"You still with us, sweetheart?" I murmur.

She blinks rapidly. "I don't know where I went."

I lean to kiss her temple. "You never have to be alone again."

Nixon's arms stay tight around her middle, holding her grounded as his knot keeps them joined. His face is pressed against her shoulder, and the tenderness in his expression guts me. I know what that bond is like now. I can *feel* its softness in the air.

It's my turn. And Finn's.

Scarlet's gaze drifts to mine, soft but filled with new heat. She reaches for me.

"Reed," The way she says my name is like a key turning in a lock I didn't know existed.

"I've got you," I say, crawling closer and kissing her gently, trying to give her all the things Nixon couldn't in that first desperate, primal claiming. She's already marked, already filled with his knot and scent. But I need her, too. I need to be inside her. I need to connect us, body, mind, and soul.

I trail kisses along her throat, across her collarbone, to her breast. She arches, still so sensitive, and when I take her nipple in my mouth, she moans my name again. The sound is needy and touches me *everywhere.*

Nixon shifts slightly, groaning as he slides from inside her, releasing a rush of their combined release onto the comforter. I settle between her thighs, and Finn is at her side now, stroking her arm, his eyes on me.

"She's ready," he says, and he's right. Her body is slick, pulsing, and already open for me. I slide into her slowly, watching her face the whole time.

She gasps, eyes wide. "Oh…"

That sound… it floors me.

I start to move slowly and carefully. The stretch is deep but gentle, not like Nixon's raw brutality. This is different. Tender. Intimate. Every stroke into her carves my name into her existence.

And then it happens.

Her eyes flash. Her fingers clutch my arms, hard. And

suddenly, I *feel* her pleasure like it's mine. Like I'm inside her mind, not only her body. Her moans vibrate in me. Her ecstasy floods through my bloodstream like wildfire.

Reed... I hear her voice. *Not* with my ears. With thought. She's inside me.

"Did you hear that?" I whisper, panting.

"Yeah. She's opening," Nixon murmurs. "The bond is anchoring."

Scarlet's back arches, and her orgasm builds like a crashing wave. But it's not just her climax. I'm riding it, too. Her heat and her need floods me so completely that I can barely keep control.

"I can feel you," she gasps aloud. "All of you."

"I know," I choke, voice hoarse. "Me, too."

Her thighs tremble around me, and I thrust a little harder now, chasing the edge with her. My release isn't separate from hers. It's *because* of hers. As she shatters beneath me, sobbing my name into the crook of her arm, my knot flares, and I spill inside her with a groan that's a lifetime being purged from my soul.

Our foreheads touch.

Her body twitches gently beneath mine.

She's still gripping me inside, her body clenching in aftershocks around my knot. Every pulse echoes through my bones. I can't move. I *don't* want to move. We're fused in the quiet aftermath of release, given time to kiss and pet each other and dwell in the connection of our bond. Her thighs quiver, muscles spent and shaking, but she's not pushing me away. She's holding me in.

I kiss her temple, then her cheek, then the edge of her lips, and every place I touch, she softens more, melting beneath me like wax warmed by flame.

"You're so fucking beautiful," I murmur, voice raw. "I didn't know it could be like this."

She turns her face toward me, dazed and flushed, eyes soft and liquid. "Like what?"

"Like... you're sewn into me now. Like I could spend the rest of my life buried inside you and never want more than this." I kiss her again, slower this time. "I thought I understood what it meant to have a mate. But this... It's so much more than I imagined."

A tremor runs through her, her fingers brushing over the back of my neck, anchoring me there.

"I never imagined it could be like this, either," she whispers. "I didn't know I could feel this much and not fall apart."

"You don't have to hold anything back with us," I tell her. "Not ever."

She closes her eyes, and when she opens them again, there's something else glowing there. Wonder. "I love you."

My heart pauses then restarts in a wilder rhythm, as love swells inside me, ready to spill out. "I love you, too, Scarlet."

She turns to Nixon, reaching to cup his cheek. "I love you, Nixon. And you, Finn. I love you all so much."

In our minds, Nixon rumbles, *Mate, you can speak this way now.*

She laughs, then closes her eyes. *I love you.*

We love you, too, mate, we all rumble, creating a hum of emotion and happiness that connects us.

Finn kisses her shoulder, his own arousal thick in the air. She turns her head toward him, dazed but smiling, as if she's already building to what's next.

"I need you."

Finn moves with quiet reverence, shedding his pants as

189

my knot releases her. He guides himself between her thighs, which are slick with both Nixon and me, and she welcomes him like he was always meant to fit there.

He enters her slowly, and a soft cry escapes her lips. "Oh… Finn…"

He doesn't rush. His rhythm is slow and sensual, hands cradling her like she's spun glass. She moans again, and it's as though my lungs are breathing her in. Her pleasure isn't hers anymore. It belongs to all of us.

The bond floods open fully, and I swear I can taste her emotions. All her fear, her wonder, her love spill into my chest.

And the corner of emptiness I've lived with my whole life?

It's gone.

Scarlet comes again, her cries fractured and raw, and Finn follows her, whispering her name over and over like an incantation. The moment he spills inside her, the final piece of the bond slides into place, locking the four of us in a tangle of blood-deep connection.

When he pulls back, she's boneless between us, radiant and glowing.

Ours.

Her eyes snap open. They're hazel but flickering with gold. Wolf gold. And *fuck*, the sight of it nearly undoes me.

We lay with her, our bodies pressed around her like a shield. Her skin is damp, and face is relaxed, oozing contentment.

"Am I still human?" she murmurs sleepily.

"Of course," I snort, curling my hand around hers. "But you're something else now, too. Stronger. Tethered to us. Claimed by us. You're the center of our world."

And as I press a kiss to her shoulder, I know she was always the missing piece.

And now she's home.

32

SCARLET

I'm lying in the same room, surrounded by Nixon, Reed, and Finn, but the rustling of the forest is louder and the sense of small animals burrowing through the undergrowth suddenly brighter and clearer in my mind. The scent of tree sap and rotting leaf matter is so strong, even though we're inside, but over that, the scent of the men around me is a vibration against my heartstrings.

They claimed me. Now I belong to them.

It's there in the marrow of my bones, in the marks that throb either side of my throat and at my nape, in the possessiveness I now feel about them as *mine*, and the deep connection that is a rope of steel between us.

It's so much more than I could have understood before. The claim has changed me. It's so strange to feel stronger, wiser... *and connected to them in mind and body*.

I turn to touch Nixon's strong jaw. I press my forehead to his, and his sleeping thoughts whisper through my mind. *Mate. Claim. Ours. Contentment.* These are the words and emotions that spill through from my alpha. Words mirrored in my own mind. He stirs, throwing a heavy arm across my middle, anchoring me to the bed. Pushing my hand beneath his wrist, I turn to find Finn and Reed beside me. Finn is closest, lying on his back with one arm stretched above his head. Reed is by his side, turned toward me.

I touch Finn first, my fingers trailing over the undulations of his abs, drinking up his beauty, and allowing the feral intensity of my desire for him to swamp me. I thought I knew what desire was, but the intense sense of ownership and the burning, aching, craving hunger is all new. I'm sore between my thighs, but the sight of his half-hard cock is enough to make me growl in my mind. His eyelids flicker, and he slowly turns his head toward me, smiling. *Mate*, he whispers. *You don't need to yearn. Take what's yours.*

I kiss down his body, drawing the scent of him deep inside, my thirst for him only worsening as I press my nose into the hair above his thick erection. Licking him isn't enough. I wrap my lips around him and suck, tasting his pleasure until the head is deep in my throat and Finn's hands are in my hair, wrapping it around his wrists so he can control me. I moan, and Reed stirs, taking my hand and pressing it to his length. My mind is filled with images of me and what I'm doing to Finn, but the images are tinted and beautiful, and I realize that's how he sees me.

Nixon is awake, too, our minds now too connected to slumber through the swelling pleasure.

She was hungry for it, Finn says by way of explanation.

The claim is surging through her, Nixon explains. I assume it's for my benefit because they know and understand what's happening to me.

Take her, Finn says. *Fill her.*

Nixon is behind me before I register he's moved, his tongue sliding over my pussy, his nose pressing deep. The way they touch me is different from any other man who came before them. It's like they want to consume me. It's as if there's no part of me that doesn't belong to them. If they could, I think they'd climb inside me.

Reed's leaking precum, and Finn loosens his grip on my hair, just loose enough to let me lick it from his brother, taking him deep into my throat longingly before being guided back.

Behind me, Nixon thrusts into my pussy, still sore from their knots, and I sob around Finn's cock, body stretched and full, claimed and taken again.

Reed's hands are everywhere, stroking the slope of my spine, cupping my breast, circling my clit with his knuckles, teasing and worshipping and working me higher. His breath gusts against my ear as he whispers in my mind.

You were made for this. You're perfect, every part of you. I want to fuck you until you forget your name and then remind you who you belong to.

The whispers aren't out loud, but they ripple through my chest like thunder. Finn's groan reverberates not just in my throat, but in my mind.

So good, baby. So fucking sweet. That mouth was made for my cock.

Nixon doesn't speak, but he's there, deeper than the others. Like a hot wire wrapped around my spine, grounding me as he hammers into me from behind. His thrusts are unrelenting, but his thoughts are wild and *fierce.*

Ours. No one else gets to touch you now. I'll burn the world before I let it take you from us.

Pleasure pulses from the inside out, each of them touching me through this strange thread that's now wound through all of us.

The sweetest one that makes my heart ache is Nixon's desire to fill me with a child. I see the brightness of his imagined future; his pack made up of his brothers and me, Ahya grown and walking, and other cubs frolicking. I gasp, pulling back from Finn, tears welling in my eyes as I'm swamped by the purity of his need to procreate, layered over my surety that my body isn't capable of giving him what he wants.

It's okay, he says, slowing his thrusts, stroking his big, rough hands up my thighs. *Everything is going to be okay. Trust in the goddess.*

I shiver as he continues driving into me, the images of our future family replaced by what he can see: the curve of my ass, his thick cock driving inside me, my pussy stretched around him, and his brothers touching me. There's a glow around us all in his mind, like a halo that contains us, blending our forms together, softening the edges of what we're doing. It spins through my mind, driving me closer and closer to the release I'm craving, but even as I near the precipice, I'm filled with the certainty that no matter how sated I am, I'll always want more. I'll crave these men until my last breath because they're in my blood, pumping through my heart, curled around my essence, holding me close.

I come with Finn deep in my throat, gulping his orgasm down with every jerking pulsation.. Nixon isn't far behind, painting me inside with his release. I'm a panting, leaking mess when Reed climbs over me, licking my neck and clavicle, over each mark his brothers made. When he fills me, I mewl, clawing at his body, needing him close. His weight presses me into the mattress, his thrusts making the bed shake. His mind is filled with other beautiful images of us running through the forest naked and making love in a clearing lit up by the midday sun. When he comes, it's with a long, satisfied groan that echoes deep in my chest. I *feel* them everywhere, taste them and smell them, and it's like a drug that circulates inside and outside me.

I'm lost in them. And found.

We are one.

I am claimed.

But what am I going to tell my mom?

33

FINN

The morning air is sharp in my lungs as I run, paws tearing into the soft earth, tongue lolling as I gasp. My body is trembling, my mind a whirl of new connections and sensations. Scarlet is ours.

She's back at the cabin, curled up with Reed, still wearing our scent, still filled with our seed. Claimed. I've never felt so content.

But peace never lasts long in these woods.

The scent of pine and wet moss rolls around me, but underneath it is something sour and wrong. Nixon's ahead of me, his massive dark gray form cutting through the brush like a shadow with purpose. We've run this trail a thousand times, but today, I sense something wrong.

The second I smell the other two wolves, upwind and circling like they think we won't notice, I veer left, snarling. Nixon slows ahead, ears flicking. He smells it, too.

Gregory's pack.

Shift, Nixon orders.

I shift mid-step, landing hard in my human skin, already pissed.

"Come out, or we'll drag you out," Nixon barks into the trees.

They appear seconds later. Jared and Malen, two of Gregory's lapdogs, both naked and smug in that way only wolves from problematic packs tend to be.

Nixon cracks his neck as he stands to his full, imposing height. Calm, but ready. Always ready. I move closer, rolling my shoulders and tipping my chin high.

Jared raises a hand like we're old friends. "Easy, boys. No need for teeth this early."

"Speak," Nixon says, voice low and hard.

"We're delivering a message." Malen's eyes flick to me, then back to Nixon. "Gregory wants to see the baby."

I step forward. "Too bad. He's not getting near it."

He doesn't say 'her', and this way, he confirms nothing of their assumptions.

Jared shrugs like it's no big deal. "He has a right. Unfinished business with Aura. That baby *girl* is technically part of his pack. Conceived by his mate."

He emphasizes the word girl and my heart sinks.

I laugh, but it's humorless. "He made his choice. He broke the bond with Aura. She left his pack and deserted the baby. Gregory has no claim."

Nixon crosses his arms, his biceps going taut. "Tell Gregory this: the baby is part of *our* family now. Claimed by this pack when it was left to die in the woods, and this pack protects its own."

Malen's nostrils flare. "You sure you want to mark this line in the sand, Nixon? You know what'll happen."

Nixon's jaw pulses with tension, jerking his head toward

them as he spits through gritted teeth, "Let him try to challenge me."

The air goes still.

The kind of stillness, laced with menace and dark intentions, that comes right before blood is spilled.

Then Jared shifts, fast and aggressive, his wolf form bristling and snarling. Malen follows suit, hackles up, posture threatening, but they don't attack.

I don't shift. I don't need to.

I step forward, bare-chested and unbothered. "Run back to your master," I yell, voice like steel. "Tell him if he sets foot in our territory, we'll tear out his fucking throat."

They don't respond.

They hold the stare a moment longer, then turn and bolt into the trees.

Nixon exhales slowly beside me, but his eyes are still locked on the trail they vanished down.

"It isn't over," I say.

"No," he agrees, voice cold. "He'll have to kill me before he gets his hands on that child."

We shift again, muscle and fur exploding through skin, and take off into the woods.

Faster this time.

Because war never waits for anyone.

And now we have everything to lose.

34

NIXON

I stand in the lumberyard, looking over the business my brothers and I bought as a fresh start. When we made the decision to leave our pack behind, it felt like chopping off a limb and limping on the bloody stump. Still, after Matt's death and the blame that continued to hang over us, it was our only option.

I understand our parents' grief, but their blame was unfair, and it ruined our pack, rotting it from the inside. A son should never have to become alpha until his father is weak or dead, but I was forced to walk away and step up to that role, and there's no going back.

Now we need support. Gregory's pack is large, filled with all the stray wolves he can find to bolster numbers. It never bothered me in the past. We have clear boundaries that haven't been challenged, but now his goons are running through our territory, making threats to come for a baby that our mate has adopted as hers. There's no negotiation here, no middle ground to reach. Ahya is ours now, unless

Aura changes her mind. Scarlet would never break another woman's heart, but she'll defend that child like she's her own, in place of a mother too broken to do the same.

An alpha doesn't crawl or beg. An alpha doesn't plead for the support of others. Going back to my father's pack and asking for support will be challenging, but I'll do it for my mate. I'll do it for my pack. I'll do it for the safety of a little wolfling whose presence in the world must have a greater significance than any of us can comprehend.

"You okay?" Reed asks. He's leaning against our newest delivery while Finn checks on Scarlet and Ahya in our office. Leaving her at home unprotected is no longer an option.

I rub the center of my eyebrows, an ache permeating my skull. "I never thought we'd have to go back."

"I know."

"They're not going to help us."

It's my greatest fear, which I've verbalized to my brother. He looks shocked by my admission. "We're still family."

"We walked away. Left dad without a bloodline."

"He has Chris and Macon."

"His brother's sons are not his bloodline."

Reed nods. In wolf packs, an alpha is responsible for siring the future alpha, much like human kingdoms. For our father to groom his brother's sons for leadership is unusual, just like it's unusual for three brothers to take one mate.

Nothing in our lives is as we expected.

"There isn't another option," I say.

"Hunter?"

I jerk my head to stare at my brother. Is he seriously suggesting we approach a clan of bear shifters to come to our assistance?

"They have their own family and their own pack issues. They're a small unit like ours. They won't want to step into problems in a world that isn't theirs."

Reed shrugs. "We live in the same world, Nixon, and they've experienced their own wolf issues. You forget what Gregory's pack did to Goldie. Hunter would have an opinion on this situation. You could reach out, alpha to alpha. There may come a time when he would benefit from *your* support."

I stare out of the open doorway at the forest beyond. We've made peace with the bears, a peace that shouldn't have been possible. I trust Hunter and his bear clan far more than Gregory's. Wolf should ally with wolf, but our world has tipped upside down.

"I'll call him," I say. "You stay with Finn and Scarlet."

I don't need to tell him to protect our mate at all costs.

***

An hour later, I stand in front of Hunter's mansion in wolf form. The scent of bear is everywhere, rubbed into the bark of every tree, brick, and thick in the air around the old mansion. Hunter pulls open the huge wooden door, and strides forward, clutching some jeans. He's come alone as a mark of trust.

I shift quickly, taking the jeans from Hunter's hand and pulling them over my naked lower half. "Thanks for these," I say.

"Easier to talk to a man, eye to eye, if his junk isn't hanging out." Hunter smiles from one corner of his mouth.

"It definitely is," I laugh. "Shifter problems."

He smirks. "So, what's up?"

I cup the back of my neck with both my hands, the discomfort of sharing things I should be able to decide for myself clawing beneath my skin.

"Why did you leave your clan?" I ask. Maybe if I understand him better, I'll be able to work through my own issues.

If he's surprised, he doesn't show it.

"I didn't agree with the direction of the wider clan on many issues," he says. "Mostly, it was this place... I couldn't leave it behind to live in the compound."

He waves his arm at the house, and I understand immediately. He's rooted in a home that's been in his family for generations. Of course, he wouldn't want to leave.

"And now your clan is small—you and your brothers—do you feel..." I struggle with the next word but force it out anyway. "...vulnerable?"

"There is a strength in numbers that shouldn't be underestimated. That's why we're working on growing our own pack. Goldie is pregnant again, with triplets."

"Congratulations."

"Thank you." There's a flicker of wariness behind his eyes. He's still gauging me, trying to understand what I'm here for without pressing too hard.

"I wouldn't be here if I had another option," I admit.

Hunter crosses his arms over his chest, his bare forearms dusted with faint scars. "What's Gregory done?"

"He sent two of his wolves into our territory yesterday. Claimed he wants to see the baby."

Hunter's jaw tightens.

"Scarlet's ours now. Fully bonded." Saying the words aloud sends a pulse of warmth through my chest despite everything. "Scarlet won't give the baby up. Neither will we. She's part of our family now. But Gregory..." I shake my head. "He's building an army out of strays and rogues. I used to think it was for status, but now—"

"Now you think he's preparing for war."

"I can't risk him hurting Scarlet. Or that little girl. We've rebuilt after leaving our pack. I won't lose everything again."

Hunter is quiet for a long moment. Then he says, "I know what it's like to be on the outside of something you were born into. To feel like everyone's waiting for you to fail."

His words hit harder than I expected. I clench my fists at my sides. "We were blamed for something we weren't responsible for. Our innocence didn't matter. The blame stuck. We couldn't stay and be torn apart by that. So we left to build something new, but I've never stopped dreading it could all be taken away again."

"You've made something strong. The mate bond changes you. It gives you roots." He watches me closely now. "So what are you asking, Nixon? Speak plainly."

I draw and hold a breath, pride burning hot in my throat. "If Gregory challenges us, I need to know I won't stand alone. If his wolves cross the boundary line again, he'll be encroaching on your territory, too. If they come for the child, we'll fight to the death. But I want to know there's someone behind us. Just one other pack who'll say *no*, this won't stand."

Hunter tilts his head. "You're asking us to fight your war?"

"No," I say firmly. "I don't believe it will come to that. Wolves don't like to challenge bears at the best of times. There has never been a time when wolf and bear have stood shoulder to shoulder. I think the sight of us united will be enough to make Gregory think twice."

He rubs his lips slowly, eyes sharpening. "A rogue pack

on our borders is a cause for concern for all of us, especially one that believes it has the strength to overwhelm. You and your brothers have kept peace in this territory, a peace we appreciate. You'll have our support, not because I owe you, but because I trust you to do what's right."

Relief hits me low in the gut, almost making me stagger.

"Thank you," I say. "I'm returning to my father's pack with the child. Maybe she'll be enough to bring about a truce."

Hunter claps a heavy hand on my shoulder. "Going back is always hard. But in this case, it's worth it. Your new life is worth protecting at all costs."

***

By the time I return to the yard, dusk is already crowding around the lumberyard. The saws are quiet. I find Reed pacing outside the office, his arms crossed.

"Everything okay?" I ask.

He looks up, eyes sharp. "Scarlet's worried about you. She doesn't like it when we leave."

My heart stutters. "What did she say?"

Reed shakes his head. "Not much. She keeps staring into the woods."

My chest tightens. I'm not used to having a mate to worry about me while I'm away. I need to be more mindful of my communication, so Scarlet doesn't fret unnecessarily. But she also needs to understand the dangers that lurk in the shadows, and how strong we are in both wolf and human form, capable of protecting her, as long as the odds aren't too stacked against us.

There's a storm coming, but we'll be prepared.

35

REED

Our father's territory lies three hours to the north. In the truck, as the forest closes in on the pack land, a tense silence grips us all. We haven't called ahead. We didn't want to give them time to think about our arrival. This way, they'll see our mate and Ahya simultaneously. It'll provide us with a distraction before we have to broach the subject of Gregory.

"What's your mom like?" Scarlet asks.

"She has Nixon's eyes. My nose. Reed's sense of humor."

"Do you think we'll get along?"

I shrug because what can I say? I have no idea if our mother will accept our mate. Matt's death shook her to her core. When we left, she didn't say goodbye. This whole confrontation is going to be a challenge. We've been putting off telling Scarlet about our brother, but it isn't fair to let her walk into our family pack without knowing why we left.

"Matt was our oldest brother," I begin, eyes fixed on the trees as they flash past the window. "Cocky, always smiling.

He used to sleep sprawled out between Nixon and me, even after we were grown. Mom called him our protector."

Scarlet's expression softens, her fingers stilling on my chest.

"The day it happened, we were out tracking through the eastern woods." My voice thickens. "Matt was fast. Goddess, he was fast. He outran us. Got too far ahead showing us what he was capable of. The alpha in wait..." I swallow hard, the knot in my throat sharp and old. "The rogue wolf wasn't supposed to be in our territory, but it came out of nowhere. A shifter gone feral. It—" I clench my jaw. "It was a slaughter."

Scarlet's hand curls over mine.

"By the time we caught up, it was already done." My voice cracks. "We tore the rogue apart. There was nothing left of him. But it was too late. There was nothing we could do for Matt."

The scent of our old pack fills the air, the deep musk of familiar wolves. It presses against my skin like humidity. Scarlet shifts in her seat, her hand resting lightly over Ahya's chest as the little one naps in her car seat. Even asleep, she clutches Scarlet's shirt in a tight fist, as if she knows who provides safety.

"It wasn't your fault," she says softly.

"We could have been closer," Nixon mutters from the driver's seat.

"Would that have made a difference?" Scarlet challenges.

Nixon doesn't reply because we know the truth. The rogue would have taken one of us. If Nixon had been faster, our mother would have buried him that day.

"We're almost there," Nixon says. His grip on the wheel

is tight enough to make the leather creak.

No one speaks.

As the truck rumbles up the long gravel drive, the house comes into view. It's as we left it; low, stone-faced, ancient. Our father always said it was built to outlast time, and maybe it will. The main doors are already open.

They scented us. They knew we were coming.

As the engine cuts off, four figures step out of the house: our father first, then our mother, followed by Chris and Macon, our cousins who are now the chosen heirs.

All in human form. All waiting.

But they're not alone.

Standing behind them is Cami, the spiritual wolf. She doesn't speak much, but when she does, people listen. Her presence isn't an accident.

She sensed something unusual about our arrival.

I step out first, unbuckling Ahya so that Scarlet can slide from the truck. Scarlet stands tall, chin high, eyes bright. She's nervous, but she won't show weakness. Not when she's aware of our complex history and the importance of today's visit. Her flaming red hair hangs long over her shoulders, and she's radiant in a long white skirt and forest green top that brings out the color of her eyes. I couldn't be prouder.

Our father watches us approach with his thick arms folded across his broad chest. The gray in his hair has spread since we last saw him, but his expression is as hard, scrutinizing, and assessing as always.

Mother's gaze flicks first to the child, then to Scarlet, and something softens in her face. She steps forward instinctively, reaching out as if to touch our mate, but stops herself short.

"Why are you here?" Father asks.

Nixon stiffens. "Before we talk, we should make introductions first. This is our mate, Scarlet. Scarlet, these are my parents, Frederick and Angeli. Cousins Chris and Macon. And Cami. This is Scarlet, and Ahya."

He leaves Ahya a mystery, but Cami's eyes linger over her, and she steps forward to get a better view. I tighten my grip on the child as Scarlet moves closer, revealing her protectiveness.

"You brought her," Cami says, her voice gravelly but high with awe.

Scarlet answers before any of us can. "I found her. She is ours."

There's a pause, long and loaded. Our father's jaw tics. "She's not yours by blood," he says.

"She's ours by choice," Nixon grits out.

Cami's eyes flash at that. She steps forward, her silver braids glinting in the fading light. "Let me see her."

I hesitate, but when Ahya stirs and turns her cheek toward Cami, as if she knows, I adjust my grip so she can be seen. Her eyes are wide and clear as she stares out over my estranged family.

Cami extends a hand, and the moment her fingers touch Ahya, the air thickens.

Wind rushes through the trees without warning. The leaves tremble. Cami closes her eyes.

Everyone watches in silence as the spiritual wolf chants softly in the old tongue. After a minute, her eyes snap open, bright and knowing.

"She's not what you think. She is more."

Our mother steps forward, eyebrows drawn. "More how?"

"She is born of pain and violation," Cami says softly. "Of forced bloodlines."

Our stomachs twist. Scarlet's hand touches Ahya possessively, and I let her lift the child from my arms and cradle her close to her breast.

"Violation?" Reed asks, voice low. Even though we know some of Aura's story, Cami has the power to discern more.

Cami's eyes gain a sharper focus. "Her mother's pain clings to her. Two violations. A rogue wolf. And a bear with black in his heart. She survived it, barely. But this child..." She looks at Ahya who's still sleeping. "There is wolf in her. But also... bear. And something else. Something veiled. She is not cursed. She is blessed. The old powers touch her. This child may be the only bridge between what was... and what must come."

Father's face is stone. "You brought the child of a bear to this house."

Scarlet steps forward, fire rising in her. "We brought a child who had no say in what was done before she was born. No one should judge her for her bloodline."

There's silence. Chris and Macon exchange looks but stay quiet.

Then our mother speaks. "Her scent is of all of you now. Your bond is sealed."

"She's our daughter," Nixon says flatly. "And Gregory, a rival alpha, wants her."

That gets our father's attention.

"You think Gregory knows what she is?"

"He knows the child is female," I say. "That's enough to make him come for her."

Cami leans in, her voice hushed. "He will. The child's

blood sings to those who are hungry for power. You've brought her to the right place, but it will not be enough."

"We need allies," Nixon says. "From your pack. Or we walk into war with our bear allies only."

"Bear allies?" Father's face screws with disgust.

"They're good men, and they'll stand with us against a shared enemy."

"Bears?" Macon says. "You've allied with bears."

Father's eyes narrow on us all, but when his eyes lock on Ahya, something changes. Finally, he says, "Come inside."

He doesn't offer peace.

But he opened the door.

***

The stone threshold under our boots seems rougher than I remember. This house, our house, is filled with echoes that never fade. Matt's laughter. Our mother's crying. Our father's anger. And the silence that echoed behind us after we left.

Now, we bring our mate and a child made from violence and mystery back into our childhood home. Every step inside is like walking through memories we thought we'd buried.

The main room is dimly lit. A fire crackles in the hearth, but the room is as cold and formal as I remembered. No warmth here, only legacy.

Scarlet holds Ahya tightly, her shoulders braced. Our mother trails behind, glancing over her shoulder at Cami, who walks with the sure, steady gait of someone who knows where this is going. Chris and Macon flank our father like lieutenants.

We sit when offered, but the tension doesn't soften.

"Tell us everything," our mother says, gaze on Nixon.

211

"From the beginning."

Nixon rubs his brow and then sighs. "We found a child abandoned on our territory. She had a familiar scent, from a rival pack. Gregory's mate Aura ..."

"Scarlet found her first," I add, glancing toward our mate. "She protected her before she even knew what she was."

Scarlet's voice is steady. "She didn't need to prove herself special to be worthy of care."

Cami speaks again. "That instinct is important. That kind of bond, one chosen rather than forged in blood, is stronger. When this child shows her true nature, you will need that kind of devotion."

Father's face remains impassive. "And Gregory?"

"He sent two wolves across our land," I say. "Claimed he wanted to see the child. He'll come for her. I don't know what he knows. But he knows enough."

"There are whispers," Cami says, tilting her head like she's listening to something none of us can hear. "Of wolves gathering. Of rogue bears answering his call. His ambition is no longer confined to territory. He wants something more."

"He wants her?" Nixon's attention drifts to Ahya.

Chris finally speaks, arms resting on his thighs. "You think Gregory would risk war for a child he doesn't even understand... who isn't his legacy?"

Cami turns her gaze on him, eyes bright. "It's not what he understands. It's what he feels. He feels her power, and that is enough."

Macon shifts beside him. "So we're supposed to fight a war over this? Risk everything on a baby born of—"

Scarlet stands slowly, Ahya in her arms. "No one

chooses how they're conceived."

Macon's jaw tightens, but he looks away.

Scarlet continues. "But we all choose who we protect. And I will die before I let anyone hurt this child again."

Our father watches her with narrow eyes. "You speak like an alpha."

"Nixon is my alpha," Scarlet says firmly, and across the room, my brother expands with pride. "But I'm now the mother of a girl who will be hunted by men like Gregory. That makes me dangerous."

There's a beat of silence. Then Cami rises from her seat.

"There is more," she says. "She is not only a bridge between wolf and bear. She holds the echo of something old. The blood in her... it sings to the earth. To the spirits. That power will need guidance."

Mother's eyes are wide now, fear and wonder braided together. Father rises, voice low. "Then she's more than a child. She's a threat."

"To Gregory," I snap. "To anyone who thinks her blood makes her a pawn. But not to us."

He stares us down, but Nixon rises to meet him eye to eye.

"I didn't come here for your approval of my family," Nixon says. "I came because war is coming, and we're stronger together than apart."

Another long silence.

Then our father looks toward our mother, then to Chris and Macon.

"You'll stay the night," he says finally. "Cami will stay near the child. We'll talk more tomorrow."

It isn't a yes. It isn't a no.

But it's more than we expected.

Scarlet exhales slowly. I reach for her hand, and she takes it without hesitation.

We've taken the first step.

But with so much unknown, the path of our future is shrouded in darkness.

36

SCARLET

My mates' old bedroom is a little too clean now, like someone tried to scrub away memories with their scent. I can still imagine them here, playfighting and laughing, sharing hopes and dreams. I imagine them planning their futures, trying to find space in a world that didn't even know they existed.

I sit on the edge of the bed, Ahya cradled in my arms, her soft baby breath steady against my collarbone. Her fingers twitch in her sleep. Every so often, she lets out a little growl-like sound, almost human, almost not. I smooth her red hair back from her forehead.

"You don't know it yet," I whisper, "but you're going to change everything."

The door creaks softly, and I look up.

Angeli, Nixon's mother, stands in the doorway with a folded blanket in her hands. She hesitates, her sharp eyes moving from Ahya to me, then back again.

"Is she always this quiet?"

"She's exhausted. The trip, the tension. She feels it, even if she doesn't understand it."

Angeli approaches slowly and sits in the chair by the window. The blanket stays on her lap.

"This room..." She sighs, not quite meeting my gaze. "They all shared it once. I used to find Reed sleeping under the bed because Matt kicked too much in his sleep."

I smile a little.

"I'm sorry you never got to know him," she says, voice tightening. "He was a force. Bold. Loud. Too brave for his own good."

I rock Ahya gently, watching Angeli's hands clench the blanket. It's never been my way to poke at sore places or to confront situations that aren't mine, but my mates have suffered enough because of this bad blood, and if I can do something about it, I will.

"You still blame them," I say softly.

She meets my gaze this time. "Wouldn't you?"

"No. Matt was the eldest. He made a choice to run ahead... his brothers couldn't have stopped him."

"There were three of them... they could have—"

"I know the men you raised. I know Nixon. And he carries the guilt of your blame like a chain around his throat. I know Reed, who laughs even though he carries his brother's absence like a scar. And I know Finn, who hides it best but dreams like he's still watching his brother bleed out in his head."

Angeli's jaw works. She looks away.

"They didn't kill Matt," I say. "But they live like they did because you made them wear the guilt."

"You don't know what it's like to lose a child."

"You're right," I say. "But I know what it's like to live

216

with fear my mother laid on my shoulders. The burden is heavy."

Angeli swallows hard, looking at the child in my arms.

"You can grieve, Matt," I say. "You *should*. He was your child. But if you bury your heart with him, you're letting the sons still alive die by inches. And I won't let that happen to my mates. If you cannot leave the past in the past, this will be the last time you see any of us."

"You love them," she whispers.

"I'd burn for them."

She slowly stands and lays the blanket at the foot of the bed. "She'll need warmth tonight," she says quietly. "You both will."

Then she's gone.

I exhale, everything inside me still buzzing from the conversation. But I don't have time to sit with it because I sense their approach before they even open the door.

Their scent hits first—earth, sweat, musk. They've been running. The shift always leaves their bodies hot and slick and charged like they're still wolves under their human skin.

The door swings open, and there they are, all shirtless, damp with sweat, eyes glowing in the low light. There's a feral edge to their energy that makes me woozy.

"You're awake," Nixon says, voice thick.

"I've been waiting."

Ahya stirs as Reed moves to take her gently from my arms, murmuring softly as he tucks her into the basket in the corner. She sighs and curls deeper into the blankets.

I stand, moistening my lips, hungry for my mates.

"You're all sweaty," I murmur.

"We can shower," Finn grins, teeth sharp, eyes on my mouth.

217

"Mmmm." I step toward them and lick a bead of sweat from Nixon's neck. "Salty."

The scent of them—hot, sweaty and masculine—drives me insane. All I can think about is clawing at them, licking them, biting them, tasting them, taking their bodies deep inside mine in whatever way I can.

Nixon's hands snap to my waist as I press my body to his. His fingers are fast, unbuttoning my shirt and pushing it to the floor. My skirt follows, and three sets of eyes devour every inch of me.

Mine, three voices rumble in my head.

"Yes," I say out loud. "I'm yours and you're mine."

Then they're on me.

Nixon is behind me, kissing the back of my neck. Reed's mouth is on my breasts, his hands everywhere as I run my fingers through his damp hair. Finn kneels, pressing his mouth between my thighs, tongue ruthless, fingers pressed deep into the flesh of my hips.

I arch, cry out, twist, and pant, as their hungry whispers take over my mind.

Look at her. So ripe. So needy. So pretty. Her pussy is sweet on my tongue. Her body jerks when you do that. Touch her there. Fill her.

It's a bond so deep it blurs the line between our bodies and minds.

I've never been so full.

So wrecked.

So *alive*.

And in the afterglow, pressed between them, still trembling, I whisper, "Whatever's coming... we face it together."

Nixon kisses my temple.

Reed strokes my spine.

Finn touches my slick thighs lazily, eyes half-lidded. "Let them come."

37

NIXON

Scarlet sleeps wrapped in the arms of my brothers, all of them tangled together, spent, and I know I should stay. I want to stay, but something gnaws at the back of my skull, restless and unfinished. I leave them in bed, careful not to wake them, and pull on a pair of shorts before slipping barefoot through the hallway.

Every board underfoot creaks in the same places it always did. The floor still leans slightly left past the staircase. That old air vent still whistles in cold weather. The familiarity should comfort me.

It doesn't.

There are no pictures of us on the walls. No childhood photos. Not even the worn candidness of the four of us standing muddy and grinning after Reed dared us to jump in the lake mid-winter.

It's like we never existed.

Or worse, like we *died* with Matt, and the memory of our laughter was too much to bear.

In their place, Father has hung elaborate marquetry, each one carved and burned into polished wood panels, depicting places deep in the territory: the ridge trail where we used to run at dawn, the old grove that smells like thunderstorms, the firepit clearing where Matt once swore he'd challenge Dad for alpha to move dinner time earlier.

He was all teeth and swagger, smile and backslaps.

The thought of him slams into my chest like a fist.

I open the front door, stepping out onto the wide porch. The night air is crisp, thick with pine and old secrets. I walk to the railing and lean against the porch post, arms folded, barefoot and bare-chested as I inhale the scent of home. Or rather, this home that no longer feels like ours.

Blackwood Forest belongs to us now. But this place?

This place is *wedged* into the muscle of my heart, and I'll carry it, grief and all, until my last breath.

I hear the soft pad of bare feet before I smell her.

Cami. She moves like smoke.

"Couldn't sleep?" she asks, her voice a low hum.

"I think I was born tired," I mutter.

She stands beside me, her gaze set on the trees like she can see something I can't. "You carry the weight well. But it's heavy, isn't it?"

I don't answer. She doesn't need me to.

"I came to tell you something," she says, and when I glance at her, her expression is unreadable. "Your mate. She's pregnant."

My heart stutters. I look at her sharply, blinking. "What?"

Cami touches my shoulder. "Only just. Her scent hasn't changed enough yet for anyone else to notice. But the flicker of it is there. A second soul is forming."

The world tilts a little on its axis. Scarlet. Carrying our child. I was right. The doctors were wrong. All she needed was our seed, and her dreams of motherhood would be fulfilled.

"I didn't know."

"You weren't meant to yet. But you should know..." She pauses. "You're on the right path, Nixon. You left when you had to. You built something new. You protected a child not born of you. And now you've created one that is. This was your destiny."

My hands flex on the porch rail. Destiny. It's a big word and one I've struggled to accept for a long time. How can I believe that Matt's death was meant to be? How can I think that his loss and my family's lingering pain are all part of a greater plan?

"Gregory has to be stopped."

"He will be. But you can't beat him with wolves. Not alone. The only way to break his ambition is to show him that bear and wolf are no longer enemies."

"Unity?" I mutter. "I have one bear family on my side. It isn't enough."

"Exactly. But for the bears to believe in Ahya's tri-aspect, they must *see* it."

"She hasn't shifted into a bear yet. At least not in front of us."

Cami looks at me. "Has she spent time with other bear cubs?"

"No. Not yet."

"Then that's your answer. She needs mirrors for the parts of her that are still silent. You must return home. Let her spend time with bear cubs. Let her learn who she is."

"And the bears will believe she belongs?"

222

"They will feel it," Cami says. "And when she shifts, there will be no denying it."

I swallow hard. "And my father?"

Cami's mouth curves slightly. "He won't listen now. He's too proud. Too wounded. He still sees your leaving as betrayal, and his grief blinds him."

"I can't wait for him to come around. We don't have time."

"You don't have to," she says. "*I* will work on Frederick. He listens to me, even when he pretends not to. But he needs time. He needs to let go of the past before he can see the future standing right in front of him."

I exhale through my nose, watching the wind tug at the trees in the dark.

When we left our cabin, I thought we carried the responsibility of a mate and a child on our shoulders. Now, I know there's a child in Scarlet's womb. Our destiny is broadening. Our pack is growing. The weight of responsibility only grows heavier.

Ahya is destined to be a bridge between species, and she has brought us into a war we would do anything to avoid, but one we'll have to finish.

"I'll take them home tomorrow," I say. "To Blackwood... then to the bears."

Cami smiles. "Good. Every step forward is a choice. You will make the right ones."

And with that, she disappears into the trees.

I remain on the porch a while longer, listening to the night and the familiar heartbeat of this place.

Then I turn back inside, toward Scarlet and my future.

38

REED

We sit in the main room, a vast space framed with wood beams and old stone, the walls alive with family history.

Hunter sits in a high-back wooden chair that's more like a throne. Nixon paces, too keyed up to rest. Finn leans against the hearth, as if he's deliberately trying to show that at least one of us is relaxed. Scarlet sits on the couch beside me, legs tucked under her, cradling Ahya against her chest with a fierce stillness I've come to recognize as her armor.

The room quiets as Hunter's eyes drift toward her.

"So," he says, rubbing a hand over his jaw, "she's a wolf... but also a bear?"

"That's what we've been told," Nixon answers, his voice edged but even. He stops pacing to stare at our mate and foundling.

Hunter glances at Robert, his brother, who sits in a thick chair by the window. The man's been silent since we arrived, but the weight in his gaze is heavy with skepticism.

"It's not possible," Robert says. "Not biologically."

"It shouldn't be," I agree. "But she's here… a female wolf shifter. And our spiritual guide senses it in her. She's never wrong and would certainly never joke about something so serious."

Evan shifts forward in his seat, brows drawn. "The essence of three individuals can't combine," Evan says.

Hunter shakes his head. "There has never been a child born of two species of shifter."

"I know," Nixon says. "I know what I'm telling you doesn't make sense, but can we let Ahya play with your sons. If she sees them shift, maybe she'll recognize something in their appearance, in their essence. If she shifts into a bear, we'll know for sure. We're not asking you to believe us blindly." He turns toward Hunter. "We want to know for sure. Just let her spend time with your boys."

"And if she shifts into a bear?" Hunter asks, still watching Scarlet.

"Then we'll all have our answer," Nixon says.

Goldie sits nearby with the twins balanced on her lap, already wriggling toward freedom.

"Goldie?" Hunter says gently.

She nods, lifting the boys off her legs. "Connell. Coran. Go play, loves."

The twins waddle over to where Scarlet sits, their chubby legs and wild hair making me smile even in this heavy moment. Ahya watches them, her blue eyes bright and still like she knows what's coming.

Goldie moves toward the rug in the corner, where soft toys and wooden animals are scattered across a thick woven mat. The boys settle into play instantly, babbling and growling at each other.

"They don't shift often," Goldie explains, looking back

over her shoulder. "We'll need to be patient."

I glance at Evan. "Would it help if one of you shifted? Something to mirror?"

He rises without hesitation.

We all go quiet.

Evan steps into the center of the room. Then, with a deep inhale and a ripple of energy, his skin splits, fur rolls across his body, and in seconds, a massive brown bear stands where he had been.

Ahya lights up immediately.

She squeals with delight and immediately squirms in Scarlet's arms. Scarlet looks stunned but places her on the ground. The strain in her face darkens her usually relaxed features. I understand it's the human part of her that's wary of animals, especially one as big and ferocious-looking as Evan. He approaches, his long snout huffing hard enough to ruffle Ahya's hair. His eyes fix on Scarlet like he's trying to reassure her that he means no harm. He bends over Ahya, and she reaches out to touch him like he's the most magical thing she's ever seen.

The twins laugh, too, scrambling toward their father. And then it happens.

They shift into little brown bears, scampering around Ahya.

Ahya stops. Her little body goes still.

Then she shifts.

Fur spills over her skin, sleek and black, limbs thicken and shorten in a blink. Where a little girl lay, now a bear cub tumbles forward, nose twitching, paws heavy and soft. She barks, a tiny, giddy sound, and lunges at Coran, rolling into a clumsy pile of cubs.

My heart stops.

Scarlet gasps, one hand pressed to her lips. "She's... *she's a bear.*"

Finn makes a low, reverent sound from the fireplace. "No more questions."

"She's not just a bear," Goldie says softly, her voice trembling. "She's the girl from my dreams."

We all look at her.

"I saw my boys," she continues. "Running through the woods. And there was a wolf girl with red hair, laughing as she ran beside them. I didn't think anything of it, but now..."

She gestures to Ahya, who's rolling in pure joy with the cubs, her dark fur shining.

"She's real."

"You didn't tell us," Hunter says, his voice a growl that reveals his displeasure. Mates don't hold secrets. Maybe it was an innocent oversight, or maybe Goldie was worried about how her clan would react to the news of bear and wolf uniting.

When Goldie shrugs, Hunter is quiet for a long time, his gaze flicking from Ahya to Scarlet, then to Nixon.

"So, it's true," he says, voice rough, "She's the bridge between us. We need the clan. The elders. Everyone."

"Do you trust them?" Nixon asks.

"Not entirely." Hunter's hand tightens on the intricately carved arm of his chair. "But if you want your mate and your daughter safe, this is the only path."

Scarlet, who's been staring wide-eyed at Ahya as she plays, interrupts. "If it keeps her safe, we'll go."

Nixon looks at her like she's the ground beneath his feet, then he turns back to Hunter. "We'll go. But we go together. And we leave when I say."

"Okay. But before then, we want to see Ahya shift to wolf," Hunter says.

I catch the flicker of unease in Scarlet's eyes. We've all seen Ahya shift to wolf, but only in fleeting, instinctual bursts, usually when she's overwhelmed or overjoyed. We've never asked her to do it on command. She's still a baby.

But right now, she's not struggling.

She's thriving.

Still in bear form, she rolls over Connell's back, growling softly in play, then flops onto the rug with a cub-sized sigh. She stretches out, tongue lolling, and I swear she smirks. Coran nuzzles up beside her, and for a second, they breathe together. Two packs, entwined.

Finn stands. "Maybe if I shift, too?"

He walks into the center of the room, exhales, and shifts. His wolf explodes forward in a smooth, effortless burst. Silver-gray fur. Broad chest. Powerful shoulders. He stands tall beside Evan's bear form. It's a sight to behold.

We all brace.

No wolf and bear stand this close without a challenge, but here they are.

And then, without warning, Ahya shifts again.

This time, fur peels back slowly, elegant in its transformation. Her limbs stretch longer, and her paws shrink. And where a bear cub lay seconds ago, a furred wolf pup now blinks up at us with sharp blue eyes and a wagging tail.

Gasps echo around the room.

"She's so young," Robert murmurs. "That kind of control shouldn't be possible."

"She doesn't know it's control," I say. "She's just

herself."

She yips, tail whipping wildly, and bounds across the rug toward Evan, who's still in bear form. She leaps and licks at his massive paw, then spins around and skitters toward Scarlet, circling her once before flopping right into her lap. Scarlet laughs, burying her fingers in Ahya's silky fur.

"She's showing them who she is," Scarlet whispers.

And then Ahya shifts again, from wolf back to *human*, bare and glowing, her cheeks flushed from the energy. She laughs in a bubbling, radiant sound that fills the whole room with light. She claps once, then shifts right back into a cub and lunges at Coran like the chaos of existence is her favorite game.

Hunter scrubs a hand over his face, his voice stunned and reverent. "That's... evolution."

"She's showing us what's next," Goldie says softly, her eyes wet. "That division on species lines isn't our future."

I look at my brothers. At Scarlet, who is smiling through tears. At Finn, still in wolf form, his eyes locked on our daughter like he can't look away. At Evan who lowers his massive head in a slow, respectful gesture toward the cub and pup tangled on the rug.

Ahya shifts again, mid-tumble, wolf to girl to bear, and collapses in laughter.

"We'll take her to the bear clan compound," Hunter repeats, firmer this time, finally convinced.

And just like that, it's decided.

The girl born of violence and miracle will be taken into the heart of the bears' world. A place we were never supposed to venture.

39

FINN

The convoy winds through narrow forest roads as we follow Hunter's truck toward the compound. It's a thirty-minute drive, and the further north we go, the quieter it gets, like the trees themselves are braced for what's to come.

Nixon sits beside me in the passenger seat, eyes forward, one hand clenched against his knee. He hasn't said a word since we crossed into bear territory, but the tension pulses off him in waves. I don't know if it's possible to be ready to face the people you've been told are your enemy your whole life without a sense of trepidation. Even so, he gives off the silent command of a man preparing for a fight he hopes he doesn't get dragged into.

Scarlet is behind us, humming something soft to Ahya as the baby plays with the edge of her sleeve.

The compound comes into view as the road flattens. High fences wrap around a sprawling stretch of old stone buildings tucked into the base of a mountain ridge. There are watchpoints at the corners. Bears don't believe in passive defense, it seems.

Hunter's truck rolls through the gates first. We follow close behind.

And within seconds, the scent of wolf we're emanating sets the compound into a frenzy.

I see them before they shift, bears in human form gathering near the central courtyard, their nostrils flaring as our truck rolls to a stop. Their instincts hit like a tidal wave. One by one, fur rips through flesh, and massive bodies fall to four paws.

A defensive ring forms around the path ahead.

Nixon opens his door slowly, stepping out with his chin high and his eyes locked on the largest bear approaching us. I climb out the other side, rolling slightly on the balls of my feet in case this goes south fast.

But Hunter steps between the lines before the growls escalate.

His arm lifts, strong, steady, and drops over Nixon's shoulders like they've been blood brothers since birth.

"They're with me," he says.

Silence follows, thick and crackling. The nearest bears pause. Then, reluctantly, the largest among them shifts back, rising to human form. The others follow, fur sinking into skin, the tension ebbing with every breath.

We're not welcomed with open arms.

But we're not being torn apart, either.

Goldie steps from the truck behind us, cradling one twin and calling gently for the other. The moment her feet touch the ground, the tone shifts. Mates rush from the buildings to greet her with soft laughter, exclamations, and hands flying to her belly. Someone pulls her into a hug so tight, I feel it from across the courtyard.

We're led into the main hall, a vast open chamber carved from the mountain stone, sunlight filtering through a high skylight. Elders and enforcers fill the room, some seated on benches, others standing with arms crossed, the old lines of battle worn into their postures.

Hunter advances with his usual determined stride. Beside him, Nixon carries Ahya. Scarlet trails at his side, and the rest of us form a silent shield around them.

When Ahya lifts her head and waves at the crowd in human form, hair wild, eyes impossibly blue, a murmur ripples through the room.

"This is the child," Hunter says, voice echoing against the stone. "Born of both lineages."

The bearded leader steps forward, his chest bare and thick with muscle, and his long hair touching his shoulders. He doesn't look at Hunter. He looks at Ahya.

"Impossible."

The urge to roll my eyes at the similarity between my father and this bear-leader is strong. What is it about some alphas that makes them so arrogant, as though they know every secret the world has to offer and are bored with it?

"I've seen it with my own eyes," Hunter says.

There's another murmur in the crowd. As if on cue, Ahya shifts in Nixon's arms, first into a tiny wolf pup with soft fur and blue eyes that pierce the entire room, then back into her human form again. It's only when she shifts into her furry brown bear form that the crowd reacts.

She hops from Nixon's arms, lands light on her paws, and *growls*.

It's not the cry of a baby, or the howl of a wolf, or even the growl of a bear. It's something that merges all three.

A call.

A summons that charms everyone around her.

It changes everything.

The room is silent for a second, then it explodes into whispers. It can't be. Is it real? Can she be three?

A single man steps forward from the shadows. He's older than any of the others, his skin weathered like bark, eyes milky with the touch of cataracts and spirit. He carries no weapon, but every bear gives way when he walks.

The clan's mystic.

"I've seen her," he says, voice soft but resonant. "In a vision. She is the child born of pain but destined for balance. A link forged in shadow to protect the creatures of the ground from the creatures of the sky."

"What does that mean?" the leader demands, but his voice falters.

The mystic turns his gaze toward Ahya, now curled up against Scarlet's chest in wolf form.

"There is a threat," he says. "One not of fur, but of wings, claws, and fire. It will fall from the sky like hunger and tear through packs and clans alike. The only way to survive is to stand together, and she is the key."

My blood chills.

No one moves.

Ahya yawns, shifts back into a baby girl, and wraps her arms around Scarlet's neck with a happy sigh.

This child, this miracle, is the storm and the shield.

And we will defend her with everything we are.

40

SCARLET

The bear clan has moved from disbelief to debate. They pace in tight circles, talk in low, urgent tones of plans, strategies, territory lines and about nature and what it means to go against it. A collective pulse beats in the room. War is coming, and they've stopped pretending it's avoidable.

At the center of it all, Ahya plays on the rug in front of me. She seems relaxed and unbothered in her human form, but I can sense the flicker of something in her eyes, like she's listening somehow. Absorbing all of it, even if she doesn't understand.

Nixon stands like a fortress next to us, one hand resting on the back of a chair he refuses to sit in. Hunter stands across from him, nodding as they speak.

"She should stay here," one of the older bears says. "This is a compound. It's fortified and guarded. If Gregory's planning an assault, he won't get through our defenses."

"My extended family won't breach your borders," Nixon says. "And we need everyone we can gather."

"Bears won't cross into wolf territory," a rugged looking bear shifter growls.

"Unless we have to," someone says, and a ripple of laughter spreads through the room.

Nixon visibly stiffens. This is the kind of bullshit both sides need to drop if there is going to be any chance of peace. He glances around, eyes catching on Reed, then Finn, then me. There is a storm behind his gaze, filled with focus and control. This is the deadly side to him that I've yet to witness; clawing closer to the surface.

"There's space in our warehouse." He pauses, daring someone to interrupt, but they wait. "More than enough. It's structurally sound, and easy to defend. We built it up when we thought we'd be expanding our business, but now we'll use it for something more important. If you want to fight for this child, you do it on our land. With us. As one force. Bear and wolf."

I crane my head to study everyone as silence drags between the group.

One of the younger bears crosses his arms. "About damn time someone gave us a real excuse to take Gregory down."

There are a few grunts of agreement.

"He's a plague on our borders," another mutters. "Raiding food stores. Picking off patrols. That bastard killed three of our outer scouts this winter alone."

"And now we know he has a rogue bear running with him," Hunter adds, jaw clenched. "A traitor turned against his own kind."

Nixon's brow furrows. "A bear in his pack? Are you sure?"

Hunter's mouth forms a grim line. "Two of my patrols

saw him. Big. Brown. Mean as hell with a scar from his eye to his nape. His name is Bruno."

My blood chills.

Could it be connected?

Could what happened to Aura... not have been a random act of brutality, but something planned?

Nixon looks back at me like he's already thinking the same thing.

"Let's go," Connor, the bear alpha says, and the hall bursts into motion.

Everyone scatters. Some pull vehicles from garages, others gather supplies. Reed and Finn are deep in conversation with Robert and Evan, pointing toward a map on the far wall. Evan rolls up a tarp and heads outside. Reed grabs an empty crate and helps a bear shifter with long dark hair fastened low to load bottled water.

It's happening fast.

But inside I'm unraveling.

I pick up Ahya and step out of the chaos and follow Goldie, who's gathering extra blankets into a large duffel bag. I can tell her thoughts are somewhere else entirely.

Leaning in close, I say. "I need to ask you something."

She glances over, lips pressing into a thin line. "Anything."

We sit near the window, light from the sky spilling across the stone floor. When she places her hands over her belly, pain tugs at my heart that I'm never going to experience the same maternal satisfaction. I swallow thickly, then find my voice.

"Do you think what happened to Aura was something Gregory planned?" I ask. Even as I say the words, sickness tightens my belly. "Was it an accident, or did he target her?"

Goldie stills. "If history has proved nothing else, it's that men will go to terrible lengths for power and control. From what I heard, Gregory claimed Aura violently. It's not unheard of, but…"

"It was particularly violent?"

Goldie's mouth twists. "Hunter saw her while he was patrolling the outer borders after the claim. He thought she looked terrified. She was with Gregory and he had his hand on the back of her neck, pushing her forward.

"Doesn't sound like a mate bond."

"Even a forced bond should have inspired Gregory to treat Aura well. The connection is deep and should go both ways."

I twist my hands in my lap. "Do you think there could be something special about Aura? Something Gregory recognized."

"There was nothing obviously different about her," Goldie says, her eyes flicking upwards, searching through her memories.

"Nothing that we would see," I say. "But a wolf?" I chew the inside of my cheek.

"Maybe. What about Nixon and Reed? Did they mention anything?"

"No." I press my knuckles to my lips. "What if Gregory knew? What if he forced the bond with Aura not because of who she was, but what she might carry?"

Goldie's eyes darken and everything in me chills. "And if he knew what that child could be, then he'll stop at nothing to take her back."

Goldie puts a hand on mine, firm and warm. "Then it's a good thing she has you all to keep her safe."

I exhale. The fear doesn't leave me, but it sharpens into

resolve.

Outside the window, Evan slams the back of a truck closed. Reed shouts something to Finn and disappears inside to grab more supplies, and in the center of it all, Nixon stands tall, speaking to Hunter again, side by side as brothers bound by a common cause.

41

NIXON

The bears are coming.

It's a scene I never thought I'd witness but here I am, loading gear and supplies into trucks alongside men I'd have considered my enemies an hour ago. Bear shifters are dropping their lives to fight a wolf we count as a shared threat. It's humbling, in a way I can't articulate, how easily little Ahya can dissolve years of bitterness and turn hardheaded shifters into protectors.

She's our future, and she's becoming theirs, too.

I shake hands with Hunter and Connor, as the weight of alliance settles between us.

My family has gathered around our vehicle. "Gregory will have scouts," Reed says, wiping sweat from his brow, his eyes scanning the tree line. "He may know we're here already. Or, if he doesn't, he will the second we pull up with a giant convoy."

"That's the point," I remind him, clapping him on the shoulder. "We want him to know. We want him to understand what he's up against. We want him to come."

Reed's jaw is tight. He turns to Scarlet. "Are you and Ahya okay?"

Scarlet, who has been quiet since our arrival at the bear compound shrugs. "Ahya's fine. I'm... worried."

"And that's natural." I step closer, brushing her hand with mine. "Don't worry. You'll be protected."

She glances from me to Reed and then to Finn, who's leaning against the truck, arms folded, gaze intense. "And you three?"

"We'll fight." I grin sharply to hide the dread curling low in my gut. We're wolves. We know how to tear flesh from bones. We know how to outpace, outthink, and outlast. But this isn't a regular wolf pack. Gregory's pack is feral, guided by no moral compass. They act like creatures with nothing to lose.

And that makes them dangerous and unpredictable.

What will they be prepared to do for Ahya and the power she may hold?

***

The crunch of tires on gravel rolls through the quiet like distant thunder as the first convoy of bear trucks pulls into the lumberyard, their headlights flashing between rows of stacked timber and aging machinery. The sight of their arrival shifts the mood—dozens of hulking men stepping out of their vehicles with the calm authority of seasoned fighters who understand the cost of battle and are willing to pay it.

Hunter steps from the cab of the lead truck, followed by Evan and Robert, their presence solid and grounding. Behind them, more bear shifters unload crates, unroll tents and mark territory with the unspoken synchronicity of those who've battled and survived together. They carry weapons and armor, but it's the quiet way they move that holds weight.

There's a tension in the air that buzzes against my skin.

The yard springs to life with shifters humming with purpose. Bears and wolves move side by side, staking perimeter posts, erecting shelters, unloading tools and supplies. No one talks about the strangeness of it. We've moved beyond disbelief and into survival.

When I return to the cabin, Scarlet sits in the doorway with Ahya in her lap. The girl nibbles banana slices while her wide, watchful eyes scan the growing camp. She looks so small, but already the earth tilts around her.

Scarlet glances up at me, her mouth pressed into a tight line that tells me more than any words ever could.

"You think Gregory's going to come to us?" Reed asks, approaching.

"We want him to come. We want him to know our power."

Before Reed can reply, the low hum of more engines draws our attention to the road again, and I know immediately that the wolves have arrived. My father rides at the front, flanked by Chris and Macon. Their convoy rolls to a stop at the far edge of the yard, every eye trained on the unfamiliar alliance before them. The scent of our old pack hits. There's a moment of stillness, brittle and electric, until my father steps out and approaches, taking deliberate strides. I meet him halfway, flanked by Reed and Finn, and without hesitation, my father extends his hand.

I clasp it.

One by one, the other alphas follow, bears approaching to make a pact and a promise, that in this yard, on this day, we are not fractured. We're many. We're united.

"We need to send scouts," my father says.

"Bears and wolves together," Hunter agrees. "Mix the teams. Let them cover each other's blind spots. Learn to trust each other."

I nod, and we dispatch the fastest runners. As they disappear into the trees, we talk about strategy. The wind shifts as the sun dips behind the treetops, and the air stirs as Cami approaches, cloaked in ash gray, moving silently through the makeshift camp with the old bear mystic at her side. They move with gravity, drawn toward Scarlet and Ahya like iron filings to a lodestone.

They find their way to Scarlet's side, where she sits watching the gathering with the wariness of a mother bird with a single precious egg in her nest. The mystics kneel beside her without ceremony, their bodies bending like old branches, their attention locked on the child who laughs as she claps her hands and shifts, not once, but *twice*, first into a bear cub with thick fur and black paws, then into her human form again, and finally, with a glimmer of silver light, into a tiny gray wolf.

A hush falls across the lumberyard.

I watch as hardened warriors, bear and wolf alike, turn to look with wonder and awe.

"She's already growing in strength and control," Cami says softly, her voice carrying power despite its low volume.

The bear mystic's eyes never leave Ahya. "She walks the line between bloods as a guide."

"Or a weapon?" Scarlet whispers. I wince, but the mystics do not chastise her, and the rest of the gathering group are too busy to take in her warning.

***

242

The scouts return faster than expected. Two wolves and a bear sprint into the clearing, sweat shining on their chests, faces grim and hollow eyed as they dress hastily.

They cross the yard quickly, heading straight for the cluster of alphas near the center.

"Gregory's gathering," one of them reports, voice low but urgent. "They're not hiding. He wants this fight. Sixty, maybe more."

"Numbers we expected," Hunter says. "But?"

The scout hesitates, glancing up. "There's something else. Something—

"What?" I bark. "Spit it out."

"We weren't sure at first," the scout says. "But then we *heard* it. Something massive. The sound of it..." The scout swallows, his Adam's apple shifting. His head lifts, eyes wide and fearful as he scans the sky above us.

My blood runs cold. "The sound of what?"

"We don't know," the bear shifter says, rubbing the center of his brows. His barrel chest heaves, and his eyes dart upto the sky, as wide and fearful.

"A bird?" I ask. "Something in the sky?"

I sound like I'm playing charades, but no one is giving me answers.

How dangerous could a bird be?

"No feathers," the bear says.

"No feathers," I repeat, confusion surging. What kind of bird doesn't have feathers? They can't mean...

The bear mystic's head lifts sharply. "A creature of ruin."

Cami's face is grave. "No. It can't be."

"We saw it," Harry, the youngest but fastest wolf shifter in my father's pack, says. "At least, I think we saw it."

He doesn't sound sure.

"Whatever you saw, is it with Gregory?"

He shrugs and I growl with frustration. "I... I don't know, Nixon. It was a glimpse... the noise of it."

I turn to Cami, desperate to understand what's happening.

"The child is born of magic," Cami says. "And dragons were always the oldest protectors of magic. If one has awakened... maybe it senses what is to come."

"Gregory can't control a dragon," I say, searching their faces for confirmation. "Right?"

"No," Cami says. "But he may have awakened it. Or worse, angered it."

I run my hands over my face as the tense silence strangles the camp. The world seems thinner now, stretched too tight, like the membrane between what we know and what we fear is about to tear.

"We deal with what's in front of us, and we stay ready for the rest," my father says. "That's all we can do. Dragon talk isn't helpful right now. "

"Okay."

I clap him on the shoulder, relieved to have his guidance again, and move past to take Scarlet's face in my hands.

"Keep Ahya with you at all times. Don't let her out of your sight."

Her eyes swell with tears that I wipe away with my thumbs before pressing a kiss onto her lips. "You carry life inside you," I whisper. "I love you. I will come back."

Her face crumples as she shakes her head. I touch her flat belly, already sensing the change within her; the warm sweetness of her pregnant scent and the magic of life growing within. "You are strong, Scarlet. My love. My mate."

I straighten quickly and walk away before the desperate way she clutches at me fractures my heart.

**

The smell of sweat and metal lingers, the tension heavy enough to choke on. Bears and wolves stand side by side now, shoulder to shoulder, moving with purpose as the final defenses are laid. No one speaks of the dragon.

But every one of us is listening for wings.

Inside the cabin, Cami and the bear mystic draw sacred lines around Scarlet, Ahya, and the children. Reed and Finn take up posts on the outer edges. Hunter stands beside me; the weight of leadership etched into the lines around his eyes.

"I have to tell you something," he says. "I want you to understand the trust I'm putting in you by making this confession. You cannot share this information with anyone. Not even your brothers. Doing so will risk my whole family."

I nod, giving him space to find the words.

"When Goldie was in labor, she almost died. We were forced to enhance our bond, to give her our life force, but in doing so, we linked ourselves and our lives for good. If one of us dies, we all die."

I blink, stunned. I didn't even know that was a possibility. Maybe it's a solution for bears.

"So, you're worried about fighting?"

"I love fighting, Nixon. But I have two cubs and a pregnant mate. I can't risk all our lives in the thick of battle. You have to understand that this goes against who I am and what I want to be as an alpha."

"I do."

"Me and my brothers... we'll stay at the cabin to protect

the women. Leave Reed with us. We can't risk our mates being harmed. It's the most we can do."

"Yes," I say. "I understand. And I'm thankful for your support, Hunter. You didn't have to bring your family into this… especially under the circumstances."

"You have enough of a force to defeat Gregory. You will win this fight."

"Goddess willing."

We stand for a while longer, the night tight around us.

No fires are lit.

No songs are sung.

We wait.

And in the distance, rising with the mist and darkness, a scream echoes, cutting the silence like a blade.

42

FINN

We smell them before we see them; the rot of unwashed bodies and the sick-slick stench of adrenaline, blood, and hunger. It coats the air like a fog, tightening in our lungs, warning of what's coming.

I hunch lower, shifting entirely now, bones stretching and snapping as fur ripples across my skin. Pain flickers through me, but I welcome it. It sharpens my focus, floods my system with clarity. All around me, others shift in tandem, a chorus of guttural groans and growls, until the forest floor is bristling with muscle and claw, our combined forms coiling into a crescent formation. Wolves and bears together, a terrifying half-moon of fangs and fury designed to trap Gregory's rabid pack inside.

To end this.

Once and for all.

Nixon is already charging forward in his wolf form, his fur that distinctive silver-gray that flashes like lightning through the trees. Every movement he makes is calculated.

Beside him, Connor barrels forward as a monstrous brown bear, slower but brutal. You don't need speed when you're that unstoppable.

I snap my jaw shut as the first of Gregory's pack bursts through the underbrush.

A black-furred wolf lunges straight for me. I twist, dragging my claws along his flank before biting hard into his shoulder. The tang of blood fills my mouth as he howls and stumbles, but another takes his place instantly. Teeth clash. Fur flies. I duck under a sweeping paw and sink my fangs into his exposed belly. He whimpers, lurches backward, and I pounce, driving him to the dirt with my full weight.

Pain sears along my side. A red-furred wolf has latched onto my ribcage, his teeth deep. I howl, slam my body into his, then roll until his grip loosens. I manage to claw his face and push away. I'm bleeding, but I can still run... Still fight.

Another wolf comes from the side, reeking of rot. He growls and tries to crush me with his weight. I dodge too late, and his claws rake my thigh, a white-hot agony exploding through my leg. I go down hard, roll, and come up snapping. I bite his forearm and twist, hearing the crunch of bone before he slams me into a tree.

The air whooshes from my lungs. My vision flickers. But then Grizzly, Connor's second in command, is there, plowing into the wolf and dragging him away, slamming his skull into the trunk until he collapses in a broken heap.

I pull myself upright, panting, blood running in rivulets along my side and leg, sticky and hot. But I'm still standing.

We push them backward. Inch by inch, we drive Gregory's pack deeper into the trap, toward the center where Nixon and Grizzly, Dad and Connor are waiting to crush them. Bodies fall. Limbs are torn. Blood darkens the forest floor.

But Gregory isn't here.

I scan the carnage, my thoughts a mental thread reaching out to Nixon. *He's not here.*

His reply is immediate, ice-cold. *I don't see him, either. I've torn through ten of his wolves, and not one of them has his scent on them.*

He sent them to die.

That's not an alpha. That's a coward.

A pause. Then Nixon again. *The rogue bear, Bruno. Do you see him?*

No.

We're being flanked.

My blood chills. We both know it. The timing, the absence of Gregory's scent, the missing rogue. It all screams diversion.

I grit my teeth against the pain and break off, launching into the trees, leaping over fallen logs and ducking low-hanging branches, racing the wind back to the cabin.

My lungs burn. My side and thigh throb. But nothing can stop me. If they've reached Scarlet and the kids—

No. They won't get that far.

The cabin appears through the trees, lights glowing. The scent of Reed is thick in the air, which means he's still alive and defending our precious mate. But there's something else cloying in the air now. The copper stench of blood.

I skid to a halt, my paws clawing at the dirt, nostrils flaring. Nixon and Connor appear beside me, their forms hulking and bristling with tension. No words pass between us. We move.

The clearing opens ahead like a gaping wound, and time slows.

Gregory stands in the center, his fur matted and dark, his massive form crouched low. His jaws are locked around Reed's throat, and our brother hangs limp in his grip, blood pouring in rivulets over his chest, his eyes half-closed, barely conscious.

A snarl tears from Nixon, pure rage and anguish. I don't wait. I leap.

Gregory whips his head around as I strike, his fangs ripping free and leaving Reed crumpling to the ground in a heap. I smash into Gregory, claws raking across his side, and we tumble across the earth in a blur of fur and fury.

Robert crashes into him next, and then Nixon, and the three of us are a whirlwind of vengeance, of grief, of blood. Gregory fights like the cornered beast he is, tearing into us with abandon, but we are not fighting for territory.

We are fighting for family.

And he will not survive this night.

43

REED

Everything is red.

Red behind my eyelids. Heat in my mouth. Red pounding through my skull like a war drum.

I don't know if it's blood or rage, but it's everywhere.

Something wet pulses at my neck. It hurts to breathe. My body's limp, barely responsive, like I'm trapped in someone else's skin. I want to move, to shift, to fight, but the connection between will and body is severed.

And yet... I hear them.

Growls, low and deep. Snarls like thunder rolling over the earth. The scent of them slaps me, rousing the little strength I have.

REED.

My brothers howl my name together.

They're here.

They came.

Through the haze, Gregory's weight is torn away. His jaws ripped from my throat with my brother's fury.

I want to tell them I'm alive. I want to lift my head, dig my claws into the dirt, and rise, tearing Gregory apart with them. But I can't. I'm buried under the weight of blood loss and darkness, slipping in and out, barely tethered to consciousness.

The sounds of battle echo around me: grunts of impact, flesh rending, the clash of bone and claw. Nixon's wolf voice booms through the link we all share, calling commands, refusing to let Gregory win.

I try to reach out, mentally and physically, but it's like shouting underwater. The only thing I manage is a twitch of my fingers against the earth.

Gregory can't win.

If he takes Ahya… Scarlet…

No. No, no. He won't. Not while Nixon lives. Not while Finn breathes. Not while Robert fights beside them.

Their fury, their pain, the depthless well of love that drives them holds me there and keeps my soul from slipping too far.

Ahya.

Scarlet.

Reed. Fight, baby. Fight. I can't live without you. I need you. Please, Reed. Fight. Her voice echoes through my mind.

They are everything. And even if my body fails, I know my brothers will not. They will end this.

Because if they don't, the world we've built will fall with me.

And I am not ready to leave everything I love behind.

44

SCARLET

I watch through the window as a battle rages outside. Wolf against wolf. Bear against bear. It wasn't supposed to come so close. It's a bad sign, and fear and frustration war inside me like a storm in a bottle.

Helplessness isn't an emotion I'm used to grappling with, but I know my limits. I'm a human woman, and the beasts outside are fearsome and violent. If the cabin is breached, I will be unable to protect myself and Ahya.

"Come back from the window," Cami says, voice calm but firm behind me.

"No."

I need to know. If the battle is lost, I must prepare myself to fight or even be captured, because there's no way I'm letting them take Ahya without me. Where she goes, I go. I'll die before I lay her in Gregory's arms.

My hand tightens around the child in my arms. She's tense too, her body pressed against mine, ears perked, eyes unusually aware.

Movement flashes at the tree line, as a massive black wolf throws itself at one of our own. My heart seizes as I recognize Reed's familiar fur. He's fighting two of them at once, blood already soaking the earth beneath him.

"No," I whisper. My knees give out, and I sink to the floor in front of the window, my palm slamming to the glass like I could somehow stop the blood from spilling, stop the tearing of flesh.

He's hurt.

Reed.

He doesn't reply to my call, and tears spill hot and fast as I rock forward. I press Ahya to my chest and sob into her curls. It's going to happen. They're going to take her. Reed is bleeding into the ground, and Gregory's monsters are pressing closer to the cabin.

Reed. Fight, baby. Fight. I can't live without you. I need you. Please, Reed. Fight.

I don't know if he will hear me. Everything's futile. But then—

Reinforcements.

Silver, gray, and deep brown forms tear through the brush. Finn's limping, his fur clogged with dried blood, but still he runs. Nixon is a streak of steel in motion, and behind them, more. Wolves and bears. Our allies.

The tide begins to turn, but Reed is motionless and silent.

He shifts, his wolf melting back into the form of a man, bloodied and barely conscious, lying naked and pale in the dirt beyond the porch. Has he lost consciousness... or worse? He looks so vulnerable surrounded by battling animals, so weak and slumped awkwardly in the cold.

"I have to help him!"

I thrust Ahya into Goldie's arms. "Don't let her out of your sight."

Goldie argues, but one look at me silences her. "Okay." Her arms tightening around Ahya.

I sprint for the door, unlocking the bolts and yanking it open, barefoot and wild, stumbling through mud and blood until I reach him. The bolts clunk back into place as my knees hit the earth beside Reed's body, and I shove my hands under his arms to drag him toward safety.

"Come on, baby," I whisper. "Don't you dare leave me."

He moans weakly. He's alive, but barely.

I tug, groaning as I haul him a few inches, tears streaming my cheeks, the weight of him nearly too much. I yank harder, gritting my teeth, grunting with the effort. I can't stop. I won't stop.

I'm almost at the door when a shadow falls over me.

I turn as a hand clamps around my throat and hauls me upright, my back slammed to a hard, hot chest.

The man is naked, strong, his scent all wrong.

"Don't scream," he hisses.

I gasp as he pulls a blade from a strap on his ankle, the edge of it biting cold against the fragile skin beneath my jaw.

A growl explodes over the thudding and scrapping of battle. I'm spun until I'm facing Nixon, who's still in wolf form.

The knife digs in.

"Move and I'll open you up," the stranger growls.

Everything goes still.

The stranger's grip around my throat is like iron, cutting off enough air to make my body scream, but not enough to knock me out.

From the trees, a voice booms out.

"Let her go, Gregory."

Finn.

I turn my head as much as I can. He's shifted back into his human form, bare-chested, blood streaked across his ribs and thighs. He's panting, but his eyes burn with uncontained fury.

The man holding me, Gregory, laughs. It's a low, scraping sound, like gravel caught in his throat.

"You think I'd let go of my creation so easily?" he sneers. "The child is mine. She carries the bloodline I forged... wolf, bear, and magic. When she's grown, she'll be my mate. Every pack, every clan, bear and wolf will surrender their alphas and join my pack."

"Bullshit," Finn spits. "You violated her mother. You tortured her. Ahya isn't a weapon, and she'll never be yours."

Gregory chuckles again, then yanks me back another step, dragging my heels across the blood-slick ground. "Worried for your mate? I know what you'll do to keep her safe. You'd give up anything, wouldn't you?"

Behind him, Nixon prowls closer in wolf form, his silver fur rippling with tension, his low growl vibrating through the ground beneath me. Other wolves fan out behind him. Bears, too. Some shift into their human forms, retrieving weapons from concealed stashes, while others remain beasts, their dark shapes looming like shadows.

"I'll carve her open," Gregory warns. "Don't test me."

Finn lifts his hands. "You can talk, Gregory. Talk. But don't take another step toward that door."

I glance behind us.

The cabin.

He's trying to get to Ahya.

256

Finn takes a step closer, leaning in like he's about to whisper a secret. "The wolves care what happens to Scarlet. The bears? They'll trade her blood for yours in a heartbeat."

Gregory growls, dragging me closer to the porch. He's distracted now, arguing, and gloating. Finn keeps talking, pacing a little, forcing Gregory to turn as he watches him. He's almost to the door.

And then it happens.

The front door explodes outward.

I'm jerked forward so hard that I lose my footing. Gregory's arms, which were tight around me, loosen as the knife drops and spears the dirt at my feet. I stumble forward, barely catching myself before my face hits the ground. I hear the crunch before I see the blood as Gregory is lifted off his feet, his scream gurgling into nothing.

Hunter?

He shakes Gregory like a rag doll, once, twice, three times, and then the snapping sound is final. The alpha's head is torn from his body, his warm blood arcing like a fountain, soaking my chest, my face, my hands.

The head rolls past me.

And everything fades.

The last thing that fills my vision before I pass out is Nixon, covered in blood, his wolf eyes fixed on me like I'm the only thing left in the world that matters.

45

NIXON

I reach her after she hits the ground.

Her body is limp, soaked in blood that isn't hers, thank the gods, and I lift her into my arms like I've done so many times before, but never like this. Never with the copper sting of spilled life in the air. Never with the imprint of another man's violence still fresh on her skin.

Scarlet is unconscious, her head lolling against my shoulder as I stride into the cabin. Her bloodstained waves are stuck to her cheeks, and every part of me is shaking with a rage I can't unleash. Not yet. Not when she needs me.

Cami parts the way with a nod, her eyes heavy with knowledge. Goldie is in the corner, rocking Ahya and her babies, and whispering soft comforts as the children whimper.

Finn and Robert carry Reed into the kitchen, his body limp and blood-soaked. I reach out for his mind and find it, weakened but still linked to mine.

Fight, brother, I urge him. *Fight for your life, for our mate, for our family. Fight because we need you, and it isn't your time. Fight to stay with us, brother.*

"Make him strong again," I tell Cami and the bear mystic. They're already pulling poultices and potions from their bags.

I head straight for the bathroom. The door closes behind me with a snap, and I step into the shower with Scarlet fully clothed in my arms. Warm water cascades over us, washing away blood in rivulets that stain the tiles and the floor with a river of red.

Her breathing is shallow, her lips pale, but she's alive. She's mine. Still mine.

I cradle her beneath the falling spray, letting it soak us through. She stirs, a soft whimper catching in her throat as her eyes flutter open.

"Nixon…"

"I've got you," I whisper against her temple.

Her eyes search my face. "Reed? Is he… Finn?"

"Finn's with him. He's okay. Alive. Ahya's safe."

Scarlet. Reed's mind connection is weak and hoarse, but it's there.

Reed, baby. I'm okay. You're okay.

Tears spill over her cheeks, mixing with water. "I thought he was dying… I almost…"

"Don't," I growl, holding her tighter. "You were brave, Scarlet. If Gregory had hurt you… taken you…"

My voice breaks. I can't say it. I won't. I already saw her bloodied in his arms. I already felt the terror of almost losing her. I knew I'd be nothing without her love.

I kiss her hard and desperately, the kind of kiss that presses a crescendo of emotion into flesh and bone. She shakes in my arms, whether from fear or shock catching up

259

with her, I don't know. I know I need to anchor her to this moment. To me. To our lives.

She tries to stand on her own, and I let her, helping her peel off the ruined clothing. I grab a thick towel and wrap it around her shaking frame, rubbing heat into her arms before guiding her to the sink to sit while I dry off and dress. Neither of us speaks, but our eyes hold each other, only breaking the connection when I pull a shirt over her head.

When we return to the main floor, the scent of blood is more potent. The door's been flung open to allow for incoming wounded. Makeshift cots already line the walls. Finn is hunched over Reed on the kitchen table, his hands slick as he applies pressure to a wound in his side. Cami moves around him with bottles and crushed herbs.

But then Harry and Caleb appear, carrying someone between them, and ice fills my veins. My father.

His face is slack. His body is too still. His scent...

A strangled sound scrapes from my throat as the wrongness of his scent drives a stake into my heart.

Not the sharp copper of fresh injury, but—

Death.

The slow, creeping decay of life, leaving a body.

They lay him on the floor

"No," I gasp, stepping forward.

Cami rushes to him, fingers pressed to his pulse points, chanting something I don't understand.

I don't realize I'm clutching Scarlet's hand until she squeezes tightly.

My father.

Gone?

The world narrows to the ragged rasp of my own breath and Scarlet's warmth against my palm.

She's alive.

Ahya's safe.

Finn and Reed are wounded, but they're going to be okay.

But now, I have to face a world without my father.

46

FINN

This is the aftermath. The deep, haunted silence that follows chaos, when the adrenaline drains and you're left with blood on your hands and a hollow in your chest.

Reed sleeps upstairs, his breathing steady but shallow. Cami gave him something for the pain, something that dragged him into a healing sleep. I checked on him. His pulse is strong. His color is better. But still, he came close.

My own wounds are bound and aching, but they are nothing serious. Battle scars will mar my skin and remind me of all that is worth fighting for.

Scarlet is upstairs with Ahya, coaxing her into bed after the day from hell. Our mate's voice is a soft hum above us as she sings something that must've come from her human childhood, and it makes my throat tighten every time I catch the melodic sweetness.

Goldie's tucked away in the spare room with her cubs, murmuring soft reassurances, the kind only mothers can give. I don't know how she has the strength left to stand, let alone parent, after everything we've been through. But maybe that's what moms do; rise even when the world is breaking down around them.

I gather with Nixon, Hunter, Robert, and Evan around the cabin's main table, the same one we used to stack lumber orders on, back when we thought starting a business together would be the most challenging thing we ever did.

We were so wrong.

Nixon starts with the roll call. Ten wolves from our father's pack succumbed. Seven bears. Gregory's forces? Mostly obliterated. His elite guard tore through our front lines, but they went down hard. The only ones left alive are three wolves, now in custody, tied up and guarded while the bears take turns to interrogate them.

Hunter leans forward, rubbing his temple. "They're not trained. They're scared. Fanatics with no clue what they were following. Gregory used fear and power to keep them loyal."

Nixon's jaw flexes. "And Bruno?"

"Gone," Evan answers. "Slipped out during the final push. We were so focused on Gregory, we missed the bastard."

Hunter adds, "He'll be hunted. Mark my words. No rogue bear escapes a debt like that. He's a disgrace to our kind."

None of us speak for a long moment.

Hunter finally breaks the silence again. "I had my suspicions about Aura, but now Gregory's wolves have spilled what I believe to be true."

We all glance up.

"She's descended from a spiritual bloodline. A vessel of magic. That's how Gregory did it. He fused bear and wolf

263

in her womb through ritual manipulation. Magic."

The way he says the word magic makes it sound like a curse.

"How could he do that to his mate?" I ask.

"She was never his mate," Robert says. "That was a cover."

"She was used," Hunter says. "And Ahya... she's the result. A child made of pain and power."

"She's also loved," Nixon says quietly. "She's our daughter. Not his legacy."

Softness replaces seriousness across the faces of all the assembled hardened fighters, shifters who are burly on the outside but gooey as marshmallow on the inside, it seems.

Talk turns to my father, and I tense with pain.

He gave everything. Every ounce of strength. Every second of breath.

The final charge to protect our family cost him everything.

Tomorrow, we'll return to our family home. We'll bury him beside Matt. Let our cousins, Chris and Macon, step into their role as alphas. The torch passed. The line continued.

My eyes sting, but I don't let the tears fall. Not in front of the men. Not here.

Harry and three other wolves, Caleb, Marcus, and Theo, have chosen to stay to protect Ahya and find mates of their own in Blackwood Forest.

"We'll make room," Nixon says. "In the house. In the business."

They nod gratefully. It makes me proud of what we've built. What we're still building.

And relieved, too. The bigger our pack, the more chance

we have of keeping our mate and children safe from outside threats.

Robert slides a bottle of whiskey across the table. "We should drink to the fallen," he says. "And to the ones who made it back."

We each pour a glass. The clink of thick-bottom tumblers is loud in the silence.

"To my father," Nixon says, voice rough.

"To our father," I echo.

Hunter raises his glass. "To the end of Gregory."

We drink.

"To the beginning of something better," Evan adds.

I drain my glass and let the warmth burn deep into my chest, fighting the cold that's tried to settle since the moment the fighting stopped. There's still so much to do. So many wounds to heal. But we're alive, and our future is blooming in front of us.

Outside, the moon glows low and almost complete, casting silver light over the trees. The forest is quiet.

I think about Ahya, already powerful enough to motivate an army. And the cubs Goldie rocks to sleep. And the life Scarlet carries, blooming beneath her heart. New life to balance out the death.

We'll rebuild.

We'll protect them.

And we'll never let a monster like Gregory rise again.

Tonight, we drink. Tomorrow, we bury the dead.

After that?

We live.

47

SCARLET

Ahya sleeps tucked into the crook of my body, small and warm and steady as a heartbeat. Downstairs, someone rinses a glass; the water runs, stops. The wind combs the trees. Pine and soap and woodsmoke drift through my enhanced senses.

I stare at my phone for a long time, the new wi-fi connection taunting me. I've been putting off calling her through all the craziness of the past days, but I know I need to make contact before she calls for a search party.

I sigh deeply, dreading the words she'll most probably say. *Come home. Don't be crazy. You can't possibly love three men. What do you mean you're giving up your life to take care of someone else's child?*

They'd all be valid concerns a mother would have for her daughter, but they'd all be wrong.

I'm not crazy for loving Nixon, Reed, and Finn. I'm not crazy for falling in love with a perfect child who needed arms to hold her and keep her safe. I'm not crazy for following a dream I'd given up thinking could be mine.

Now, I have to convince her.

I hit call.

Mom answers on the second ring, panting like she's been carrying groceries up the stairs. "Scarlet? Are you okay?"

The worry permeating her voice makes my heart ache. I wish she could let go of all the anxiety she has around me living my life, for her and for me.

"I'm okay." I swallow, eyes stinging. "I'm... actually really good."

"What kind of good?"

"The best kind, Mom." I exhale, and it shakes on the way out. "Mom, I have to tell you something."

"That tone," she says softly. "Go on."

"I fell in love." The words are huge and right. "In Braysville. And I'm... I'm staying."

She lets out a surprised gasp. "Tell me about him," she says, careful. "What's his name?"

I press my mouth to Ahya's curls. "It's... not just *a* him."

Another breath on her end. My mother has a talent for not making me defend myself before I've had a chance to explain. "Okay."

"It's three hims," I say, choking on a laugh that's half terror, half joy. "Nixon. Reed. Finn. They're brothers—" I search for the right shape, the truest one. "They're good men. The best kind. They run a lumberyard and build beautiful furniture. Their cabin is in the forest, and we're surrounded by the most beautiful trees. It's peaceful, and they love what I love... they see me... All of me."

"Three," she repeats, voice even. "Is this safe?"

"Yes." I don't let the word wobble. "I feel safer than I have in years. Not because they're... big and ridiculously

267

strong—though they are—but because they protect me and listen. They're the best men I've ever met. And there's a little girl, this baby, here who needs us. I know you're about to tell me to beware of strangers, and you're not wrong. I heard you in my head the whole time." A huff of a laugh. "But they're not strangers anymore."

"A baby?" Her gasp is watery, and if I had any doubts that she would accept this, they fly out of the window. She knows how hard I grieved after my diagnosis, and how devastated I was to have to let my dreams of a family slip through my fingers.

"Ahya," I say. "She's got red hair like mine, and she's the sweetest little thing. Hang on. I'll send you a picture."

I flick to my photo app and forward the picture to my mom. It's of me, holding Ahya, a close up where I'm staring at her beautiful sleeping face.

"Oh, Scarlet." My mother makes a sound I've heard in kitchens and car rides and doctor offices—when she changes gears from protection to support. "She's gorgeous… and look at you."

"She's happy with me, Momma. She looks at me like I light up her world."

"It's the best, isn't it?"

I smile at Ahya, holding her a little closer.

"Do they love you, baby?" Mom asks. "Do they put you first? Do they support your dreams? Do they make you feel like you can grow and thrive with them?"

"They do." My throat gets tight. "I love them."

"Okay," she says again, and I can hear her smile now, thin but real. "Then I'm happy for you, baby."

I bite my lip. "I'll still need to come back and pack up my life. Tools. Contracts. The ugly chair I keep because it was my first commission."

"You can take your grandmother's quilt," she says, practical through the emotion, like always. "And the muffin basket."

"You're giving me the muffin basket? I thought I was only getting that in your will."

"Someone has to fill it with muffins," she laughs. "Sugar isn't my friend these days." A pause. "When are you coming back?"

"After... some things settle here." My voice dips. I don't tell her about the battle or the danger I was in. I'd never hear the end of it. I can't tell her about Nixon, Reed, and Finn and their true nature yet. There will come a time when I'll have to if I want her to be a grandmother to Ahya, but that'll be up to my wolves to decide. I won't do anything to put their lives at risk. "Maybe next week? Finn offered to drive me. He's the artistic one. You'll like him."

"I'll like all of them," she says dryly, "if they keep my girl safe and treat her right."

"They do."

"And they understand I'll have questions," she adds. "Pointed ones. Over coffee."

I smile into the dark. "Deal."

"And Scarlet?"

"Yeah?"

"I don't care if it's one or three or a whole basketball team as long as you sound like this." Her voice goes slow and sure. "Happy. You sound happy, and that's all I've ever wanted for you."

I press my hand flat over my sternum, where a new kind of warmth blooms. "I am."

"Then call me when you have dates. Will you bring the

baby?"

"Maybe not this time. She's still small," I say.

"Okay, tell me their names again?"

"Nixon. Reed. Finn."

"Okay," she says. In the background, pen scratches against paper. My mother, making a list of my big, good wolves. "It's late, baby. You should sleep. I love you."

"I love you, too."

When I end the call, the house seems different, like I opened a window and allowed two worlds touch for the first time. I tuck the phone under my pillow and inhale a new calm. Downstairs, the water runs again. Somewhere outside, an owl calls.

"This is our home," I whisper. "This is our home."

48

REED

I run through the forest like it belongs to me, my paws sinking to its moss-soft floor and jumping its ancient roots. The ache in my side is dulled now, a shadow of the pain that nearly ended me. Cami's potions were bitter as sin, but I drank them without flinching, because I had no choice. The world wouldn't have stopped turning because I bled all over it. I could fight or die.

I chose to fight.

My breath moves steadily and deeply, filling my lungs with life as my limbs stretch in time with the wind. The scent of pine and damp earth fills my nostrils. This is peace, or something close to it. But peace has edges now. War made sure of that.

I circle back to a place I haven't visited since before the final battle. A grove by the cliffs, shadowed by rock and overgrown trees. This is where Aura hid. The woman who brought Ahya into the world disappeared like mist at sunrise.

271

Her scent is gone now. Rain washed it away long ago. But I remember it. She left more than a child behind. She left questions that no one can answer.

Does she wonder about Ahya? Does she think about the child who shifts between forms as easily as water slips through fingers? Does she lie awake in the dark and ache with regret? Or did she give Ahya up in her mind long before her body walked away?

I don't know. I may never know.

But Scarlet? Scarlet has taken that child into her heart, wrapped her around the twins growing inside her, as if she were born to be her mother. And maybe she was. Fate is strange like that. The goddess's plans are a constant source of mystery.

Scarlet's love for Ahya is fierce and selfless, but it comes with a fragility I recognize, because if Aura ever returns, if she tries to reclaim what she abandoned, Scarlet's heart could break.

The forest shifts around me. Quiet becomes stillness. Stillness becomes tension.

A cry rings out across the sky.

I lift my muzzle, curious.

It's not a wolf.

It's not a bear.

It's not anything I've heard in my life.

A heavy rush of air follows, like sails snapping on an old ship, but faster, larger. I stop dead in my tracks, eyes scanning the tops of the trees that sway and bend, and the clouds that merge and blend as they drift into the horizon.

There's nothing.

But there's a scent in the air. Faint. Foreign. Burnt metal and ozone.

All that talk of dragons was nervous mouths painting myths with fear. I told myself they were wrong. That was panic talking. Ahya's existence had suddenly made the impossible possible. But the age of monsters is over.

But what if it isn't? What if those scouts saw something real.

What if the creature Cami feared was in the skies over Blackwood? What if it was never Gregory who summoned it… but something else? Something like Aura's magic?

My skin prickles beneath my fur. My wounds may be healed, but the past still clings to my bones. I shake it off. Not today.

Today, I turn away from the ghost of Aura and the imagined wings in the sky.

Today, I run back to my family. To the warmth of Scarlet's hands. To the wild spirit of Ahya. To the babies waiting to be born and the legacy we'll build with love.

Today, I run home.

***

The scent of the cabin reaches me before it comes into view. Smoke and pine, honey and jasmine from Scarlet's hair, the faint sweetness of Ahya's skin, the steady scent of my brothers. I crest the last ridge and find Scarlet waiting, seated on the front step, her hair loose around her shoulders, a shawl wrapped around her shoulders.

She stands when she notices me, barefoot in the dirt, and walks toward me with her palm outstretched and a fond smile playing at her pretty lips.

I don't shift. I don't want to yet.

I press my muzzle into her palm, and she gasps, then smiles, her other hand sliding through the fur behind my ear, her fingers small and warm.

"Reed," she whispers.

I nuzzle into her neck, breathing her in, licking the edge of her jaw where her pulse beats fast. She laughs softly and presses her forehead to mine.

"You're beautiful like this," she murmurs. "All soft fur and soft eyes. *Mine.*"

I let her hold me, wrapping her arms around my furry neck, grounding me in a way nothing else ever has. When I finally shift, I do it slowly, letting my body melt back into human form, still crouched in front of her, bare and vulnerable.

I rise to my feet and pull her against me, wrapping my arms around her and tucking her close. She's warm and smells like home, and I bury my face in her hair, inhaling deeply as I let the rhythm of her body pull the tension from my shoulders.

Her hands move over my back, stroking gently, lingering on the ridges of old wounds and new scars.

"Come inside, baby," she whispers. "It's cold."

***

Nixon and Finn murmur over papers strewn across the table. We're expanding the business, and Finn is pushing to make furniture production a greater part of our business. He's worked on plans with Scarlet that look solid. Now, he has to convince Nixon.

They both glance up, their eyes softening as they take in Scarlet, bundled up in the thick, red, oversized cardigan she practically lives in now, her cheeks pink from the cold and her boots dusted in frost. Their posture relaxes. Hell, I feel it, too. The bone-deep satisfaction of having a mate has changed us all. She doesn't have to ask for anything. We'd give it all to her before the thought even leaves her lips.

I yank my sweater off the back of a chair and pull it over my head. "Colder than a witch's tit out there."

Scarlet snorts, eyes gleaming. "How many witches' tits have you fondled, exactly?"

I grin. "Do you want the honest answer or the one that keeps the mystery alive?"

She lifts her hands, laughing. "Forget I asked. Between the shifters, mystics, and actual wolf-bear-babies in this house, I'm maxed out on supernatural weirdness. Let's not add witches to the mix."

I stalk toward her, a slow prowl, sliding my arms around her waist. "Good. Because the only tits I want to fondle..." I cup her breast through the fabric, my thumb teasing her nipple until it pebbles beneath my touch and she gasps against my throat, "are yours."

Her hands go to my hips, and she raises a brow. "You're not wearing pants."

"All the better to fuck you," I murmur, pressing my hard length against her stomach.

Scarlet's laugh is half-moan now, her nails dragging lightly up my spine. She's always been this way; fire and humor, sweetness and hunger. Every time I touch her, it's like discovering her all over again.

Nixon groans from the table, scrubbing a hand over his face. "Can we please get through one day without the big bad wolf references?"

I bare my teeth and snap them gently near Scarlet's neck, earning a squeal and a giggle as she tugs me closer. "Our mate tastes like heaven," I growl. "I'd huff and puff and blow down this whole fucking cabin to get to her sweet pussy."

"Reed," Finn says without looking up, "for the love of

all that's holy, put on some goddamn pants."

Scarlet leans into me, her voice low and teasing. "Don't. I like you like this."

I grin wickedly. "See? She's the boss."

With one smooth motion, I scoop Scarlet into my arms and turn toward the table, ignoring the groans behind me as I brush the paperwork and plans onto the floor with a casual sweep of my arm. Finn curses. Nixon sighs.

I lower her onto the table like she's the offering, and I'm the one who's seeking the goddess's favor. Scarlet's breath hitches, but she doesn't protest. She watches me with that soft, glowing gaze that says she's mine in every way that counts.

"You're beautiful," I whisper, kissing the curve of her cheek, the pulse point beneath her jaw, the place behind her ear that always makes her tremble.

I tug open the cardigan and push it off her shoulders, followed by the soft cotton tee she's wearing. Her skin is warm under my palms, her belly round with our children. I kiss it gently, again and again, trailing my lips along the rise of it, marking her with my scent. Scarlet moans, fingers tangling in my hair as I move lower, my mouth mapping her like a man memorizing home.

"Reed," she whispers, the word catching like it's too big to hold inside.

My chest tightens, too full of love, too heavy with gratitude. I undress her slowly, reverently, peeling away the last layers of fabric to reveal the woman who carries our future and holds our past together like it's nothing. I don't rush. She deserves more than hunger. She deserves worship.

She reaches for me, pulling me down, and I go willingly, bracing myself over her, fitting my body to hers like we were shaped by the same stars.

"Make love to me," she whispers, her eyes glossy, her hands reaching for my brothers, too. "I need all of you."

Nixon moves first, coming to her side, brushing hair from her face, and kissing her forehead. Finn's slower, more hesitant, always the careful one. But he steps close, dragging his knuckles along her arm and lifting her hand to his lips.

And then it's the three of us.

Our clothes fall away, scattered like the papers we swept to the floor, and we come to her with love spilling from our lips. Scarlet gasps as Nixon kisses along her throat. At the same time, Finn's hands explore the curve of her hips, and I take my time at her center, tasting her, coaxing pleasure from her until she's bucking against me, wild and out of control.

She arches beneath us, body trembling, so close to breaking, so close to flying apart, and we catch her with mouths, with hands, with love so fierce it burns through the past and binds us tighter to the present.

She cries out as we bring her over the edge again and again, her voice a song that only we know the melody to. When I finally push inside her, she sighs like she's finally home.

And I am home. Here. With her. With them.

Her lips find Nixon's as I move inside her, and she reaches for Finn, drawing him closer so his mouth can discover her breast, swollen and sensitive. It's all tenderness. All heat. All trust.

Scarlet lies beneath me, her skin glowing in the soft amber light spilling from the hearth, her eyes wide and dark with emotion. She gasps as I move inside her like I'm carving my name into her soul.

"I've got you," I whisper, my hand splayed across her belly. "I'll always have you."

My wolf rises with the need to bind us together. My knot pulses, swelling with every thrust, threatening to breach her tight entrance and seal us.

Her body trembles, her gasp caught between pleasure and something more primal. She's mine now, in every way that matters.

When I pull back, her eyes lock with mine, and she touches my face, lips parting in a soft moan. "Reed."

"You feel so good," I grind out, hammering into her. "Like you were made for my cock."

I grind my hips into her, dragging my pelvic bone against her clit, giving her the pressure she needs as she grunts and whines, begging to come.

"Fuck, Reed. Oh, fuck."

She's so slick that it's coating my balls as they draw tighter.

"Give it to me, Reed. Give me your knot."

"You want it? You want this big dick to fill you up and seal you shut?"

Her fingernails rake my spine. "Yes. Give it to me. Give it to me…" She arches her neck, grabbing hold of Nixon's arm on her left and Finn's hand on her right. "Like that. Fuck. Please… oh, fuck, please…"

I thrust hard, my pulsating knot driving inside her, stretching her wide, hips snapping like a machine, and she cries out, her pussy clamping in waves that are so tight, my vision becomes white light as I fill her with my seed. My climax punches through me so hard, I lose connection with the world around me, yanked into blackness that spins with pinpricks of light, pleasure roaring through my body as she clings to me.

I press my forehead to hers, staring into her lust-glazed eyes, as she contracts around me again.

"Feels. So. Good," she gasps, gripping the back of my neck and wrapping her legs around my waist, sealing us together in her own way.

Sweat drips from my pecs to her breasts and coats our skin where we're joined. Her scent rises around us, making Nixon and Finn growl for their own turns.

They have to wait at least twenty minutes for my body to release her, and this time is mine. I relish her around me, peppering her face with kisses.

Her body bears three marks, proof of what she is to us.

Scarlet. Mate. Mother. Magic.

My brothers will take their turns to show her what she means to them, and after, we'll curl around her, our hands resting on her belly, over the lives we've created. Her skin will glow. Her eyes will flutter closed.

With every kiss, every touch, we remind her, and ourselves, that love can rise from ashes. Sometimes, fate takes the shape of a woman with fire in her hair and passion in her soul.

Once, we ran wild beneath the moon, all teeth and fury. But now, we sleep with Scarlet's heartbeat beside ours. The big bad wolves still live in us... now, they have something to protect.

And in that perfect moment, clasped tightly inside my woman, I whisper the only truth I know, accompanied by my trademark smirk.

"Even big bad wolves can be tamed by the right woman."

EPILOGUE

SCARLET

The babies in my belly squirm, their limbs creating moving hills and valleys of my skin. I'm huge and swollen and sore, but so damned happy, I can barely keep the smile from my face.

A week after the battle, Finn drove me back to the city. We boxed my life, including tools, the ugly first-commission chair, Gran's quilt, and the muffin basket, and loaded the truck while Mom pressed cinnamon rolls into our hands and told my wolves to drive safe.

She loved them, whispering about how handsome and strong they are, and how the adoration in their eyes when they look at me is as clear as day. She flushed happily as they kissed her cheek goodbye, telling her they'd bring me home whenever I wanted. It was a happy day, and it gave me the courage to broach the subject of their unusual nature three months later.

Maybe I would have waited longer if I hadn't found out about my pregnancy.

I'm still reeling that they managed to get me pregnant the first time we had sex. Mom was baffled, but that bafflement became wonder when I introduced her to Ahya for the first time, and my little girl chose that moment to shift into her wolf form, leaving me clutching an empty pink princess dress, and my mom chasing a wild wolf around her living room. I think it was the cat that prompted the shift.

Nixon sits on the rug, building tall towers for Ahya to knock over. She yells 'more' and 'higher' and 'no Daddy', making all my big, bad wolves' hearts melt.

Reed responds to a knock at the door, and Goldie's smiling face appears. She's dressed in jeans and a canary yellow jumper, and clutching a container of something that smells delicious. "I made my pineapple cake. I know it's supposed to be a myth that pineapple helps to bring on labor, but I thought it couldn't hurt. At worst, you get to eat something sweet. At best, you'll be free of that massive bump."

"Gimme," I say, beckoning with both hands. These babies have made me feral for sugary treats, and Goldie has become an excellent baker in recent months, despite having five small children to take care of.

"I'll make coffee," Finn says, as Ahya toddles away from the tower towards the box of cake. She may not be my biological daughter, but she shares so many of my traits that she may as well be.

I slide my feet off the couch and bend to help her eat tiny bites of cake, all while avoiding a crumby mess. "More," she says.

I stroke her halo of soft red curls. "My little red riding hood." I smile softly as her sweet cupid's bow mouth purses as she chews.

"She's not afraid of the big bad wolves," Nixon says.

"She's going to grow up to be one," Reed says proudly. He follows Finn into the kitchen and returns with two cups of coffee for Goldie and me.

"And a big bad bear," Goldie reminds us.

It's still strange to think of my sweet little girl as a wolf or a bear. She shifts when her daddies shift, mainly into the little wolf I've gotten more accustomed to seeing. When she's in wolf form, she's inquisitive and playful, bounding into the forest with Finn at her side, sniffing out small prey, and frolicking in the fallen leaves. She comes back filthy but happy, as though the freedom of her small furry body gives her a more profound sense of connection to who she is.

When Goldie brings her older boys around, Ahya will shift into a bear to play with them. Last week, however, she transformed into a wolf partway through the afternoon, and they played like that, wolf and bear together. We found them curled in a tired heap in our yard, surrounded by leaves. Goldie's expression was wistful, and I suspect her dreams have shown her a future for our children that she hasn't yet felt ready to share.

Already, I have a picture in my mind of Ahya as a woman, running barefoot through Blackwood Forest to meet her mate, or mates. She'll be carefree and connected to the forest in a way that no other shifter has ever been, understanding the strengths and limitations of two animal forms. In my mind, she has mates of both species, living in a blended harem that will challenge the fixed beliefs from both sides. They'll cement the fragile peace that the war with Gregory's wild pack forged.

"Are you ready?" Goldie asks.

She's been careful not to talk too much about her own

birth experiences, but I know her first labor was hard because, by the time she was eight months pregnant with her second brood, she had a full-blown panic attack about going through labor again. Hunter, who's usually gruff and aloof, scooped her into his arms, and reminded her that they would all be there with her, that they are all connected, and that she doesn't have to fear anything. He pressed his forehead to hers and continued to talk to her silently through their minds as Robert and Evan drew close. They didn't seem to care that I was watching it all.

I know their connection is what got Goldie through it, as I trust my connection with Nixon, Reed, and Finn.

"I'm ready to be less swollen," I say. "But I'm still enjoying their little bodies moving and safe inside me. Who knows if I'll get to go through this again."

Nixon fixes me with his 'don't get comfortable because I'm going to breed you again look' that makes me flush. If he had his way, we'd have to extend the cabin to accommodate twenty little wolf cubs, and he'd be stuffing me full of his seed and his knot whenever my womb was vacant.

Being a momma is everything I ever wanted, but I'm not sure my body could cope with going through many more nine months like this. Growing the next generation of wolves is seriously hard work.

I gorge on the pineapple cake, washing it down with my caffeine-free hot beverage, as Goldie talks about how grateful she is to have three men to help her with all her bear cubs. Her business is going from strength to strength, although I'm yet to put in an order. Thankfully, my wolves keep me more than satisfied, so I've no need for any battery-powered assistance. She showed me around her stockroom, and I was fascinated to find vibrators shaped like fruits and vegetables. Things have changed a lot since I was last forced to shop for one.

"So, how are the babies sleeping?" I ask her.

"They're not. I'm dealing with constant hunger and constant wakefulness, and that's just Hunter!"

We both laugh and she continues. "The only way we get through is that two of us take an early shift and the other two handle a late shift, and that way, we all get at least five hours of uninterrupted sleep. Add in a nap at lunchtime and we're just about functioning."

"Has it put them off having any more?"

"Are you crazy?" Goldie says. "These shifter men want to make babies night and day. If I didn't have to incubate them for nine months and I was popping them out every seventy-five days like a bear, we'd have a houseful!"

Nixon laughs, surprising Ahya, who giggles along with him. "Seems like we have even more in common with our bear friends than I previously thought."

"I'm not a baby-making machine," I tell him in a low warning tone. "Don't even think about coming near me until I've recovered from this batch!"

He holds his hands up and looks to his brothers for support. "We want to build a big family. And we're here to support you all the way."

"Great. Maybe you should handle the next pregnancy, then. See how much you enjoy the swollen ankles and inability to tie your shoelaces."

"But you look so beautiful all rounded with our pups," Reed says, staring at me with a hungry, feral look in his eyes. "If you weren't already pregnant…" He shakes his head.

"Down, boy." Goldie puts her hands up defensively. "I

284

know how to handle three bears. Don't think I won't take down three wolves."

The laughter is still hanging in the air when it happens.

A sudden warmth spreads between my thighs. It's not a trickle, but a full release, like my body has decided it's *time*. I freeze, blinking fast at the dark patch growing beneath me, and then lift my eyes to Goldie, wide with realization.

"I think it's starting," I say, calm only on the outside.

"It worked!" she gasps, clapping her hands. "I told Hunter it would, but he was all, 'it's a stupid myth'. He was less smug when I reminded him that most people think he's a stupid myth."

I laugh reluctantly, clinging onto my belly, as though the babies could follow with the speed of the amniotic fluid. Goldie's expression shifts in an instant. The lightness is gone, replaced by practiced urgency. She sets her cup onto the coffee table, already moving. "Okay. Let's get you settled. Reed, towels. Finn, clear the floor. Nixon, call for your midwife, but don't expect she'll make it in time. We may be doing this ourselves. "

The first contraction hits hard, and it's like the air is knocked from my lungs. I curl forward instinctively, pressing my hands to the top of my thighs, breathing through the deep, low pressure.

"She's early," Nixon says, voice too tight and too loud. "Is that normal? What does it mean? Is it safe?"

"Nixon," Goldie says, sharply but kindly, placing a hand on his arm. "This is happening. Focus."

He swallows hard and then paces back and forth in front of the hearth like a caged wolf who doesn't know whether to fight or flee. Ahya stares at him with wide eyes from her spot on the rug, sensing the shifting energy in the room.

He's poking his finger at his phone like he wants to smash the screen, then he's growling orders at the poor midwife.

I lose concentration, funneling all my attention to my body.

Finn's behind me, a strong and steady presence, hands pressed to my lower back in broad, comforting circles. He murmurs something low into my hair, something meant to soothe, but I can't hear it over the rush of blood roaring in my ears.

Reed returns with towels and blankets, laying them out calmly under Goldie's supervision. His face is pale but focused. He kneels beside me, brushing a damp wave from my forehead, his other hand bringing a cool cloth to my neck.

Goldie guides me to my knees, urging me to bend over the sofa for support. "This position will help with the pressure. Breathe, Scarlet, and try to relax. That's all you have to do. Let your body do the rest."

I close my eyes and lean forward, fists clenching into the cushions, hissing through clenched teeth. Relax? Is she high?

The next contraction comes sharp and fast, and I cry out, but Finn's hands don't leave my back. Reed murmurs soft encouragement from beside me.

"We've got you" Nixon says. "We're here. All of us. You're safe. "

I nod, a slight motion, as another wave of pain grips me and I moan through it, loud and primal and utterly unconcerned with anything but the need to *push*.

Goldie peels away my wet underwear, and I'm so grateful to have another woman who's been through this to support me that it isn't weird.

Time seems to blur the space between my birthing pains like I'm underwater as I pant and focus to regain my strength, then the tightening agony grips me so violently, I lose all connections to the world around me.

Goldie hands Finn something. "It's a sex toy. Use it on Scarlet to improve her pain. I'm going to take Ahya outside and call Hunter."

"Are you sure?" Finn says, his voice high with disbelief.

I pant like a crazy person, eyes fixed to a crumb on the sofa.

"I'm sure. Trust me. It's all about happy, pain-relieving hormones."

"Okay." He doesn't sound sure, studying the thing like an unexploded bomb that's suddenly appeared in his palm.

Goldie closes the door behind her, and then Finn kisses my temple and whispers, "Goldie has recommended helping you to orgasm to help with pain relief. She's given me one of her weird fruit-shaped toys."

"Nothing's going up there," I gasp. "Somethings about to come out."

"It's for your clit," he laughs.

"It'll help," Nixon says firmly. "The power of the female orgasm. It's the goddess's gift to women."

"Maybe she should have focused on painless childbirth instead," I grumble. Then, as I'm almost flattened by another gripping wave of pain, I gasp, "Anything… just… oh fuck."

Finn's hands move between my legs. His finger searches out my clit, then he latches a clit sucker on and holds it to me. It's strange when the first flutters of pleasure rise from beneath so much pain, but as the contraction subsides, the pleasure overtakes its clutches and I moan, rocking into

287

Finn's hand. "That's it, Scarlet," he says. "Let yourself feel good."

I moan, low and deep, more like a cow than a woman, but the toy is clever, and it varies its sucking action, edging me closer. Another contraction builds, but the pain is muted by pleasure. Reed's hand caresses my back in long, slow swoops, and I moan again, gripping the edge of the sofa cushions desperately.

"Let go," Finn says, and I'm so close, I can taste the release on the back of my tongue. I clamp down, my pussy constricting in wave after wave of pleasure that swamp the next rising contraction, making it bearable.

"Was that good?" Nixon asks.

"So good," I murmur.

"You want more?" Finn asks, easing it from between my legs.

"Maybe. Give me a few minutes. "

He chuckles, lowering the toy and placing it on the towel between my legs. I hang my head, letting my hair pool around me, imagining my sons making their way into the world, trying to picture the boys and wolves they will be. Will they be stoic and controlled like Nixon, funny and clever like Reed, or caring and insightful like Finn? Will they have my creativity, or my desire for adventure? Will they have my mom's caution or my father's fiery temperament? Maybe they'll be unique: dreamers, poets, pioneers. Perhaps they'll challenge the status quo like their sister.

As my belly contracts again, the movement and pressure between my legs intensifies. "Get Goldie," I groan.

When she returns, Ahya is handed to Nixon, and she kneels behind me with her phone in hand. After two contractions, she declares, "The contractions are only a minute apart. She's close and doing beautifully. "

"Where's the damn midwife?" Nixon huffs.

"I'm here," a breathless voice answers from the door.

Our wolf pack midwife, Annie, rushes in, her bag slung over one shoulder, followed by Caleb, who scoops Ahya into his arms. "I'll take her for a while, until the babies are here."

Nixon hands her over gratefully. It's a whirlwind, and I'm at the center of the storm, keening lowly as the pressure crests into fire.

Annie's instantly in motion, slipping beside Goldie, eyes sharp and sure as she glances over my trembling form. I'm so grateful Caleb chose her as his mate. It's been such a blessing to have a friend take care of me throughout my pregnancy.

"You're almost there," she says. "Just a little more, Scarlet. You're ready to push."

I bear down with everything I have, breath held, body shuddering. Over and over, I work with the contractions, rocking with the pain as my wolves whisper words of encouragement and rub my back in circles that alleviate some of the pain.

Then the pressure breaks, replaced by a ripple of inferno, release, and the high, *piercing* cry of a newborn fills the air.

"One," the midwife says with a soft smile. I look at the perfect baby resting between my legs. "A strong, healthy baby."

But before I can fully register his presence, another contraction tightens in my core.

"The next one's coming," Goldie says gently. "One more, Scarlet."

My head swims. I blink back tears, exhausted but

incandescent. Reed strokes my arm. Finn kisses my shoulder. Nixon grips my hand, holding it to his chest like a lifeline.

I push again, shaking now, crying with effort, and after three more contractions, and the last of my strength sapped by pushing, a second cry joins the first.

"Two," the midwife says, awe in her voice. "Smaller, but fierce."

My legs are shaking as I stare at our sons. Their little faces are red and creased as they cry. Tears of happiness spill from my eyes in hot streaks.

Annie is gently wiping their faces and covering them with a blanket. I want to hold them so much but it's more important to let them continue to benefit from their connection to the placenta. Only when it's born and has stopped pulsing to deliver nutrients will its cords be cut.

"They're so beautiful," I gasp, stunned to realize that one has my red hair and the other the intense dark color of his fathers'. I thought they'd be identical, but I'm relieved to discover they're not. I want them to forge a path of their own rather than live in each other's shadows.

"I want to name him after my grandfather, Thoren," I whisper, touching the face of my copper-haired son. "And this one... Fredrik after your father," I say, looking at Nixon.

His eyes shine, no trace of his usual control left. "He would've been proud."

It's a peace offering and a promise, wrapped in the name of a man who stood beside us when the world threatened to split in two. I know what it means to Nixon to carry his father's name into the next generation. He kisses my hand, his eyes lingering with warmth and wonder.

The next few minutes pass in a blur. Eventually, I'm helped to the sofa, covered with a blanket, and handed two slippery perfect babies to hold against my chest. They're warm, soft and impossibly real. One of them lets out a tiny grunt. The other curls into my collarbone and immediately quiets.

They're perfect.

Ahya is brought back in, toddling shyly into the room with Goldie and Caleb at her side. Her eyes go wide at the sight of me, then the babies. She tiptoes forward, cautious but curious, and then she nestles against my side, resting her head gently against my hip.

"You want to meet your brothers?" I whisper.

She nods and strokes their tiny fists with one finger, her expression soft and solemn in a way that's so much older than her years.

"I think you're going to be the best big sister in the world."

She doesn't answer with words but with a smile that could melt even the coldest heart.

And like that, my heart splits wide open, overflowing.

Here I am. A mother with her children, her bonded mates surrounding her. My heart is full of wolves. My home is filled with the sounds of joy and life and new beginnings.

This… this is everything.

My mom always warned me about strangers. But if I never allowed three men to show me the path to my future, I'd still be trapped in the past.

This is the life I never knew I was allowed to dream of.

And it's all mine.

ABOUT THE AUTHOR

International bestselling author Stephanie Brother writes high heat love stories with a hint of the forbidden. Since 2015, she's been bringing to life handsome, flawed heroes who know how to treat their women. If you enjoy stories involving multiple lovers, including twins, triplets, stepbrothers, and their friends, you're in the right place. When it comes to books and men, Stephanie truly believes it's the more, the merrier.

She spends most of her day typing, drinking coffee, and interacting with readers.

Her books have been translated into German, French, and Spanish, and she has hit the Amazon bestseller list in seven countries.

Find her at stephaniebrotherbooks.com